Black
Beans
&
Vice

Books by Ellery Adams

The Secret, Book & Scone Society

The Secret, Book & Scone Society
The Whispered Word

The Book Retreat Mysteries

Murder in the Mystery Suite
Murder in the Paperback Parlor
Murder in the Secret Garden
Murder in the Locked Library

The Charmed Pie Shoppe Mysteries

Pies and Prejudice
Peach Pies and Alibis
Pecan Pies and Homicides
Lemon Pies and Little White Lies
Breach of Crust

Antiques & Collectibles Mysteries

A Killer Collection
A Fatal Appraisal
A Deadly Dealer
A Treacherous Trader
A Devious Lot
A Killer Keepsake

More Books by Ellery Adams

Supper Club Mysteries

Carbs & Cadavers
Fit to Die
Chili con Corpses
Stiffs and Swine
The Battered Body
Black Beans & Vice
Pasta Mortem

Hope Street Church Mysteries

The Path of the Crooked
The Way of the Wicked
The Graves of the Guilty
The Root of All Evil
Fate of the Fallen

The Books by the Bay Mysteries

A Killer Plot
A Deadly Cliché
The Last Word
Written in Stone
Poisoned Prose
Lethal Letters
Writing All Wrongs
Killer Characters

Black
Beans
&
Vice

ELLERY ADAMS

Black Beans & Vice
Ellery Adams
Copyright © 2010 by J. B. Stanley, copyright © 2018 by Ellery Adams

Beyond the Page Books
are published by
Beyond the Page Publishing
www.beyondthepagepub.com

ISBN: 978-1-958384-70-1

Black
Beans
&
Vice

Chapter One

Black Jelly Beans

Head librarian James Henry held the brochure as if the glossy trifold paper covered with photographs of happy, healthy people might suddenly ignite in his hands. "You want us to get *hypnotized*?" he asked, his voice rather shrill.

High school art teacher Lindy Perez nodded calmly. "Hypnotherapy is a *very* effective weight-loss method. Or so I've read. There are loads of testimonials on the Internet."

Tossing the brochure on the circulation desk, James reached for a glass bowl filled with jelly beans. Picking out two black ones, he popped the candies into his mouth and chewed thoughtfully. "I'm having a moment of déjà vu, Lindy," he declared once his mouth was empty. "It doesn't seem too long ago that I met you right here for the first time. You had schemes then too, remember? You were asking for permission to hang a flyer on the bulletin board—"

"In search of folks to join a dieter's supper club!" Lindy finished for him, her brown eyes glimmering at the memory. "You were mighty nervous about becoming a member, and look how *that's* turned out!"

James couldn't help but grin. "It was one of the best decisions of my life, no doubt about it. What would I do without all of you? You're my best friends." He gestured at the brochure. "Still, this is a bit out there. I could picture Gillian appearing at one of our meetings with this brochure, but not you, the ever-so-sensible Lindy Perez. You're too levelheaded to be reaching for these mumbo-jumbo straws."

Lindy's eyes flashed and James shrank back a little, worried that his friend was about to unleash her fierce Brazilian temper. "I may be Ms. Practical, but I've also gained fifteen pounds over the last three months. I was maintaining my weight until your stepmother's sister had to go and get herself murdered. After that, *plop!*" Lindy smacked her palms together. "I fell off the wagon in a big way. I'd like to gain control over the way I eat once and for all. I'm sick and tired of food controlling *me*, James, and I'm not looking for another diet plan." She pointed a finger at her temple.

"We're never going to change our bodies until we fix what's going on in here."

"And a hypnotherapist can do that?" James was doubtful.

Lindy nodded enthusiastically. "What's the one thing you can't seem to resist? When you go on a diet, what food do you miss most?"

"Cheese puffs," James answered right away. "And in a close second, anything made with sugar." He held up another jelly bean. "Like these, for instance."

"Exactly!" Lindy cried and several library patrons sent frowns in her direction. "Sorry," she whispered and gave a self-effacing wave to those browsing the New Releases section.

"We're *all* addicted to sugar. Candy, cake, soda, ice cream, cookies—"

James held out his hand. "Enough! Do you want me to drool all over the barcode scanner? I don't think it's waterproof."

Lindy picked up the brochure and gave it a triumphant wave. "See? Sugar is ruling you even as we speak. How many of those jelly beans have you had?"

Embarrassed, James shrugged. "I don't know. Enough to turn my tongue black?"

"Pick a number," Lindy insisted.

"Well, since I've only been eating one color out of five possible shades and I bought a jumbo-sized bag, I'd say twenty-five."

"Okay. Let me give you a brief lesson in mathematics. I might be an art teacher, but I can demonstrate some basic addition that will have your black tongue hanging on the floor." Lindy dashed over to the shelving cart, grabbed a few books, and pushed them against James's soft paunch. He automatically reached out to grab them. "Feel those books? Would you say they weigh somewhere between two and three pounds?" Lindy asked.

James tested the weight by bobbing the tomes up and down. "I'd say that's accurate."

"*That's* how much sugar the average American eats *every* week! Sugar weakens our immune system, rots our teeth, and makes us fat!" Lindy looked down at the ground and murmured, "I think it's why Luis isn't proposing. He's watched me grow bigger and bigger over the past few months. I've stopped going to the gym and my portions are the size of a linebacker's. He must believe I have no self-discipline, no self-respect. He might even wonder how big I'd get after having a few kids. With that unpleasant visual, it's no wonder he's had second thoughts about popping the question."

"Oh, Lindy." James put an arm around his friend's shoulder and squeezed. He hated to see sadness etched on her face. "Anyone worth his salt would be lucky to call you his wife. You're smart, kind, funny, and easy on the eye. And Luis is not so shallow that he'd stop loving you because you put on a few pounds. You wouldn't be in love with *him* if he were. Have you two talked about your future recently?"

Sighing, Lindy nodded. "He wants me to fly to Mexico to meet his mama when school is out. His treat, of course."

"There you go!" James proclaimed boisterously "He's taking you home to Mother. You're halfway up the aisle already."

"Yeah, *if* she likes me!" Lindy snorted. "I'm not her first choice, remember? That honor goes to the daughter of her best friend. Luis's mama set her sights on that girl to be her daughter-in-law, so how am I, an outsider and a woman who is half South American, half Brazilian, supposed to compete with Miss Mexico?"

Leading Lindy to the lobby door, James said, "You're going to dazzle her just like you dazzle everyone you meet."

"Well, I only have two months to look dazzling, so I'm going to book us an appointment with the hypnotherapist. She can explain the process to all of us at once. Do you have Eliot this weekend?"

At the mention of his son's name, James felt a rush of pleasure that seemed to increase in intensity whenever he thought of his little boy. Six months ago, James hadn't even known he had a child, but when his ex-wife introduced him to a sweet, shy four-year-old named Eliot Henry, James had instantly fallen in love. Since then, James had been spending most of his free time with his son, and every time Eliot ran into his arms, James felt like his heart would burst with joy.

"Jane's taking Eliot to visit her parents in Tennessee for the better part of spring break," James said. "I was invited to go along, and while Jane and I are really enjoying getting reacquainted, I'm not quite ready to spend five days with my former in-laws. So I'm completely available to be put under a spell."

Lindy swiped at him with the hypnotherapy brochure. "You'd better not show up at the consultation with that kind of attitude, mister."

"Yes, Ms. Perez." James used a high, squeaky voice to mimic one of Lindy's students. "I will be on my best behavior. Just don't expect me to get acupuncture next if this experiment fails. I have no desire to resemble a human pin cushion."

Backing up a few steps, Lindy helped herself to a handful of jelly beans and smiled self-effacingly. "A few for the road. And don't worry about the other lifestyle gurus at the Wellness Village. We can bypass the masseuses, acupuncturists, and yoga masters. We're only interested in one therapist: the woman who is going to kick our sugar craving for good!"

Visualizing the new complex south of town, which consisted of six offices built to resemble a row of small cottages surrounding a courtyard, James grew pensive. "If we let Gillian near this place, we may never see her again."

Lindy laughed. "We should tell Lucy to bring a pair of handcuffs. She'd better cuff Bennett to Gillian because that's the only way we'll get our favorite mailman within a mile of those pink and purple 'health' houses!"

"Yes, I believe it's quite likely he'll balk at the idea of being hypnotized, especially in a setting that looks like it was teleported from Disneyland." James gave Lindy his sternest look. "The first sign of an oversized mouse wearing gloves and suspenders and I'm leaving."

Lindy snorted. "The only oversized creatures there will be us!"

• • •

Later that week, James met Bennett at the local YMCA. It had been a long time since the two friends had worked out together and they spent the first few minutes in the weight-training alcove simply studying their images in the mirror. While they unhappily examined their protruding bellies and flaccid limbs, a pair of younger men with hard, streamlined bodies entered the room.

After greeting James and Bennett with friendly waves, the two men opened a notebook and began to discuss their goals for the day's workout. They debated a variety of different exercises until they agreed to complete five rounds of three hundred jump ropes, twenty-five weighted front squats, and fifteen shoulder presses. The men gathered their equipment, picked up their jump ropes, and synchronized their watches.

"Ready?" the first one asked.

"Let's do it," the second replied. When the subtle beep of his watch indicated the commencement of the stopwatch feature, the two twentysomethings began to jump.

James and Bennett watched in awe. The jump ropes whirled so quickly that the blue plastic cords blurred in the air. The men held their bodies rigid, their wrists circling with incredible speed as the jump ropes passed under their feet again and again. Their even rhythm never altered, and neither man missed a jump or got tangled in the rope. Not once. The sound in the room was like two small helicopters in hover mode.

"Hey, man. How about some bicep curls?" Bennett suggested after turning away from the athletic jumpers.

"Yeah. Let's go *heavy*," James said in a deeper voice than usual. He and Bennett selected the largest dumbbells from the rack. As James curled the weight toward his shoulder, he compressed his lips to bite back a groan. He couldn't believe how weak he'd become.

And that's my strong arm! he thought.

After two pathetic reps, he switched to his left arm. Meanwhile, Bennett was focused on lifting a forty-five-pound Olympic bar in one motion from the middle of his thighs to over his head. Normally, he would conduct this motion with slow deliberation, being careful to maintain correct form, but the intense pace of the younger men encouraged him to increase his speed. Bennett now raised and lowered the bar as fast as he could, his back rounding as he lost his good form. Suddenly, the bar became unbalanced. With an anguished yelp, Bennett dropped it right onto his shoe.

"*Aaarrrgh!*" he shouted in pain and began to hop on one foot. In his awkward dance of agony, he bumped into James. The heavy dumbbell in James's left hand lurched, forcing him to pitch forward. He reached across his body with his right hand to keep his grip on the weight. In doing so, he twisted his entire torso. The motion caused a painful wrenching of his back.

"Ooooo!" James howled and immediately sank down on the carpeted floor. Digging his fingers into his lower back, he moaned and winced in acute discomfort. Bennett dropped next to him, took off his sneaker and white tube sock, and gingerly bent the toes on his right foot to make sure none were broken.

When James was finally able to speak, he turned to his friend. "Are you hurt?"

Bennett eased his sock back on. "I don't think my little piggies are gonna be running all the way home for a real long time."

Feeling clumsy, weak, and old, James glanced in the mirror and was relieved to see that the younger men were far too busy lifting superhuman amounts of weight to have noticed their inelegant collapse.

"So much for our workout." Bennett mopped his face with a towel. "It'll take me twice as long to deliver the mail tomorrow, since I'm going to be limping every time I have to carry a box to someone's door."

"And I'll be the Hunchback of the Shenandoah Public Library," James said. "Bennett, I think this may be a sign that we should give Lindy's hypnotherapist a shot. We're clearly floundering on our own."

Bennett mulled the proposition over as he retied his shoe. James witnessed his friend's internal debate as Bennett's expression changed from a frown to a look of hopefulness and back to a frown again. "You really believe this woman can change our minds without turning us into zombies or making us—I don't know—squawk like parrots whenever we stop at a red light? Because I sit through lots of lights every day."

James clapped Bennett on the back, though the motion made him grimace in pain. "Don't worry, my friend. I doubt anyone intends to turn you into a parrot."

With a sigh, Bennett helped James to his feet. The two friends hobbled toward the locker room just as the younger men removed their shirts and began to jump rope again.

Bennett gazed at their rippled abs, the bulging muscles in their arms, and their rock-hard pectorals. "Okay, man, I'm in. Let this woman brainwash me. If I end up looking half as good as those two, she can even sneak in the parrot squawks."

Sharp stabs exploded across James's lower back. He placed his palm on the wall for support. "Don't make me laugh!" he cried. "It hurts too much!"

• • •

The next day, the five friends gathered in the parking lot of the new Wellness Village. Lucy Hanover, dressed in her brown and beige sheriff's deputy uniform, stood with her hands on her hips, looking rather nervous. To her left, Gillian O'Malley, the owner of the Yuppie Puppy Pet Grooming and Pet Palaces, grinned in buoyant expectation. She gazed at the sign reading YOUR MAP TO GOOD HEALTH with an expression bordering on rapture.

Lindy pointed at the map. "Harmony York's office is in Health House Number Four. This way." She began to march down a cobblestone pathway.

"Harmony?" Bennett spluttered. "That's her real name? Is she one of those Flower Child types."

Gillian looped her arm around his and beamed. "Not only is it a lovely name, but I find it *very* symbolic. Isn't our goal to rebalance our bodies and minds? To create an inner harmony? I have *complete* faith that we are not meeting a woman named Harmony by coincidence. This is the cosmos working on our behalf!"

"Pink Health Houses! Hrmph! Where's the yellow brick road," Bennett grumbled, clearly apprehensive. "I never thought I'd want be whisked away by a flying monkey, but if I see a chimp with wings, I'm going to wave him down and hitch a ride away from here."

Gillian nearly yanked his arm off as she dragged him up the path toward one of the purple cottages bordered by a garden of riotous and fragrant wildflowers.

Next to the light blue front door, a simple placard bearing the name A BETTER STATE OF MIND hung by a gold chain. Letting Lindy take the lead, the rest of the supper club members entered the waiting room and took in their surroundings.

"Something smells funny," Lucy whispered, and James pointed at a burning stick of incense in the far corner. The opposite corner was occupied by a small wall fountain, which gurgled pleasantly at a slightly lower volume than the instrumental music being piped into the space through a set of speakers resembling gray stones.

"Do I detect the sound of pan pipes?" James whispered in hopes of making Lucy grin. Ever since Jane and Eliot had become such a significant part of his life, Lucy had become more distant around James. She was always polite, but he knew that she was still coming to terms with the reality that their romance would never be rekindled.

Not only did Lucy place law enforcement at the center of her life, but she also wanted to be free of dependents other than her trio of gargantuan German shepherds. And though James knew that the gift of fatherhood had forever changed him for the better, Lucy viewed his new role as a personal slight. Because James understood the crushing weight of loneliness and the pain of rejection, he tried to make his former flame smile whenever he could. He wanted Lucy to be as happy as he was.

Unaffected by his attempt at humor, Lucy skirted around the mauve sofa and approached the coffee table. She investigated each magazine, but James knew she wasn't really interested in the office's reading material. She was merely nervous and was looking for clues about Harmony York. Eyeing a gold-painted Buddha on the receptionist's desk, James had to admit he shared Lucy's trepidation.

Eventually, he settled down on the sofa with a copy of *Body + Soul* magazine and had just flipped to an article on the best workout for one's body shape when a pretty woman in her mid-twenties entered the room from deeper within the cottage.

"*Namaste,*" she said and, folding her palms together, bowed her upper body. A curtain of shiny brown hair fell over her shoulders as she did so. Gillian immediately returned the greeting, while the rest of the supper club members merely smiled.

"My name is Skye," the young woman said. "I'm Harmony's assistant."

Bennett rolled his eyes at the name and Lindy quickly stepped in front of him. "I spoke with you on the phone. Thanks for mailing me the brochure. It sure convinced us to give this a try."

Skye swept her arm around the room in an encompassing gesture. "I'm afraid we don't offer group hypnotherapy. Are you *all* here for the consultation?"

"Yes," Lindy answered. "We have the same goal, and since the first session is free, I figured we'd save Harmony's time by coming together." She smiled warmly at her friends. "Besides, we like to support one another when it comes to our issues with food—"

"So it makes sense for us to embark on this exciting new journey as one entity," Gillian interrupted. "We believe we'll have better success this way."

Skye appeared to have no objections. "Let me just tell Harmony that she has five clients waiting for her." She gazed at each of them warmly and then said, "Please, help yourselves to some spring water flavored with organic orange slices. I'll be back in a sec."

James watched the poised young lady walk away and then pivoted. "Where is the water?" He found that he was suddenly very thirsty.

Bennett licked his lips and pointed at a stainless steel pitcher on Skye's desk. "Man, I could slurp down a lake right about now. Was that the power of suggestion or what?"

Fortified with glasses of cool and refreshing citrus-flavored water, the five friends made themselves comfortable. They'd barely sipped from their recycled cups when Skye returned. "Harmony would be delighted to talk to you together. It would be a tight squeeze in her office so she'll meet with you here, in our Welcome Space."

Skye returned to her desk. James watched her sit with the straight-backed posture of a ballerina. Her fingers moved with deliberate gracefulness over the computer keyboard and her face seemed infused with a serene glow. There was an air of calm assurance about her, which James found to be an unusual trait in one so young. It was as if she already knew the answers to life's most significant questions.

I certainly didn't feel that way when I was twenty-five, James thought.

His attention was distracted by the arrival of Harmony York. James had expected someone with waist-long hair, a flowing skirt, and leather sandals. Someone who dressed, looked, and acted a bit like Gillian. Harmony and Gillian might have been cut from the same cloth, but while Gillian was outfitted in a vibrant tangerine-colored sundress, which echoed the orange shade of her frizzy hair,

Harmony wore a plain gray suit and a blue blouse. Her hair was silver and fashioned in a sleek bob. She was in her late fifties, James guessed, though her age was difficult to approximate, as her skin was mostly smooth and shone with the light of good health.

"It's a pleasure to meet all of you." Harmony went around the room, shaking hands with her five potential clients and asking for their names. She then pulled one of the side chairs positioned near Skye's desk to the center of the room. She sat, smoothed her pants, and studied each of them. Normally, such scrutiny would discomfit James, but Harmony's gentle gaze actually encouraged him to relax.

"Now." She smiled. "Let me tell you what we do here. I will be your therapist and Skye will take care of scheduling, billing, and the creation of your daily listening CDs. I'll explain how those work in a moment. First and foremost, allow me to assure you that anything you tell me will remain in the strictest confidence. During your therapy session, I'll talk to you, but I will also ask you questions. I'll be taking notes on your answers, but none of my movements will interrupt your relaxed state."

Bennett cleared his throat. "So we're not *under*? We know what's happening to us?"

"Absolutely," Harmony said. "This isn't sideshow hypnosis where you're tricked into submitting to another person's suggestions for the sake of entertainment. You will enter a deeply relaxed state so that your mind can become incredibly focused while your body rests. I will ask your mind to do something for you and, with repetition, your mind will respond."

Lindy wiggled on her seat in excitement. "Well, like I explained to Skye, we don't want to be controlled by sugar any longer. Can you help our bodies stop wanting it so badly?"

Harmony laughed. Her voice was low and melodious. It reminded James of the seductive pitch shared by so many female actresses from the forties and fifties. "Yes, if *you're* willing. You see, you *cannot* be hypnotized unless you're willing to be hypnotized. Some people want to change, but they can't trust enough to let go. I often can't get through to those clients and have to suggest another method of treatment for them."

"What other things do people get help for besides food issues?" Lucy asked with an edge of skepticism to her voice.

If Harmony picked up on the tone, she didn't let it show. "All kinds of things. Many clients want to stop repeating bad habits like smoking, overindulging in alcohol, gambling, drug abuse, and even nail biting. Others seek freedom from phobias such as a fear of flying or of confined spaces. And many want relief from chronic pain, depression, or destructive attitudes."

Gillian, who'd been hanging on Harmony's every word, sighed in delight. "This is so *enlightening*. When can we start?"

Harmony rose and walked over to Skye's desk. She returned with a cup holder filled with pens and several pieces of paper. "Like everything else, we have to begin with paperwork." She distributed two sheets to each of them. "The first is a consent form. This basically states that you understand the meaning of hypnotherapy. If, at any time, you wish to stop your session and leave the hypnotic state, you have the right and the ability to do so. *You* are in control." She grinned as Bennett sighed in relief. "We'll have three sessions together. Every night, as you get ready to go to sleep, you'll listen to your reinforcement CD. That's the gist of this form."

Lucy's pen hovered over the signature line. "Will any of this be covered by health insurance?"

"I'm afraid not." Harmony shook her head in genuine regret. "Payment is required at the end of each session and I'd prefer to receive twenty-four hours advance notice in the event of a cancelation. Once you sign, feel free to schedule your first session with Skye."

"What's this? Homework?" Bennett joked as he flourished the second sheet of paper.

Harmony laughed again. "That's just a diagram to show you how hypnosis works. My goal is to bypass the conscious mind, which is where your short-term memory operates, and target the subconscious mind, where permanent memory resides."

The five friends studied the drawing for a moment. Gillian actually traced her finger around the rings representing the different levels of the mind. James watched her in amusement, wondering whether she'd try to line up an appointment that very day. "So we're going to *retrain* our mind's memory into believing it doesn't crave sugar?"

Harmony beamed at Gillian. "Precisely. We're going to rewire your permanent memory in order to get a positive reaction from your short-term memory. In this case, your short-term memory will wonder if you feel like a piece of cake. Your mind will check with your long-term memory and come back with the answer, 'No, I don't want to eat cake. That's no longer a taste I'm interested in.'"

Whipping out her checkbook and pocket calendar, Gillian leapt out of her seat and stood at attention in front of Skye's desk.

"When is the next opening? I simply cannot *wait* to begin this journey!"

"How's Tuesday at four thirty?" Skye asked.

"Sublime!" Gillian cried.

Bennett rolled his eyes again. "Like a pig in mud."

Lindy jabbed him in the arm with her capped pen. "Not the best of analogies there, Romeo."

Having booked her preliminary session, Gillian practically skipped over to Bennett, yanked him out of his sofa seat, and led him over to Skye. "Give him the five thirty. This way, I can drag him by the mustache if he gets cold feet."

"That's right, my friend." James winked at Bennett. "Think about those *feet*. Especially the one with the bruised toes."

A scowl bloomed on Bennett's face and James knew his friend was picturing their failed workout at the gym. "Five thirty it is," he told Skye with the despondency of one being led to the electric chair.

Chapter Two

Sausage and Pepperoni Pizza

James was in a good mood the following morning. The sun was shining, he could smell freshly brewed coffee wafting down the hallway of his yellow house on Hickory Hill Lane, and Eliot and Jane were driving down from Harrisonburg for dinner.

Sliding his feet into his leather slippers, James filled a mug embellished with the slogan I'M A LIBRARIAN: ASSUME I KNOW EVERYTHING and took a leisurely walk to the end of the driveway to collect the Saturday paper. Sliding the *Shenandoah Star Ledger* into his robe pocket, he examined the flower bed at the base of the front porch.

According to last night's garden report on the community television channel, Quincy's Gap and its environs had safely moved past the season's final frost. The announcer proclaimed that it was officially time to begin spring planting.

"Work hard now. Rest all summer," the Master Gardener had suggested.

James decided to heed the expert's advice. He sat at his kitchen table and searched the paper for sales on tulips, daffodils, phlox, and azalea bushes. After showering and dressing in his yard clothes, a faded William & Mary sweatshirt and jeans that had gone thin in the knees, James hopped into his old white Bronco and headed north.

He deliberately selected one of the two-lane highways, doubling the length of the drive time to the nearest Lowe's, but as he eased the vintage truck around curve after curve, he could feel his spirits rise as the road steepened. In his opinion, there was no place else on earth as beautiful as the Shenandoah Valley. The rugged line of the Blue Ridge Mountains, the wild forests, and the crisp, untainted air had always been a source of strength to James. After driving for twenty-five miles, he pulled over at one of the lookouts and parked the Bronco next to a minivan from Ohio.

He walked to the edge, leaned on the iron rail, and inhaled the scents of spring. The trees were covered with plump buds or newly unfurled leaves, highlighted by dappled sunlight. Everywhere he looked there was a glow of verdant green that existed only at the end of April.

A red-tailed hawk circled overhead, and as James watched the raptor adjust its wings to a draft of wind, the bird cried out with a hunter's primeval call.

"This is God's country," the mother from the minivan said to her children.

James couldn't agree more. He got back in the Bronco and spent the rest of the trip fantasizing about the trips he would take with his son. Like the family at the overlook, he wanted Eliot to see the wonders of his own region. Sure, there'd be a visit to Disneyland at one point, but it was important to James to foster a sense of state pride in his child, and he couldn't imagine a better way to do that than to embark on a series of short road trips.

On the other hand, the idea of pitching tents and spending the night in bug-infested woods didn't appeal to James. Though he hated to admit it, he'd grown rather soft now that he'd entered his middle years and wondered how he could create the intimacy of the camping environment without having to resort to sleeping bags, canned food, and the absence of plumbing.

"Jane will come up with a plan," he said with confidence.

Over the past few months he'd spent every weekend and several weeknights with his ex-wife, but they'd never been alone. Eliot was always present, and Jackson and Milla were often around too. James's normally irascible father melted like a pat of butter in the frying pan whenever he was with his grandson, and Milla was in danger of completely spoiling the child. She never stopped by the house empty-handed, and should Eliot visit her store, Quincy's Whimsies, he was allowed to pick out any candy he wanted from the bulk bins. For the price of a kiss and a hug, Eliot could procure more sugar than his mother would allow over the course of a week.

At first, Jane had smiled indulgently. She'd longed for a loving reception from James's family when it came to her only child, but she didn't want Eliot's new grandparents to coddle Eliot too much. After holding her tongue for a month, Jane convinced Milla to settle for giving Eliot two pieces of candy instead of twenty and begged the older woman to ease off on the gift giving unless it was a special occasion. Milla had respectfully promised to obey Eliot's mother, but James knew that she slipped Eliot little treats on the sly. Fortunately, Eliot seemed more interested in spending time with his grandparents than in garnering material goods, and since he was a polite and helpful little boy, James decided not to tell Jane about Milla's infractions.

All in all, James and Jane were united when it came to how they wanted to raise their son. Intent on molding a person of strong character, they'd spent several long evenings agreeing on a set of rules for Eliot to obey in both of their homes. James had told his ex more than once that he was extremely impressed by her mothering skills. Jane had blushed at the praise, her pretty face — now fuller and rounder than it had been when they were married — tinged pink with pleasure.

Thinking of her now, James experienced a powerful and completely unexpected wave of lust. Now that their friendship had been renewed, James was reminded of the year they'd dated before becoming engaged. Every time he and Jane got together, James recalled all the reasons he'd proposed in the first place. He loved her sense of humor and quick wit, and he enjoyed discussing books with her. As he had back then, he wanted to touch her as well. He wanted to kiss her. On the lips, the neck, the soft skin on her shoulder.

Though James knew such feelings would complicate their lives, he couldn't help himself. Jane was no longer the skinny, somewhat angular woman he'd wed, but a softer, curvier, and totally enticing woman of forty. She was growing out her hair and her thick waves of lustrous walnut brown now reached her shoulders. James longed to touch the silky locks and then slide his hand down the nape of her lovely neck. Her body, once familiar to him, would be intriguing new territory. Territory that he was eager to explore.

"Stop it!" he chided his stimulated libido. "I'm supposed to be focusing on plants!"

But as he wandered through the rows of vibrant blooms at Lowe's, he tried to remember which flowers Jane preferred. Eliot loved the color yellow, so James selected a flat of daffodils to plant along the front walkway. He noticed that Jane often wore a lavender sweater set. In hopes of pleasing her, he picked out a flat of light purple phlox. He skipped the tulips, knowing the deer that meandered through his property would make a quick meal of the bright red and orange flowers. In fact, the Master Gardener on last night's television program had also listed skunks, squirrels, mice, rats, and voles as tulip destroyers, and James assumed that his spacious lot harbored these creatures in droves. Instead, he selected a few bleeding hearts for the corner of the porch bed and pushed his loaded cart to the checkout counter.

When the sales associate rang up his purchases and the total flashed upon the register screen, James nearly passed out.

"That's *with* the coupons?" he asked.

The young woman didn't bother to look up from the register. "Yep. If you're using a credit card, you can slide it now, sir."

Outside, he carefully examined his receipt and saw that the sale had been tendered correctly.

"I wanted my own house," James muttered as he loaded his plants into the Bronco. "I wanted independence and privacy and to own something other than a bunch of dog-eared paperbacks and comic books. I agreed to humbly accept all the gripes and grievances that go with home ownership. Well, here's a big fat gripe. Plants cost *way* too much money."

His bright mood a bit dampened, James decided to return home for lunch instead of treating himself to a burger and fries.

I'll have to save for years to pay for a vacation for three to Disneyland, James thought sourly. It wasn't like his bank account grew larger with each paycheck. Librarians weren't exactly in the upper echelons of the salary scale and there were always so many bills to pay.

Driving home, James reflected that he had earned a great deal more money as an English professor. He could always return to that field, but such a change could mean moving farther away from Eliot and Jane, his parents, his friends, and his beloved library.

"Quincy's Gap is my home. I'll just have to find ways to trim costs wherever I can," he declared.

James's spirits were slightly restored by a lunch of salami and cheese on sourdough, Granny Smith apple slices, and a generous handful of cheese doodles. Following this feast of comfort foods, he spent the afternoon cleaning leaves and dried stalks from the garden beds, planting his new flowers, and spreading hardwood mulch. Singing along to the local country music station, James delighted in his outdoor work. He didn't mind that his job at the library kept him inside five days a week, but during his time off, his favorite activity was to walk around his property and make a list of chores that needed to be done over the weekend.

"I practically had to chase after you with the danged chain saw to get you to mow the lawn when you were a boy," Jackson had remarked one evening as James described how much he enjoyed yard work. "And *now* look at you! Mr. John Deere himself."

"Don't badger him, dear," Milla had chided. "He still drives to our place to cut the lawn twice a month. You should count your blessings that you have such a fine son."

Jackson had made a noise somewhere between a snort and a huff and had quickly focused on his plate of pot roast.

This evening, James didn't have to concern himself with cooking, as it was the Henry Family Pizza Night. He was relieved to be ordering pizza because he was too worn out to cook. His lower back and legs were sore after a day of physical labor. He imagined that Jane would also be tired from her flight back from Nashville. The idea of sitting down to a casual supper was sure to appeal to her, and James went to extra lengths to tidy up the house before her arrival.

For months, the only pizza place that would deliver to Quincy's Gap was Papa John's. James liked their pizza just fine, but ever since Luigi's Pizzeria had opened two doors down from Quincy's Whimsies, James had felt obliged to patronize Milla's new business neighbor. Besides, Luigi had six children to feed, a fact he repeated to his customers at every opportunity. Just thinking of the photo of the adorable kids tacked behind Luigi's cash register made James feel doubly compelled to order all his Italian food from the eatery.

"Aha!" Luigi shouted when James phoned to place his order. "The professor is calling for two pepperoni and sausage pies and a Caesar salad, no?"

James smiled. Luigi didn't seem capable of regular speech. Everything he said came out as an exuberant yell. One day, he'd reprimanded James for being too soft-spoken on the phone. "I cannot hear your mumbles, Mr. Librarian!" Luigi had hollered.

"I'm calling from the library," James had answered in a hushed tone. "I'm used to speaking quietly."

"I've got six kids, Professor! There is *no* quiet in my life, capiche?"

"That's right, Luigi," James now informed the boisterous proprietor using a raised voice. "Can you have the order delivered to my house around six o'clock?"

"Certainly!" Luigi screamed and hung up.

James had just showered and put on a pair of loose-fitting chinos and a long-sleeved collared shirt when he heard Eliot's impatient footsteps on the front porch.

"Daddy!" he cried, his freckled nose wrinkling in delight.

James knelt down and opened his arms wide. Eliot flew against his father's arms, permitting a longer embrace than usual. James smelled the aroma of childhood on the boy: fresh grass, Ivory soap, Johnson's Baby Shampoo, and the promise of things to come.

"Did you have a nice time in Nashville?" James asked, reluctantly releasing his son.

Once freed, Eliot stepped aside and commanded, "Say hi to Mommy first."

Smiling, James reached out to Jane. She hugged him and gave him a kiss on the cheek. "We missed you," she said warmly. She was wearing her lavender sweater set.

"Five days never seemed so long," James answered, and was unable to say more as Eliot demanded his full attention from then on. The four-year-old prattled on and on about his grandparents' house, the day spent at the zoo, the tour of the Grand Ole Opry (which he referred to as the place where the cowboys sang), getting to meet Fay Sunray (whoever she was), and the set of wings he was given by the pilot of their "ginormous airplane."

"And Granny and Grandpa Steward have a pool! It was warm. Like a bathtub. And I have my own room in their house with tons and tons of toys!"

Jane must have noticed the fleeting expression of jealousy that crossed James's face. She knew he could never provide Eliot with an equitable amount of material goods or entertainment, but to her, that didn't matter. He'd quickly proved to be a loving and devoted father and no amount of money would make him a better parent.

"And how many times a day did you say, 'I wish Daddy was here'?" Jane poked Eliot in the side.

He giggled. "A *million!*"

James shot Jane a grateful look, knowing full well she'd asked their son that question to make him feel good.

"I can't believe how gorgeous the flower beds are!" She gestured toward the front yard. "Purple phlox are my favorite spring flowers. Won't it be nice to sit out on the porch with a glass of sweet tea come summertime?"

The doorbell rang and Eliot ran off to see who was waiting on the welcome mat. Jackson and Milla greeted their grandchild as though he'd been away for months. Milla scooped him into her arms and covered the little boy with kisses until Jackson finally intervened.

"Ease up there, Milla! The boy can't breathe!" he grumbled with false sternness. His eyes were twinkling at the sight of his grandson.

Jane also received a warm hello from Milla, while Jackson remained polite but aloof. James knew that his father still wanted to punish Jane a bit for breaking James's heart years ago. Right after Jane had resurfaced, Jackson had counseled James to distrust her and to seek legal advice regarding Eliot's custody.

James had ignored his father's suggestion, however. Jane had never denied James the opportunity to spend time with his son. In fact, she was the one who routinely made the drive down from Harrisonburg, where she was a professor at James Madison University, so that the three of them could be together.

Often, while James and Eliot built LEGO towers or Lincoln Log fortresses, she busied herself grading papers, enabling father and son to make the most of their time together. She and James took turns cooking and they both strove to gather around the dinner table as a family whenever possible. The result of this schedule was that on weeknights, Jane had to drive home in the dark with Eliot falling asleep to the sound of a children's lullaby CD, arriving home with little time to do anything for herself. She never complained, though. Unlike the Jane of old, who was rather self-centered and impatient, motherhood had softened her heart as much as it had softened her body.

"You're a different woman now," James had told her one night.

She'd nodded in response and covered his hand with her own.

"When we were married, I cared about insignificant things, like the brand of car I drove or fitting into a size six dress. I had a great guy, but I couldn't see you for what you were. I thought our life didn't measure up somehow. I was a fool, James. A fool who didn't understand what defines true happiness. With you and Eliot in my life, I understand the meaning of that word now."

Looking around at his enlarged family, James recalled Jane's words. He too was amazingly content and the feeling scared him a little. Suddenly, after years of being unsure of his future, his life was full of love and hope. What could he do to ensure that nothing changed?

Luigi's arrival interrupted his trepidations. "Aha!" he boomed as his stout form filled the doorway. "I think you no have enough food for all these people, eh?"

James handed him some cash and received the pizzas and Caesar salad in return. "I have dessert if we're still hungry. Thank you, Luigi. Have a nice evening."

"But you no order cheesecake from me! I've got six kids to feed!"

"Good night!" James called out and shut the door. The adults tried to stifle laughs.

"What's so funny?" Eliot asked. "Does Mr. Luigi think cheese-cake is yucky?"

Jane put an arm around her son's shoulders and pivoted him toward the bathroom. "We're laughing because Luigi is what we call a loud talker. March down the hall and wash your hands, please."

While Eliot complied, James poured cold bottles of beer into chilled pint glasses. Jane placed slices of pizza on the plastic red-and-white-checkered plates that were held in reserve for the Henry Family Pizza Night. Milla distributed napkins and forks for the salad. These tasks were completed amid a stream of chatter, and by the time Eliot joined his family at the table, his plate had been filled and a glass of cold milk rested on top of his napkin.

After clinking pint glasses together in a toast, everyone tucked into their food. The pizza had a thin, crisp crust, mounds of melted cheese, and tender pieces of pepperoni and sausage. It was perfection.

"I *love* pizza night," James declared after swallowing a bite of crust. At that moment, he looked across the table at Eliot in order to elicit his son's agreement, but Eliot hadn't eaten a bite. Instead, he was performing surgery on his pizza. He was clearly trying to remove the round discs of pepperoni and the lumps of brown sausage while keeping the cheese intact.

"What are you doing, buddy?" James asked. "Is there something wrong with your meal?"

Eliot shrugged but didn't say a word.

Jane frowned. "Your father asked you a question, mister."

Tears sprang to Eliot's eyes, and though he fought against them, his effort failed and two little rivulets slipped down his cheeks. With trembling lips, he cried, "May I be excused?" and without waiting for permission, he jumped off his chair and ran down the hall. The stunned adults heard the door to his room close with a thud.

"What in Heaven's name . . . ?" Milla started to rise.

"I'll go," James told his family. "Go ahead and eat. The pizza will get cold."

Though he was as flummoxed as the rest of them by Eliot's outburst, James was secretly glad to have the opportunity to listen to his son's troubles and offer comfort. Knocking respectfully on the door, James didn't wait to be invited in. After all, his son was four years old and too young to merit privacy.

"What's going on, Eliot?"

The boy, who had been lying facedown on his bed, rolled over and sniffed. "I don't want to eat meat anymore, Daddy. Are you gonna make me?"

James hadn't expected this. He was so surprised by Eliot's statement that he had no idea how to reply. "Why don't you want to eat meat? You've always eaten it before."

Clearly relieved that his father planned to calmly listen to his reasons, Eliot sat up a little straighter. "Fay Sunray never eats it. She says it's mean to kill animals for food." His eyes threatened to spill over again. "I don't want cows to die for my Happy Meal."

Oh boy, James thought. He had no idea how to handle the current scenario. *Maybe I should have ordered* Idiot's Guide to Parenting *for the library,* he silently mourned. To stall for time, he said, "Can you tell me about Fay Sunray? I don't know her."

"She's on TV," Eliot said, his expression quickly morphing from despair to adulation. "She sings, and shows us yoga, and explains how to take care of the earth and stuff."

"She's the one you saw perform when you were in Nashville, right?"

Eliot bounced up and down on the bed. "Yeah! We went last night. It was *awesome!*"

"I'm sure it was, son." James looked around the room. "Do you have a Fay Sunray book or movie or something? I'd like to get to know her better."

"Mom bought me the movie, but it hasn't come in the mail yet." Eliot had been greatly cheered by discussing the entertainer. "So I'm not in trouble?"

"No, you're not," James reassured the boy. "Come back to the table. I'll make you a grilled cheese. We're going to talk about this some more, but I'd like to tell your mother what you told me first."

Shifting nervously, Eliot gave James his most plaintive look. "But she might get mad. Do you have to tell her?"

James nodded solemnly. "Yes, I do. Your mother and I are a team, remember? Different houses, same rules."

Eliot stuck out his bottom lip. "I wish we had just *one* house. I wish we could be together all the time."

Surprised by his son's words, James put his hand on Eliot's back and gently pushed him toward the door. "You can never tell what the future will bring, kiddo. You can never tell."

Chapter Three

Chocolate Iced Glazed Doughnut

On Monday morning, James was still reeling over his son's decision to become a vegetarian. At a quarter to nine, he unlocked the library's front doors, rolled the cart of sale books gathered by the Friends of the Library out of the supply closet and into the lobby, flipped on the main light switch, and booted up all twenty computers. While the machines hummed and blipped into life, James made a beeline for the parenting books and began to scan the shelves. He was foolishly hoping to find a quick and easy answer on how to handle Eliot's request.

James selected several books with chapters on children and eating, but after reading several paragraphs on how parents should give their progeny a choice about what they'd like to eat for each meal, he grew frustrated. James planned dinners ahead of time. He didn't wait to ask Eliot what he was in the mood to eat. He just cooked the boy the same food he was eating and served it to him.

He wondered if he'd been handling dinnertime incorrectly. After all, he was fairly new to parenting and had decided to follow the same rules and guidelines established by his parents. The book in his hands clearly discouraged such old-fashioned child-rearing methods.

"You should encourage a child's natural curiosity about foods by providing a colorful plate. Make their food look fun to eat! For example, create a vegetable pizza with a face made of broccoli and mushrooms, or use a cookie cutter to make a heart-shaped tuna and sprout sandwich. Many children prefer their different foods to be separated on their plate. Try serving the meals in a Japanese-style divided box or three colorful bowls," one psychiatrist advised. "If a child still resists sampling something on his plate, you should respect his wishes and take the unappealing food away. Respect and dignity are an integral part of the parent-child relationship."

James chuckled ruefully. "I'd like to read that paragraph to Pop. He'd uncap his pen and write this PhD a letter about how parents are meant to be benevolent dictators and kids are meant to be polite and obedient, not the other way around. I can't even imagine what he'd think about the recommendation to serve Eliot's dinner in a Japanese box."

Jackson had given James some parenting advice a few weeks ago. "You be sure to do the right thing by Eliot," his father had told him. "Don't be too soft. He won't grow into a man if you're a lily-livered father. Draw the line and give him hell when he crosses it. That's what makes a man. Not these long-winded reasons why he can't do this or shouldn't do that. You say, 'because I said so,' and leave it at that. Worked for you and millions of kids before you."

It had taken every ounce of Jackson's willpower to stay silent regarding his grandson's decision to become a vegetarian. He merely shook his head with wonder and gave James a look that said, "You'd better nip this one in the bud."

Jane had also been nonplussed by her son's determination to change his diet. After Eliot was asleep in James's house and she'd driven back to Harrisonburg, she and James had spoken on the phone until late in the night. They decided not to do anything until they'd both done a little research on the nutritional effects of vegetarianism on such a young child.

Tired as he was, James had been unable to fall asleep afterward and so he perused the hypnotherapy brochure until he could practically recite the content verbatim.

"At least I'm prepared for my afternoon session with Harmony," James murmured as he examined another parenting book. "Because I'm not finding an ounce of practical advice on how to handle this situation with Eliot."

At the sound of someone clearing his throat, James pivoted to his left and looked up. Scott Fitzgerald, one half of the amiable twin brother team working at the library, wore a solemn expression.

"Good morning, Professor." Scott spoke in his "business hours" whisper, though no patrons were inside the building.

Francis Fitzgerald stepped around the corner of the stacks and stood next to his tall and lanky brother.

Running a hand through waves of untamed brown curls, he whispered a sedate hello. Silently, the twins exchanged worried glances and then, as if they'd rehearsed the movement in a mirror, each young man reached up to push his tortoiseshell glasses farther up the bridge of his nose. If their expressions hadn't been so mournful, James would have found the synchronized gesture amusing, but he recognized the signs of impending trouble in the body language of his two employees.

"Gentlemen. There appears to be a problem." He smiled at the brothers, letting his fondness for them show through his eyes. "We've tackled some tough challenges before, so let me know what we're dealing with and we'll come up with a plan."

Shoulders slumping slightly in relief, Scott held out a sealed envelope. "This is for you. It's from Mrs. Waxman."

James raised his brows in surprise. He certainly hadn't expected an issue involving his former middle school teacher. Mrs. Waxman was his only part-time employee. She worked weekday evenings and every Saturday, managing the library as efficiently as she'd once run her classroom. A few months ago, James had noticed that Mrs. Waxman was moving slower and looking more fatigued than she had in the past. She was nearly his father's age, and because he was worried that she might be overdoing it by working so many hours, he'd asked her if she'd like to cut back.

"This is my home," she'd responded, waving her arm around the library. "I love this job. No, I do *not* want fewer hours!" That was the end of the matter as far as James was concerned. Mrs. Waxman knew her limits, and since he felt exactly as she did about their work, he'd accepted her answer without argument. But now, as he tore open the letter and read the first few lines, he saw that even though Mrs. Waxman would never retire by choice, circumstance was forcing her to resign.

According to the letter, her younger sister had recently been widowed and was having a difficult time due to complicated health issues. After giving the matter much thought, Mrs. Waxman had decided to move into her sister's condo in Phoenix.

"Therefore, it is with no small measure of regret nor shortage of gratitude that I tender my resignation. This is my official two-week notice," she'd written in her tidy script. "It has been an honor and a joy to be an employee of the Shenandoah County Library and to share many wonderful years with Francis and Scott and with you, James Henry. For those who believe library work is dull, they've never had the privilege of working in your employ. Thank you for making my golden years so fulfilling. I'm very proud that I had the chance to know you as a bright young boy and now, as a fine man, community leader, and father. I wish you the very best."

Mrs. Waxman's signature became blurred as James's eyes grew misty. He blinked hard and inhaled a giant breath in an attempt to gain control of his emotions. Folding the letter into a small rectangle, he avoided looking at the twins until he'd collected himself.

"What's that song our local Brownie troop sings at the end of their monthly meetings?" he asked the brothers. "The one about friendship?"

The twins answered in perfect unison. Without the slightest hint of shyness, their bass voices lifted together in song, "'*Make new friends, but keep the old. One is silver and the other gold.*'"

James nodded. "That's it. Let's look at this as an opportunity to make a new friend while keeping in touch with an old one. I'll put an ad in the paper right away. We have only two weeks to find someone to meet our high standards." The brothers didn't seem overly cheered by the idea of a new employee. "You two know as well as anyone how much I dislike change. But the biggest surprise of my life, finding out that I had a son, was also the most wonderful. Who knows? Your new coworker might just be a sci-fi-loving, video-game-playing bibliophile. She might even be your age. That wouldn't be so horrible, would it?"

As he was already dating Milla's business partner, Willow Singletary, Francis just shrugged. Scott, however, instantly brightened. "You make an excellent point, Professor. We have the chance of a lifetime to pick the perfect coworker. Can you put all the requirements you just mentioned in the classified ad?"

James swatted the younger man with a parenting book and the men moved off to continue with their duties.

After prepping the coffee machine in the break room, James pushed the brew button and went into his office to compose an ad for a part-time librarian.

"Wanted. Part-time library assistant," he spoke to the empty room. He paused, sharpened his pencil, and resumed. "Must be available weeknights from 5 to 8:30 p.m. and Saturdays from 9 a.m. to 6 p.m. High school diploma required. Customer service and computer experience a plus." Placing the eraser nub against his lips, James hesitated again. "How can I say that the suitable candidate should love books, be able to assist even the most aggravating patrons with courtesy, and have the ability to soothe crying toddlers and communicate with surly teenagers? How can I say that each book must be treated like a crown jewel, and though the salary isn't very high, it's worth every meager cent to be able to serve the public as we librarians have served them for hundreds of years? The ad would cost a small fortune if I could ask for what I truly want!" James tossed the pencil down and sighed.

He then picked up the phone and dialed the main number of the *Shenandoah Star Ledger*. "I'd like to place a classified ad," he told the woman on the other end of the line. When she gave him the go-ahead, he dictated the words.

"Have you heard the big news, Professor Henry?" the young woman asked breathlessly after their business was concluded.

"I don't think so," James said.

"Your famous ex-girlfriend is back!"

Frown lines furrowed James's brow. "What do you mean? Has she released another book so soon?" He struggled to recall if the library had received a postcard similar to the one he'd been mailed at his father's address announcing the debut of Murphy Alistair's thrilling mystery, *The Body in the Bakery*.

"Not yet. I think the sequel comes out a week before Christmas, but she can tell you all about her future bestseller in person."

Though James knew he was being baited, he couldn't stop from asking, "Why would that be the case? I thought she spent her time in New York or *on tour*."

"Not anymore! She's come back to Quincy's Gap!" the girl cried. "In fact, she bought the *Star*! She's moved into one of those big old houses off Main Street and is working on her third book. She's a real celebrity! Can you believe it?"

The news hit James like a punch in the gut. It was bad enough that his former flame had written a novel portraying him and the rest of the supper club group as overweight amateur sleuths, bumbling their way through a small-town murder investigation. Whether out of spite for having been dumped by James or for the sake of comic exaggeration, his character was especially inept and spineless. Though he'd refused to read the book himself, he'd heard more than enough about it from friends and library patrons to be angered and embarrassed by his fictionalized persona.

"Professor?" The young woman's voice penetrated his unpleasant thoughts. "Are you there?"

"Please place the ad as soon as possible," James said as if it didn't matter that his ex-girlfriend and local-reporter-turned-celebrity-novelist had returned to stir up more strife. "Thank you and have a nice day."

James hung up and walked over to his window. He let his eyes rest on the brilliant green hue of the spring grass bordering the tidy sidewalk and then lifted his gaze toward the parking lot, as if expecting to see Murphy Alistair sitting out in her car, plotting the next chapter in which she would make certain to depict him as a fat fool once again.

"Why did she come back?" he asked the pink dogwood blossoms at the edge of his vision. "Half the town hates her because of how she described them in her book." On the other hand, he had to admit that many citizens were pleased with Murphy, citing her novel as the reason so many tourists had flocked to Quincy's Gap over the course of the year. In truth, the number of visitors had nearly doubled, bringing much-needed income to small-business owners. Milla had told James several times that she'd made sales to tourists who'd asked her numerous questions about the "real" people described in *The Body in the Bakery*. Of course, Milla always tactfully replied that she hadn't been around when the actual events occurred, so she couldn't attest to the truth of Ms. Alistair's version.

James turned away from the window and strode out to the circulation desk, his fists balled in irritation. The morning had gone from bad to worse. There was Eliot's declaration followed by Mrs. Waxman's unexpected retirement. And now, James had to face the return of his vexing ex-girlfriend.

"Are you okay, Professor?" Francis asked as he passed by with the shelving cart.

A hunger pang awoke in James's belly and he looked at his watch without really seeing the time. "Hold the fort, Francis. I'll be right back."

"Aye, aye, Captain!" Francis saluted and gave the cart a mighty heave toward the open space where patrons lined up to wait for assistance checking out. Scott darted from behind the Information desk and deftly caught the cart. In a continuous and fluid motion he pushed it toward the Children's Corner while giving his brother a thumbs-up behind his back.

James never left the library during the morning. He'd occasionally meet one of the supper club members for lunch at Dolly's Diner or he'd eat a sandwich in the Bronco while running a few quick errands, but he and the twins had a system for handling midmorning coffee breaks. James would brew the coffee around ten o'clock. When the coffee was ready, he'd take a mug to his office to review emails or complete necessary paperwork, such as balancing the budget or placing orders to the library supply company. When he reappeared at the circulation desk, it was Scott's turn in the break room. He'd repair a few hardcovers while bolting down a Twinkie and a cup of milky coffee or a Mountain Dew. Francis would go last.

Using this system, all three began the workday in a relaxed manner. They never fell behind because they all worked during this respite. No one kept track of the length of these sit-down times and no one took advantage of them.

Yet now, James Henry, Head Librarian, was blatantly leaving the building just as the coffeepot finished percolating. Despite the fact that he was tampering with their flawless system, he jumped into the Bronco and drove to the nearest Wawa. Inside, he filled up a takeout cup with French Vanilla–flavored coffee and selected half a dozen doughnuts from the Krispy Kreme display.

"Were these baked this morning?" James asked the clerk.

"Yessir. The truck came in at five thirty. They were still warm enough to fog up the glass after the deliveryman unloaded them."

James pulled the bag to his chest and inhaled the scents of chocolate, cinnamon, powdered sugar, baked dough, and glazed icing. "That's exactly what I wanted to hear."

Inside the privacy of the Bronco, he reached into the bag and pulled out the doughnut on top. He didn't care which of the six varieties his fingers closed around. Any one of them would do. Unhinging his jaw like a python attempting to swallow his oversized prey, James sank his teeth through the layer of chocolate icing and into the soft, cake-like dough. An explosion of sugar coated his teeth, gums, tongue, and the roof of his mouth. For a moment, he was completely lost in the overwhelming power of the sensation. It was heavenly.

It was, he thought, a total high.

It took all of forty-five seconds for James to consume the doughnut. He then licked his fingers, took a sip of coffee, and leaned back against the seat with a sigh of contentment.

"I needed that," he murmured, noting how much of his anxiety had drained away. He felt calmer and more optimistic. Turning on the engine, James pulled out of the Wawa parking lot and headed back to Quincy's Gap. He breezed through the lobby doors as if it was completely normal for him to have left work for a doughnut run. Still, when James raised the white and green Krispy Kreme bag in the air so that Francis could see it over the head of the elderly patron he was assisting, the young man's eyes sparkled with delight.

James placed the bag in the center of the round table in the break room, removed a blueberry cake doughnut from the bag, and placed it on his desk blotter for later. Returning to aid the patron waiting at circulation, James looked over his shoulder and smiled as the Fitzgerald brothers circled the pastry bag like sharks, bickering good-naturedly over which one to try first.

"We'll cut them in half, bro," Scott suggested. "That way we get to sample every flavor."

"Totally!" Francis happily agreed. "Do you think this will become a new tradition? The Monday morning sugar rush?"

After a pause in which James imagined his employee's mouth was crammed with a glazed cruller, Scott said, "Nope. The professor is being hypnotized after work today, remember? This might be the last time we'll walk into this break room and find one of Milla's cakes, Mrs. Waxman's pies, or Mrs. Goodbee's brownies."

Francis groaned. "That would be a total tragedy for us, bro." He sighed. "Well, at least we have Willow's chocolates to eat at night."

"The perfect gaming food!" The brothers exchanged high fives while James loaded the last two books in the Harry Potter series into a Friends of the Library canvas tote bag.

He smiled at his patron. "You're going to enjoy these, Mrs. Gibb."

"Oh, I *know* I will!" The old woman cackled. "I saw the boy who played the movie Harry Potter onstage in England." She lowered her voice to a conspiratorial whisper. "What a play! That boy was as naked as the day he was born! Cute little tush on him too." She patted her tote bag. "It's gonna be real hard to picture him back in the old Hogwart's robes again, but I'll do my best!"

Doing his best to hide a grin, James set to work on the hold and transfer requests until Scott reappeared from the break room. His upper lip was lined with chocolate frosting and a sprinkling of powdered sugar covered the front of his navy polo shirt.

"I don't know how you're going to live without it, Professor. Sugar, I mean. The best-tasting food is loaded with sugar or salt. Your giving that up would be like Francis and me being hypnotized to stop loving video games."

James indicated his protruding belly. "Video games aren't bad for your health the way sugar is. Being a sedentary gamer is, but you boys get plenty of exercise. I need to do this so I can live a fuller life with my son."

Scott nodded. "For what it's worth, Francis and I think it's really cool of you to give this alternative treatment a shot." He fell silent for a moment and then began brushing the flecks of sugar from his shirt. "And you've given me something to think about. Maybe I'm not living a full life either. Francis has been spending more and more time with Willow and they're super happy together. I think they might be the real deal. But me? I waste so many hours trying to complete missions with a bunch of online friends I've never met face-to-face."

"It's a hobby. I don't see any harm in that," said James kindly.

"But life's about making connections," Scott continued. "For example, there's this person I team up with every night. She even lives around here somewhere, because her User ID is Shenandoah Shutterfly. For an entire year we've messaged each other about all kinds of stuff, but I don't even know her name."

James shrugged. "Can't you just ask?"

Scott shook his head. "That would be poor gaming etiquette, Professor. We're all on there pretending to be brawny barbarians or powerful mages. For example, I've never told anyone that I'm a librarian. I need to stay in character. When I'm playing, I become Fitz the Fierce!" He brandished his right arm as though it held a sword.

"Excuse me, Fitz the Fierce," a middle-aged man carrying a thumb drive interrupted. "Could you help me with the computer? I keep trying to open a file and the danged thing won't let me."

Smiling, Scott thrust out his arm again. "Lead the way, sir. No stubborn Word doc or paltry PDF can withstand the lightning-quick fingers of Fritz the Fierce!"

Between the chocolate-glazed Krispy Kreme and Scott's playacting, James discovered that his bad mood had been wiped away like the powdered sugar from his employee's shirt.

• • •

James opened the blue front door of A Better State of Mind's office at half past five that afternoon. He was too nervous to read the selection of magazines stacked on the end table, so he just sat on the sofa and stared at the bowl of purple crocuses on the credenza near the door.

Skye appeared a few minutes later, carrying a CD in her hand. "Hello, Mr. Henry. Would you like to settle up before your session begins?"

"Sure." James pulled out his wallet and handed Skye a credit card. "Is my friend Bennett in there now?"

"No. He switched appointments with Ms. Perez. She and Harmony just finished. After I label your friend's nighttime CD, it'll be your turn." She smiled in encouragement.

"I guess you hear lots of interesting things working here," James said as Skye ran his credit card.

She swiveled abruptly in her chair, her eyes stormy. "I don't listen in on Harmony's sessions, Mr. Henry. They're strictly confidential."

"Of course! I didn't mean to imply . . ." He trailed off, feeling like an idiot. He was relieved to hear the sound of Lindy's voice. She called out "thank you" from farther down the hall. When she entered the reception room, she seemed calm and slightly groggy.

"How was it?" he whispered to her.

"Great." Lindy's voice was quiet and relaxed. "I feel like I had a long nap, but I heard every word Harmony said." She touched James on the arm. "You're going to be just fine."

Lindy collected her CD from Skye, and James noticed that his friend continued to speak in a slow, sleepy voice, as if her tongue could not move any faster.

James would have liked to ask Lindy more questions, but Harmony glided down the hall. She greeted James and asked him to follow her. After giving Lindy a nervous wave, he trailed behind Harmony and entered a dimly lit room. As his eyes adjusted, he noticed that a large indigo sofa and a beige recliner took up most of the space. Watercolors of lush gardens hung in a set of three above the sofa, and a pair of midnight blue curtains covered the room's large picture window.

Expecting he'd be lying on the sofa, James was just about to stretch out when Harmony gestured toward the recliner. "Clients are usually most comfortable sitting here."

As soon as James sat down, he began to relax. He pushed against the chair back and the footrest gently popped up. Harmony reached into a nearby cabinet and removed a cotton throw. She handed it to James. "I keep it a little chilly in here. If you're under a blanket, it helps your body think that it's rest time."

The blanket smelled of lavender and laundry detergent. James spread it over his legs and wriggled farther into the chair's yielding cushion. Harmony switched on her CD player and the sounds of instruments and wind chimes piped through the speakers. It wasn't exactly music, as there wasn't a clear melody, but the noises were very tranquil. James recognized the sounds of flutes, running water, and occasionally the chirping of birds and the gentle clanging of a small metal gong. The overall effect was the feeling of being at repose in some isolated Japanese garden.

"Let's begin by taking several deep breaths," Harmony said. "Breathe in through the nose and out the mouth. One. That's good. Two. Annnnd, three." She smiled as though James had accomplished a great feat. "Well done. Now, if you feel comfortable, go ahead and close your eyes."

James was delighted to oblige. Suddenly, the idea of spending an hour in the recliner, listening to the soothing music and Harmony's melodious voice, became very appealing.

"I'd like you to allow your body to become *very* heavy," Harmony quietly directed. "Your muscles are going to relax. Your body doesn't have to work anymore. Imagine that you're on a lounge chair by a pool. Or by the ocean. There is a gentle breeze blowing across your face and you feel very warm and *very* relaxed."

Snuggled in his blanket, James did feel warm. He gave his shoulders leave to sink farther into the chair cushion.

"Now imagine a current of warm air flowing down your body starting with the top of your head. As it moves down your face, to your neck and your shoulders, you can feel any tension, any stresses or worries that you might have walked in with today, start to melt away."

For a moment, his concerns about Eliot, finding a replacement for Mrs. Waxman, and Murphy's return flitted through his mind, but James turned from those thoughts and centered his attention on the vision of a sparkling ocean lined by a pristine white beach and a few stands of palm trees.

"A warm, gentle flow of air now moves down your arms and down each and every finger. It flows across your chest, over your stomach, over your lower back and your hips, and down each leg. As it moves, you feel more and more *relaxed*, while your mind stays focused on the sound of my voice." She inhaled deeply. "And now, as that air moves over your calves and your feet, let any anxiety flow out with it through your toes. Let your body rest. It feels *very* heavy in the chair, but your mind is very clear. It is actually at a heightened state of awareness."

It was true. James felt like he'd never possessed such mental focus before. He was certain that, if asked, he could suddenly solve complex mathematical algorithms or balance the library budget without a calculator. He believed he could also recite all the Shakespearean soliloquies he'd made his students memorize when he'd been a college professor.

"Take your mind to that pool," Harmony continued in her lulling voice. "There's a set of steps leading down into the pool. The water is very warm and inviting and there's a floating lounge chair waiting for you. Try to picture this peaceful place in your mind. Nod if you can see it."

James nodded.

"Okay, you're going to walk down those steps slowly, one at a time, as I count backward from ten. With every step, your body is going to become *more* and *more* relaxed. Ten . . . nine . . . eight . . . seven . . . six . . . five . . . four . . . three . . . two . . . one. You can rest on that float now, James."

He could practically hear the water lapping at the side of the pool. The sun bathed him with its gentle, nourishing rays and a breeze cooled his heated skin. It was paradise.

"James." Harmony's voice drifted to him across the pool. "I want you to ask your mind to give up this craving for sugar. I want you to pretend that your mind looks like the inside of a control center. I want you to climb up a ladder into the middle of that control center."

Reluctantly, James switched his visual away from the pool and focused on a wooden ladder.

"You're going to climb up into a room. It's filled with lots and lots of lights. There are lights of every color and there are switches all around you. Walk around your brain's control center and observe it carefully."

Harmony was right. There were buttons and levers and switches. Rows of bare bulbs dangled from the ceiling and the whir of machinery filled the air. Despite the sense of endless industry, the room was neat and tidy.

"Look at the switch closest to you," Harmony intoned. "Put both hands on the switch. This is the machine that sends your brain a message that you want to eat sugar. You're going to turn it off, James. And as you do so, tell your brain that you don't want to crave sugar anymore. You're turning that craving off for good right now. Go ahead, James."

Reaching both hands forward, James gripped the metal lever and pushed it down with all his might. He whispered the orders Harmony had given him to his brain and felt a surge of accomplishment rush through him as he urged his mind to believe what it was being told.

Next, Harmony directed him to return to the pool. She repeated over and over that he no longer needed sugar, that he was free of his addiction to the substance, and that he'd been released from his craving. Eventually, she led him back up the stairs from the enticing water and asked him to open his eyes.

"That was amazing!" he croaked. "I saw everything as if I actually experienced it! The pool, the float, the control center. But the session was so brief. Are you sure it can work that rapidly?"

Harmony laughed lightly. "Most people lose all sense of time when they're in a highly relaxed state. How long do you think we've been in here?"

James eased himself upward and shrugged. "Twenty minutes?"

"Try fifty minutes," she said with a smile.

"Wow," he replied in surprise. "So what happens next?"

"You must listen to your CD every night." She held his gaze. "The reinforcement is very important, James. Please don't skip any nights, especially since we've had only one session together. When I see you next Monday, we'll see how things are coming along."

James collected his CD from Skye and walked to his Bronco. At home, he ate a healthy meal of roasted chicken breast, green beans, and brown rice. When he opened up the freezer to get some ice cubes for his diet Dr. Pepper, he glanced at the pint of Caramel Crunch ice cream and waited for the desire to compel him to reach for the carton.

"I really don't feel like anything sweet," he whispered in astonishment. He then dug out a package of Eliot's snack-sized Oreos, a bag of chocolate-chip morsels, a tin of candied pecans, and a Charleston Chew that he kept hidden in the freezer for an emergency. He examined each of the goodies for several moments, but nothing happened. He didn't want any of them.

Staring at the food, James shook his head in disbelief. For the second time that evening, he whispered "wow" in complete and utter astonishment.

Chapter Four

Chickpea Burger

The rest of the workweek passed quickly for James. Between the high school students researching topics for their senior projects and the flood of incoming applications for the part-time librarian position, time zipped by.

On Thursday, just as James was about to duck into his office to review the paperwork on a fresh batch of candidates, a middle-aged woman with a very long ponytail of blond hair going to gray walked up to the circulation desk. She had several rolled posters tucked under her right arm.

"I was wondering if you could hang this in the lobby right away?" Her tone was friendly but determined. "The Wellness Village is sponsoring a Fresh Food Festival this weekend. I know it's late to be promoting the event, but we don't have much of an advertising budget and we're hoping to attract people through word of mouth."

James reached for the poster. "May I?"

The woman unfurled one and laid it on the counter. The central graphic showed a picnic basket overflowing with fruits, vegetables, and a loaf of bread. Each corner was embellished with drawings of a farmer's life. One showed him plowing his field, another featured him selling wares at an outdoor market, the third was a close-up of him handing a peach to a little boy, and the final picture depicted him sharing a meal with his family. James thought the farmer bore a close resemblance to Santa Claus. Though the red suit had been replaced by denim overalls and a straw hat, the man had the same merry face and laughing eyes. In addition to the date, time, and location of the event, a stream of text ran around the perimeter of the poster. It read, *Save Our Farms! Buy Fresh! Buy Local!*

James couldn't agree more. Having lived in the Shenandoah Valley most of his life, he rubbed shoulders with members of the agricultural community every day. He believed there were few individuals who worked harder or with more dedication than the farmers he'd come to know in his years as head librarian.

"I'd be glad to hang this for you. In fact, if you have any extras I can promise that they'll be prominently displayed in the windows of Quincy's Whimsies and the Yuppie Puppy. Both of those proprietors support the farming community. As do I."

"Thank you!" The woman beamed at him. "My name's Roslyn Rhodes, by the way. I'm an herbal healer. I have an office in the Wellness Village." She handed him a business card. Under her name were the words *Holistic Medicine* and the slogan *Let Nature Heal You.* Her phone numbers, address, and hours were also listed. James noticed that Roslyn's Health House was right down the path from Harmony's.

For some reason, James wanted to show how open-minded he was, so he informed Roslyn that he'd recently received a hypno-therapy treatment from her neighbor at A Better State of Mind.

"Good for you!" Roslyn's praise was genuine. "I've heard lots of positive feedback about Harmony's sessions. She's a lovely person and has been an incredible help putting this festival together." She laughed. "Us go-with-the-flow types aren't always the best at organization. Ask me about any herb on the face of this green earth and I can tell you about its properties, but ask me where my checkbook is and I'm at a total loss!"

They continued to exchange small talk while James hung the poster. "It says here that we can buy lunch at the festival. My son has recently become a vegetarian. Will there be something else for him to eat besides farm stand fruits and vegetables?"

Roslyn nodded in excitement. "Oh, yes! There will be dozens of wonderful dishes to choose from. Trust me, I've been a vegan for fifteen years and I'm already daydreaming about the tasty things I'll be sampling on Saturday. Your whole family is in for a treat. Come hungry, my friend."

After Roslyn left, the Fitzgerald twins wandered into the lobby to examine the poster. The two brothers consumed more food than James deemed humanly possible for individuals with such lean frames, and the slightest reference to anything edible caused a glimmer to appear in their hazel eyes.

"A food festival! Sweet!" Francis said, trying to peer around Scott's shoulder. "What kind? Greek? Italian? Lebanese? Barbeque?"

"Locally grown," Scott answered. "You know what *that* means?"

The brothers exchanged hungry grins and in perfect unison shouted, "Pie!"

Francis elbowed his brother away from the bulletin board and gazed at the poster with a dreamy expression. "Apple Brown Betty, peach crisp, pear crumble."

"Blueberry cream cheese, lemon meringue, chocolate peanut butter pie!" Scott finished the list and then turned to James. "Sorry, Professor. We didn't mean to torture you."

James gave a lighthearted shrug. "Believe it or not, I'm not drooling onto my tie. Three nights of listening to my hypnotherapy CD has really helped me control my sugar cravings."

"That's good, Professor," Francis said. "Because that's the tie we gave you for Boss's Day last year and it's dry-clean only."

Looking down, James picked up the end of his tie and gave it a shake. "I know. It's my all-time favorite. I became a librarian hoping that one day I could wear a garment that says Don't Make Me Shush You."

Scott poked his brother in the side. "*I* wanted to get you the Librarian Drinking League tie, but Francis said Mrs. Waxman wouldn't approve."

"Probably not," James agreed with a laugh. "I'd better get back in there and look over those applications. So far, no one's worthy of licking Mrs. Waxman's boots, let alone filling them."

As James reviewed applications from college students in search of an easy summer job, retirees who wanted a permanent part-time position but didn't want to work the hours the position required, and a young mother who wanted to bring her three-month-old infant to work, he began to despair.

Finally, near the bottom of the stack, James came across a very promising application. A graduate student from UVA who had classes every weekday morning was looking for a job with evening and weekend hours. The young man was working toward a master's in English Literature and was not only well read, but also mentioned an interest in pursuing a career in public service. Feeling optimistic, James was just reaching for the phone to schedule an interview when his gaze fell on the application line reading *Wage Sought.*

The young man had written that he needed to make a minimum of twenty-five dollars an hour to cover his cost of living.

Spluttering, James slammed the phone back into the cradle. "Where are you living? In a mansion? With a butler and a personal chef? The nerve!"

He was just warming up to his indignation when the phone rang. It was Jane calling to assure him that Eliot's pediatrician said that their son could receive all the nutrition he needed from a balanced vegetarian diet.

"As long as he's eating plenty of protein, taking his vitamins, and not subsisting on potato chips and fruit roll-ups, he'll be fine." James heard a hesitation in her voice. "The doctor was also of the opinion that this was most likely a phase. Apparently, it's quite common for kids to experience feelings of guilt about eating animals at some point in their development."

"What do we do?" James asked. "Encourage him to be a vegetarian or try to convince him that he doesn't need to feel guilty?"

"I think we should support his decision, but we need to sit down with him this weekend and explain animal husbandry a bit. I want him to realize that raising livestock or eating meat doesn't make a person bad."

An idea formed in James's mind. "Why don't we let him talk to a farmer? There's a food festival in town this weekend and a bunch of local food producers have been invited to sell their products to the public. After we give Eliot his Livestock 101 talk, we can bring him to the fair."

"Sounds good to me," Jane said. "But, James, we have to be honest with him. You and I both know that animals raised for food consumption don't always have decent lives or humane deaths. I know he's only four, but I don't want to deceive him."

James felt uneasy over the direction the conversation was headed. "We're not going to tell him baldfaced lies, but I'm not going to go into detail about slaughterhouse practices either. He's too young for graphic detail. I think we should focus on the message he got from this Fay Sunray person. I'll search around on the Internet and see if someone posted a recording of her Nashville performance. She started this whole thing, so I want to know *exactly* what she said that upset Eliot so much."

"I wish my parents could remember. Of all the times for me to have gone to the restroom!" Jane lamented. "I feel like I've lost my mind since he made his announcement. I wouldn't be so worried if my friends at work hadn't freaked me out by recommending links to a dozen parenting websites." She grew quiet for a moment. "I've never second-guessed my maternal instincts until now. I just don't want to emotionally scar this kid by mishandling this situation."

Though James knew precisely how Jane felt, he suspected they were both overreacting. "First of all, we won't be perfect parents. That's okay. Eliot doesn't need perfection. He needs the love and guidance you've given him since birth. Secondly, I've been perusing several parenting books in my spare time. If these people had their way, the three of us would be in therapy until Eliot has a family of his own! Don't buy into the insanity. Stick to your instincts — you and I will figure out what's best for our son."

"There's something else you should know," Jane added reluctantly. "Eliot's been having nightmares about dead animals. Someone played a really cruel prank on us before we left for Nashville and it's affected him more than I'd realized."

James brushed aside the pile of job applications and sat forward in his chair. "What kind of prank?"

Though Jane was clearly reluctant to speak of it, she finally began to talk. "Someone put a dead robin in our mailbox. It was probably a disgruntled student. You remember what it was like during midterm exams. Between all the overnight cram sessions and cans of Red Bull, the kids can lose their heads. Didn't a freshman vandalize your car with shaving cream?"

Recalling the words *Professor Puff Sucks!* written across his windshield as if it had happened yesterday, James muttered something about entitled youth and told Jane to go on.

"Unfortunately, Eliot was expecting his wildlife magazine, so he opened the mailbox," Jane continued. "The bird was way in the back, but when he pulled out the magazine, the body fell right on his chest. I've never heard such a scream."

James shook his head in dismay. "Poor little guy. That would have spooked anyone."

"I know, but after Fay Sunray's comments about animals, whatever they were, Eliot now has this illogical fear that they'll come after him if he eats them." She made a growling noise. "You know, if I had a backstage pass to the next Fay Sunray show I'd choke her with her own guitar strings. Child entertainers should leave their personal platforms out of their performances. I don't care how noble the cause!"

The parents discussed their son's meal selections for the weekend and said their goodbyes. James stuck the sheaf of job applications into a folder, dropped it into his desk drawer, and sighed.

Change is never easy, he thought.

• • •

That night, he had his own frightening dream about birds. These weren't robins like the red and blue body Eliot had found in the mailbox, but black crows with malicious eyes and sharp beaks. A mass of them congregated on a leafless tree in the front yard and suddenly flew toward James — an ominous cloud of shadows. Their caws grew louder and more aggressive as they raced toward him through the night sky. James's dream self darted inside his house and slammed the door. Terrified, he ran to his bedroom, hoping to draw the curtains before the crows could reach his window. But just as his fingers closed on the cotton drapes, the impact of dozens of beaks smashing into the glass made him cry out in fear.

James bolted awake in his bed, his heart pounding. He glanced nervously at the window, exhaling in relief as he realized that the rapping on the glass was caused by raindrops. He wasn't being attacked by a murder of hostile crows.

The spring storm persisted for most of Friday, but by Saturday morning, the sun was bathing the Shenandoah Valley in warmth. The flowers James had planted the week before had produced new buds, inviting the attention of honeybees, monarch butterflies, and hummingbirds. Squirrels chattered at him from the dogwood tree while he swept the front walk and raked stray leaves and pine needles from the lush grass.

After his outdoor chores were done, James took a shower and settled at his computer with a large glass of iced tea. After searching for Fay Sunray on YouTube, he clicked on a video called

"We Love Our Earth," and sat back to watch. Fay had golden hair styled in pigtail braids and big, bright blue eyes. She was in her late twenties, but sang with a very high and girlish voice. She wore a navy dress with a sunflower design and a pair of green galoshes. As she sang about recycling and water conservation, a group of flower puppets with smiling faces provided background vocals.

"Nothing offensive there," James mumbled. "She's pretty and sweet. The little boys probably all have crushes on her." He scrolled farther down the page. "I need to find a link to that Nashville show."

After watching several videos, James heard nothing untoward in the verses or in the silly knock-knock jokes her sidekick, Dew Drop, liked to tell.

Finally, he clicked on a video for the song "Animals Are Our Friends (Nashville Version)" and listened closely as people dressed in a variety of farm animal costumes sang along with Fay. The song was clearly one of the children's favorites, and whenever the entertainer pointed the microphone at the audience, the kids shouted the appropriate animal noises at the top of their lungs. As another chorus reached a crescendo, the flower puppets James had seen on previous clips popped up onstage.

"This has to be the finale." James tapped the mouse impatiently. He preferred shows like *Sesame Street* or Mr. Rogers and wished Eliot could watch old episodes of *Captain Kangaroo* or the *Muppet Show* instead of the bizarre cartoons he enjoyed. Fay Sunray was certainly a welcome throwback to the good old days of television, especially when compared to shows like *SpongeBob* or the *Teenage Mutant Ninja Turtles.*

As James waited, the computer screen filled with blinking lights. Rainbow-hued confetti rained down on the Nashville stage. The animals and flowers bowed. Most of them waved and wiggled off stage to a roar of applause. However, the actors dressed in the cow, chicken, and pig costumes remained. Fay carefully laid her guitar on her stool and put an arm around the cow and the pig. The chicken snuggled up to her legs and gazed up at her with adoration.

"And remember, boys and girls," she spoke melodically into her headset microphone. "Animals are our friends. We need to protect them. I don't eat meat, because *I don't eat my friends*. I am proud to be a ve-ge-ta-ri-an." Fay sang the word as she squeezed the cow, which hugged her fiercely in return while the pig nodded in agreement. "Good night, children! Thank you for coming and remember to be kind to our planet! It's the only one we have!"

The video clip ended and James shook his head in disgust. '"I don't eat my friends!' What kind of thing is that to say to a bunch of little kids? No wonder this woman influenced Eliot. He probably idolizes her and wouldn't want to disappoint her."

For the most part, James agreed with Fay's pro-environmental messages, even though he was certain that kids between three and six years old had no idea what she meant by "eco-friendly measures." He'd have no issue with the entertainer had she stuck to her usual montage, but he was aggrieved by how she chose to close her Nashville show. He was sorely tempted to write her a letter expressing his disapproval.

He'd just begun composing an opening line in his mind when Jane and Eliot arrived.

"We had chocolate chip pancakes for breakfast! At my favorite truck stop!" Eliot shouted as he jumped into his father's open arms. "With a strawberry mouth and bananas for eyes. And guess what the nose was?"

James scrunched up his face and pretended to give the matter serious consideration. "A grape?"

"Nope!" Eliot shouted, delighted to have stumped his father. "A cherry! Like the ones they put in Shirley Temples."

"Your mom is awfully good to you, buddy." James winked at Jane over Eliot's head. "Do you think you'll be hungry enough for lunch at the food festival?"

Eliot nodded. "Will there be cotton candy?"

Jane ruffled Eliot's hair. "Not for you, young man. You had plenty of sugar at breakfast. I'm sure there'll be some delicious and healthy food for you to eat." She took James by the arm. "I only had a bowl of oatmeal, so let's head downtown. We could walk around for a bit and then grab some lunch. I could eat a hor—" She stopped herself just in time. "A humongous sandwich!"

The three of them climbed into the Bronco and drove south into town. James told Jane about the lack of suitable candidates for the part-time library position while she shared her concern about the disrespectful attitude that some of her students had displayed during the final marking period. The former spouses reminisced on how work ethics and family values were the norms of their childhoods while Eliot amused himself by counting all the red cars he could spot.

As they approached the pink and purple cottages of the Wellness Village, James could see that the food festival had drawn a huge crowd.

"I don't think we're going to find a parking space close by," James informed Jane. "We'll find a spot behind the ABC Store. Danny won't mind, especially if I pick up some Cutty Sark for my father before we leave."

James wasn't the only one with that idea. A mix of pickup trucks and hybrid sedans filled up most of the lot. After running in to the liquor store to make a purchase, James lifted Eliot onto his shoulders, cherishing the burden of his son's weight. Jane took a picture of them with her cell phone before the threesome jogged across the street.

The courtyard of the Wellness Village was covered by a large tent. Enticing aromas drifted into the parking lot. Here, vendors had set up tables to display information on their health-conscious businesses or to sell wares like reusable shopping bags, beaded jewelry, yoga equipment, or inspirational music CDs. Skye waved at him from the Better State of Mind table.

In the cool shade of the tent, James and Jane studied the menus of the food vendors and debated over what to have for lunch.

"All the food here is good for vegetarians," Jane told Eliot. "How does a chickpea burger and sliced peaches sound?"

Eliot curled his lip a little. "A pea burger? That doesn't sound very good."

Though James silently agreed, he decided that Eliot needed to know that he couldn't subsist on French fries, pasta, and pizza as a non–meat eater. "Son, being a vegetarian will mean eating lots of fruits and vegetables."

"I know," said Eliot quite seriously. "Are you going to get one, Daddy?"

Stepping closer to the sizzling patties, James decided that they smelled quite good. "I am. We'll take three chickpea burgers," he informed the vendor.

"With cheese?" the man asked.

James told the man yes and waited for the burgers while Jane took Eliot to the neighboring booth to order fruit smoothies made from locally grown produce.

The family sat at a picnic table and James made several trips to the condiment counter to collect packets of ketchup, mustard, relish, and salt. After grabbing a few napkins and three straws, he picked up his chickpea burger and took a large bite, knowing Eliot was watching for any adverse reaction. But the burger was very tasty.

"Yum!" James declared. "Go ahead, buddy. You'll like it."

Eliot took a tentative nibble. He chewed several times and then reached into his mouth with his thumb and index finger and pulled something out. "What's this?" he inquired.

"Eliot, don't take food out of your mouth," Jane reprimanded and then peered at the object on his plate. "That's a piece of tomato."

"Oh." Eliot examined the interior of his burger. "There's corn in here too." He squirted on another dollop of ketchup. "It doesn't taste like McDonald's."

The three of them ate their lunches and watched the crowd. James spotted Roslyn Rhodes working her way through a knot of people. She looked utterly frazzled. Her long hair was tangled, her face was shining with perspiration, and her eyes darted wildly around.

"That's the woman who came to the library with the event posters," James told Jane.

Jane followed his gaze. "She looks a little freaked out."

In a few minutes, the reason behind her anxiety became clear. A group of grim-faced farmers barreled past, clearly following in Roslyn's wake. Concerned that Roslyn might need assistance, James darted after them.

Just outside the tent, James found Roslyn, Harmony, Skye, and two men standing on one side of a folding table while five farmers shouted at them from the other side.

"We're locals too!" one of them hollered with a clenched fist. "You kept us out because we're livestock farmers!"

A second one slammed his hand on the table. "Your fruit-loopy friends are gonna make us lose business! It's bad enough you didn't invite us to this damned fair, but now you're tryin' to ruin our livelihood too!"

Roslyn held out her hands in supplication. "I did *not* invite those demonstrators, and I don't have the authority to make them leave! They're on public property."

The man standing next to Harmony put his arm around her in a protective gesture. James assumed he was her husband. "Gentlemen, the Wellness Village merchants decided to promote vegan and vegetarian lifestyles during this festival," he said with admirable calm. "It was their prerogative to make that call. None of the organizers are speaking against your farms, so please stop yelling at us."

The young man next to Skye, who wore a tie-dye Grateful Dead shirt, frayed denim shorts, and an armful of beaded hemp bracelets, flicked a sandy-colored dreadlock off his shoulder and said, "Yeah. Chill out, dudes."

Skye smiled at him and took his hand.

Temporarily derailed, one of the farmers glanced around as if looking for support from members of the public. He called out someone's name and a man in a purple polo shirt and tan chinos halted mid-stride and turned to face them. James recognized him. It was Ned Woodman, one of the town councilmen.

Seeing the standoff in progress, Ned continued moving as though he hadn't heard his name. More enraged than ever, the farmers hurried after him, and before James could offer his assistance to either group, the situation had been diffused. At least for the moment.

"Everything okay?" James asked, stepping up to the table.

Roslyn sank into a metal chair "For now, but I'm afraid those men are too upset to behave rationally. The picketers out front . . . they really taunted those men."

James didn't like the sound of that. "Who are they? Animal rights demonstrators?"

Harmony nodded. "Yes. They often congregate at fairs like ours because they're able to recruit volunteers and solicit donations from a receptive public. But it's a shame today couldn't have been more peaceful." To change the subject, she introduced her husband, Mike, and pointed at the young man standing next to Skye. "And this is Skye's boyfriend, Lennon Snyder. He's in charge of maintenance here at the Village."

James shook hands with the men before focusing on Roslyn once again. "I'm going to call my friend. She's a sheriff's deputy and will know how to restore peace and order."

Roslyn and Harmony readily agreed to the suggestion and James went off to find a quiet corner behind a budding crepe myrtle tree. He dialed Lucy's number and was relieved when she answered on the first ring.

"I'm on my way!" she exclaimed when he finished relaying his concerns. "I have Lindy with me and I'm not in uniform. We'd planned on a girls' day out, but I do have my badge and my gun, so I can handle the situation. Just hold the fort until I get there." Returning to the picnic table where Jane and Eliot waited, James hastily told his ex-wife what was going on.

"We didn't see any protestors on the way in," she said, perplexed.

James put a hand on his son's shoulder. "They're here now, and I think you two should stay put until I check things out."

Jane nodded. "No problem. We'll work on the 'Healthy Kids' activity book the smoothie lady gave us."

Thankful for her composure, James marched toward the entrance. The closer he got to the large mounted map of the Wellness Village, the more the sounds of loud chanting assaulted his ears. When the protestors came into view, James was unsurprised to find Gillian among them. She was busily writing a check while Bennett shifted uncomfortably beside her.

James took a brief glance at the posters being brandished by the picketers. They read "Meat Is Murder," "Be Human, Not Inhumane," "Help Animals. Don't Be One," and "Live and Let Live."

"Animals have souls too!" a young woman screamed, her face red with exertion. "Dominion does not mean domination!" She pointed a finger at an old man trying to scuttle past her toward the parking lot.

None of the other demonstrators seemed to possess this woman's fervor. With brown spiky hair and ears pierced by rows of silver hoops in ascending sizes, she appeared to be the group's leader. James took in her baggy beige dress and gaunt arms before his gaze was drawn to her poster. It portrayed a headless chicken spouting blood from its neck as it ran around in an aimless, pathetic circle.

James felt anger rise within him. "That's a bit graphic for little kids to look at, don't you think?" he asked the woman when she paused for breath.

Her dark eyes crackled with intensity. "And what about the *graphic murders* humans commit every second? Of helpless animals! It happens right here in Shenandoah County!"

Before James could reply, a cluster of teenage boys materialized in front of the protestors. They carried take-out bags from Dolly's Diner and wore smug grins. Sitting on the ground, they unwrapped bacon double cheeseburgers with deliberate slowness, waved the food around, and shouted, "Carnivores rock! Carnivores rock!" before sinking their teeth into the thick burgers.

Spurred on by the teenagers, other members of the community began to trade insults with the protestors. Both sides were egged on by the female leader. She got right in people's faces, shouting and spitting as she described slaughterhouse practices in very explicit terms. At one point, a pregnant woman who'd paused to gawk suddenly dashed off, her hand on her swelled stomach. Concerned, James followed her and saw her doubled over behind the bushes lining the parking lot. Afterward, she straightened, wiped her mouth with a tissue, and fled.

Bennett, who'd appeared from a knot of people to join James as he checked on the pregnant woman, shook his head in dismay. "I hope she's all right."

"Where's Lucy?" James looked around for his friend's Jeep.

"I don't know, but she needs to fire a gun in the air when she gets here." Bennett looked miserable. "Man, I know where these folks are coming from, but this is not the way to change things. How am I going to get Gillian out of here before folks start throwing punches?"

James didn't have an answer. Gillian was as passionate about animal rights as the rest of the demonstrators, but she preferred to champion the cause in a calm and quiet manner.

At that moment, James saw Ned Woodman heading for the exit. He looked as frantic as Roslyn had earlier, but James stepped in the councilman's path.

Pointing at the increasingly hostile throng, he said, "Ned! Can you disperse these people? Don't protestors need some sort of a permit? This is going to get out of hand if someone in a position of authority doesn't act quickly!"

Ned shot a panicked look over his shoulder. He seemed fearful. Not of the protestors, but of something or someone near the main tent. Suddenly, James's attention was drawn by the wail of a siren. Deputy Keith Donovan pulled his sedan within inches of the demonstrators and jumped out of the car, his face set in a fierce scowl. When James turned to speak to Ned again, he saw only a glimpse of purple shirt as the councilman rushed back toward the heart of the Village.

Lucy parked her Jeep right behind the surly deputy, and though Donovan strutted up to the protestors and began to order them around in his typical mulish manner, Lucy and Lindy were able to gently pull the female leader aside and speak to her. Donovan, who'd become obsessed with weightlifting over the past few months, now had such a thick neck that he looked more like a redheaded bulldog than ever. He had long been Lucy's nemesis, and the supper club members did their best to avoid him whenever possible.

While Donovan mildly scolded the burger-eating teenagers, James lured Gillian away from the protestors. He captured her attention by telling her about Eliot's recent conversion to vegetarianism.

"What an honorable decision to make at such a tender age!" Gillian was delighted. "Where is he? I'd love to congratulate him and offer *my full* support."

Bennett shot James a grateful look as the three friends headed back into the Village and rejoined Jane and Eliot at the picnic table. Bennett and Gillian had barely said their hellos when Eliot tugged on James's hand. "Daddy! I need to go to the bathroom."

James noted that his son was doing little hops from side to side. "It was a pretty big smoothie, wasn't it? Come on, we'll ask Harmony if we can use the restroom in her office. You and I aren't going near those port-a-potties by the entrance."

The Better State of Mind booth was unmanned, but Roslyn was more than happy to lend James the keys to her office. James and Eliot trotted to her blue door. As it turned out, they didn't need the keys. The door was unlocked and slightly ajar.

"Hello?" James called out. The office was silent. "I guess Roslyn really *is* absentminded."

He glanced around a reception area similar to Harmony's. Judging by the number of closed doors off the hallway, Roslyn's office unit contained a few more rooms than the hypnotherapist's. Luckily, the restroom was clearly marked. James opened the door and turned the lights on for his son.

"I can go by myself," Eliot told his father.

Despite his son's declaration, James listened at the door as Eliot conducted his business and washed his hands. When he didn't come back out after turning off the water, James opened the door by an inch.

"All done in there?"

Eliot reappeared, wearing a befuddled frown. "Daddy? Why is that man sleeping on the ground?"

James frowned and entered the bathroom.

On the floor of the handicapped stall was a man's body. James recognized the figure in the purple polo shirt and tan pants right away.

"Ned?" he called and stooped over the prone form. Even in the shadowy restroom stall, James could see that Ned Woodman's eyes were open. They were glassy and unblinking, their still gaze fixed on the peach-and-green tiled wall.

James checked for a pulse but didn't find one. As he pulled his phone out of his pocket and dialed Lucy's number, he ushered Eliot into the reception room. When she didn't answer, he punched in Bennett's number next.

"Bennett!" James whispered urgently into the speaker. "Tell Jane to come get Eliot from the Health House. It's two doors down from Harmony's. And call 911. Councilman Ned Woodman is in a bathroom stall back here." He lowered his voice even further. "He's dead."

"Damn." Bennett whistled. "When it's my turn to pass on, that is *not* how I want to go!"

Chapter Five

Blueberry Dream Pie

It took less than five minutes for Jane to enter the office and collect Eliot. James gave her the Bronco keys and insisted she drive back to his house while he waited for the authorities.

The authorities turned out to be Donovan and Lucy, since they were already at the festival. The two deputies were having a full-scale argument as they walked across the threshold.

"You're not even in uniform, Hanover," Deputy Donovan sneered and hitched up his utility belt to emphasize her lack of nightstick, handcuffs, or firearm. "Leave this to the *men!*"

Lucy rolled her eyes. "If a man was here, I would. All I see is the same know-it-all jerk I knew back in high school. When are you going to grow up, Keith? Didn't you turn forty a few months ago?" She jerked her thumb at his thinning red hair as she brushed past him. "It's too bad you don't shed your bad habits the way you seem to be shedding your hair."

Donovan snorted. "Go on, then. Be your aggressive, sarcastic self. That's why you can't hold on to a man, Hanover. Guys don't like pushy women."

The last comment struck home, especially because Lucy's fellow deputy knew full well that she still mourned the loss of her relationship with James. To spare Lucy any more embarrassment, James avoided her gaze as he led the pair of squabbling deputies to the bathroom.

"He's inside," he said before Lucy opened the door. "I checked for vital signs but found nothing."

Donovan shook his head in disgust. "Would it have killed you to try CPR before pronouncing the man dead? Or is M.D. one of your dozens of degrees?"

"I didn't need a degree to see that Ned was gone," James answered, doing his best not to rise to Donovan's bait. "He wasn't even warm to the touch. There was no trace of life left in him."

Before Donovan could continue berating James, his radio crackled with the announcement that Sheriff Huckabee was on his way. Donovan snapped to attention and ducked into the bathroom.

He and Lucy reappeared a few minutes later, just as the paramedics entered the office. They eased a gurney into the reception room, and after exchanging professional greetings with the deputies, went into the restroom to examine Ned Woodman's body.

Lucy dug a notebook out of her cluttered purse and began searching for a pen among the gum wrappers, wadded tissues, and crumpled receipts. She finally found one, but the cap was gone and it had dried out. James smiled at her customary untidiness and handed her a pen from a cup holder on the coffee table. The pens were mauve and bore the name, phone number, and address of Roslyn's business.

While Lucy asked James for details about his discovery of the body, the EMTs carried Ned out of the handicapped stall and carefully lifted him onto the gurney. Donovan stood behind the paramedics as they strapped Ned's inert form onto their wheeled cart.

"What do you boys make of this?" he asked in a conversational tone.

The man cinching the belt around Ned's legs replied, "This isn't official, but it looks like your standard heart attack."

James listened with interest. He recalled how Ned's left hand had been balled into a tight fist and how his right arm had been stretched across his chest, as if he'd held his left side before falling onto the floor.

"It's a shame," the second paramedic murmured. "Guy can't be more than sixty."

"Yeah, it sucks to be him," Donovan said without an iota of genuine sympathy.

The paramedics were about to exit when the doorway was suddenly blocked by the arrival of Sheriff Huckabee. Huckabee, who was stocky and wide-shouldered like Donovan but had fifty pounds on his deputy, strode into the room. Twirling the ends of his splendid mustache, which had turned dark pewter over the years, Huckabee had never looked more like a walrus than he did now. His meaty hand scratched the stubble sprouting on his second chin while his small eyes carefully surveyed the scene. He approached the gurney. "What's the verdict, gentlemen?"

"Looks like a heart attack, Sheriff," Donovan said before anyone else could. "At least it was quick, sir. I know he was a friend of yours."

"Thank you, Keith," the sheriff said and placed a palm on the side of the gurney. "Ned was a good man. I'll head over to his place and tell Donna myself." He turned to the closest paramedic. "Where you boys taking him? I'll drive his wife over whenever she's ready."

As the men reviewed the procedural details concerning the care of the councilman's body, James found that he couldn't take his eyes off Ned's face. Less than an hour ago he'd seen this man walking around the festival. He was now dead. It happened without warning, without witnesses, and without the presence of a single loved one. James hadn't known Ned well, but he'd spoken to him minutes before the man had taken his last breath.

Feeling discomfited by Ned's death, James glanced around. He wanted to look at something other than the body on the gurney. Leaning toward Lucy, who was still seated on the sofa, he whispered, "What happened with the protestors?"

"They were relocated," she said with a ghost of a smile. "I figured if we tried to shoo them away they'd call us fascists and get even more riled up. I told them they were harassing the folks trying to enter the fair and that they were free to continue their demonstration, but they'd have to move farther down the street. There's no shade in that spot and half of them left before Donovan got the call about Mr. Woodman."

They both fell silent and James reflected that he and Lucy had been in this position several times before. There'd been an unexpected death and the two friends had done their best to remain composed despite their feelings of shock or sorrow. Lucy had always handled such situations with professional aplomb, even before she'd become a deputy. James wondered if her ability to be so emotionally detached had prevented her from experiencing intimate relationships.

James wished she could find a suitable partner. If she found happiness, he could let go of the guilt he occasionally felt for telling her they'd never be a couple again. James didn't expect his wish for Lucy to be granted so quickly, but that's exactly what happened when Huckabee plodded over to the sofa and told Lucy that he'd like to speak to her in private.

As Huckabee and Lucy moved down the hall to talk, James waited for someone to tell him that he was free to leave.

The paramedics wheeled Ned's corpse from the room and Donovan tagged along, undoubtedly hoping to shout at anyone standing too close to the ambulance. In the silence, it dawned on James that he'd neglected to tell Lucy about Roslyn's office being unlocked. When she returned, her face was filled with such joy that he forgot all about the omitted detail.

"Good news?" he asked.

Lucy waited until Huckabee went outside before flashing a jubilant smile. "Yes! Do you remember Sullie?"

Of course, James remembered the hunky deputy. He'd been the reason James and Lucy's relationship had failed the first time around. Lucy had become obsessed with Sullie and turned her back on James. Because of her actions, James had sought comfort in the arms of the reporter, Murphy Alistair. Thinking about the two women who'd caused him such heartache, James became instantly cross.

"Who could forget Sullie the Magnificent?"

Too happy to notice James's peevishness, Lucy went right on talking. "He's transferring to our station! The sheriff wants me to arrange a welcome party. Isn't this wonderful news?"

Recalling that only moments before he'd hoped for this very thing to happen, James forced his mouth into a smile. "It's great, Lucy." He then churlishly asked, "Do you think he's still single?"

Lucy was unfazed by the question. "I know he is. I became friends with one of the female deputies in Sullie's station during the last tri-county department bowling tournament. *She* said that Sullie talks about me all the time."

James put a hand on her arm. "I hope everything works out for you, Lucy."

"Me too. I feel like it's finally my turn," she said.

Together, she and James walked out of the office.

• • •

By the time Monday rolled around, James had recovered from the unsettling experience of Ned Woodman's death. Fortunately,

Eliot continued to believe the man had decided to take a nap on the bathroom floor. His four-year-old brain reasoned that the man had been really hot and sought relief by resting on the cool tile floor. James and Jane said nothing to correct this notion.

The workday was refreshingly uneventful. James discarded more unpromising job applications, manned both the circulation and information desks while the Fitzgerald twins put on a Dr. Seuss puppet show for a group of kindergartners, and made it through eight hours without a single sugar craving. That afternoon, he nearly hugged Harmony when she invited him into her office for their second session.

"I've lost two pounds!" he told her. "I know that isn't much, but I feel like this treatment is exactly what I needed."

Harmony smiled in encouragement. "Kicking your sugar addiction is a great start, but remember, you still need to eat balanced meals and exercise regularly if you truly want to be healthy."

James didn't want to admit that he hadn't been to the gym once over the past week so he merely nodded in agreement.

After gesturing for her client to sit in the recliner, Harmony took her place on the sofa and gazed at him with friendly concern. "I heard that your son discovered Mr. Woodman's body on Saturday. Is he okay?"

James wiggled in the chair until his body weight felt evenly distributed. "Eliot thinks Ned was just resting. He's forgotten all about it by now." He spread the blanket Harmony handed him over his legs and belly. "Did you know Ned?"

"No," Harmony answered. "Not personally, I mean. I knew that he was a councilman and I've seen his wife around the Village. She's a regular at Knead Your Cares Away. That poor woman. Her husband's death must have been such a terrible shock."

Staring at one of the soft watercolors above Harmony's head, James nodded. "I hope stress wasn't what killed him. The last time I saw him alive, he was standing near the protestors. He looked utterly panic-stricken. I asked him to keep the crowd calm, but he disappeared as soon as Deputy Donovan showed up."

Harmony didn't seem surprised that Ned had dodged his responsibility as a town official. "Not everyone is comfortable handling volatile situations. The noise, the escalating emotions, the possibility of violence. I'm sure several people were upset by the protest, but I'm still grateful to live in a country where our opinions can be voiced."

Wanting to avoid a political discussion, James changed the subject. "Tomorrow night is the first meeting of our new and improved sugar-free supper club."

"Well, let's make certain you stay that way," Harmony said. "Are you comfortable?"

"Very."

Harmony turned on her CD player and the tranquil mixture of birdsong, running water, and wind chimes drifted into the room. James closed his eyes. The session was similar to the first one. However, instead of visiting his brain's control room, Harmony asked James to picture the sugary treats he'd loved most when he was boy.

One at a time, he called the images to mind. Charleston Chews, chocolate chip cookies, ice cream sandwiches, Twinkies, his mother's homemade doughnuts, and bowls of Halloween candy floated across his vision, and he couldn't help but grin over the variety of sweets his memory had been able to bring forth. With great detail, James made a spread of the delicacies he'd succumbed to for nearly forty years and then turned his back on the entire display. When he awoke, he felt a sense of freedom, as if he'd reprogrammed his long-term memory. That memory would no longer have the power to make him believe that he wanted to cave in to the sugary temptations of his boyhood.

Once again, James collected his reinforcement CD from Skye before leaving the office. Skye's boyfriend, Lennon, was raking a swath of white pebbles in the Japanese rock garden in between Harmony's office and her neighbor, the massage therapist. Watching the young man's steady and deliberate movements, James realized that he was raking in time to music. He then spotted the white wires dangling from his ears and disappearing into the neck of another tie-dyed T-shirt.

James glanced around the tidy garden, the spotless cement walkways, and the carefully trimmed bushes. Bluebirds flitted about the treetops and the sun fell through the leaves, dappling the ground with patterns of light and shadow. The Village was incredibly serene compared to Saturday's boisterous scene.

The feeling of relaxed empowerment dissipated the moment James returned home and hit the Play button on his answering machine.

"It's me," Jane's voice trembled slightly. "I was really hoping you'd be home. I . . . I need to know how worried I should be about what happened today. Someone left another dead bird at my house, James, but this one wasn't in the mailbox." She paused to collect herself. "It was nailed to the front door."

James called her right away. "Honey, are you okay?" He didn't notice the use of the endearment. It just rolled off his tongue.

"I actually had a shot of whiskey to settle my nerves. I'm better now. Luckily, Eliot didn't see it because we always come inside through the garage." Jane sounded exhausted.

"You've had quite a shock," he told her. "I can hear it in your voice. But sweetheart, you have to call the police. This has moved beyond the realm of prank to vandalism. A person sick enough to nail a dead bird to your door could be capable of much worse."

Jane sighed. "I'll do it in the morning. I promise. Right now, I just wish . . . well, I wish you were here."

It was all the invitation James needed. "Give me an hour," he said and hung up.

By the time James reached Harrisonburg, Eliot was already asleep. Jane was clad in a pair of blue cotton pajamas covered with designs of bacon and eggs. After hugging her, James pointed at her nighttime ensemble and smiled.

"You like my 'breakfast in bed' PJs?" She laughed and then her face grew serious. "Thank you for coming, James. It's not like me to feel insecure in the house by myself, but with you here, I feel much safer."

James pointed at the sofa. "Should I make this up?"

"No," Jane said. She stepped closer, her eyes shining with invitation. "You'd be a much more efficient bodyguard in my bed."

Without the slightest hesitation, James scooped her into his arms and kissed the exposed skin of her neck. "Why do I hear Whitney Houston music playing in my head?"

Jane's lips found his. After their kiss, she murmured, "Get that other woman out of your mind. Tonight, you're mine."

Whispering into her hair, James answered, "I always have been."

• • •

The next morning, Eliot was delighted to find his father standing at the stove, cooking scrambled eggs with cheese with one hand and drinking coffee from one of Jane's purple JMU coffee mugs with the other. However, his initial pleasure quickly soured when he realized that he'd missed James's arrival the night before.

"I didn't know we were having a sleepover!" Eliot whined. "I missed it!"

At that moment, Jane entered the kitchen and distributed good morning kisses to both males. "It was a grown-up sleepover," she said and winked at James. Pointing at the stovetop clock, she said, "You'd better get going or you'll be late for work."

James cast an anxious look toward the front door. "Are you sure you want to deal with this alone? I can take a sick day."

Jane nodded and lowered her voice. "I'll do it after I drop Eliot at day care. Having cops at our house might freak him out. Then again, he might love it. Either way, he won't be here."

"Will you call me later? I have an interview scheduled for two this afternoon, but otherwise, I'll be available to talk." He hugged his ex-wife and presented his son with his breakfast. "An egg monster for the coolest kid in the room."

Eliot examined the lumpy pile of eggs forming an oval face, the apple-slice mouth, the baby carrot nose, and the four eyes made out of cheese cubes and laughed. "I like this monster, Daddy."

James gave his son a kiss on the nose, picked up his overnight bag, and waved goodbye. Before leaving, he snuck around to the front door to get a firsthand look at the dead bird.

This was no pathetic robin resting on a pile of mail, but a big black crow, like the ones from James's nightmare. Both wings had been spread wide. Nails had been driven through each wing bone. The bird's head and neck sagged sideways and its feet curled inward.

Repulsed, James took a step backward. He glanced around the

stoop, looking for a note or any indication that would explain the gruesome display. His eyes swept the property. As he walked to his truck, he thought about how difficult it would be to have arranged the macabre display in Jane's neighborhood. The houses were relatively close together and there weren't many mature trees dividing the yards. Most of the neighbors were two-parent families, and though many of the mothers worked outside the home, the women living on either side of Jane did not.

"Who walks up to the front door of someone's house, nails a dead bird on it, and gets away without being seen?" he asked the quiet street. "And just as important as the who is the why. Why do this to Jane?"

James put his hands on his hips and glared in every direction as if he could frighten away the perpetrator with his presence. Putting his faith in the abilities of the local police, James backed out of the driveway and headed south to Quincy's Gap.

• • •

The Fitzgerald twins were in a buoyant mood when they met James on the library steps at a quarter to nine. In fact, both of the young men, who'd taken to riding their mountain bikes to work, were so impatient to share their news that they dismounted and let their bikes drop onto the grass.

"Guess what, Professor?" Francis was flushed from exercise and excitement.

Hoping the announcement would distract him from the image of the dead crow, James paused in the act of unlocking the front door. "You won the Mega Million jackpot?"

Scott shook his head. "It's way better than that! We entered a contest for people who have ideas for groundbreaking new video games and—"

"We won!" Francis shouted and the brothers exchanged celebratory chest bumps.

James smiled at them. "That's terrific. What was your idea?"

Francis beamed. "This is why you're awesome, Professor. Everybody else asked us about the prize, but *you* want to know what we dreamed up."

"Our proposal stemmed from our experiences working here, at the library," said Scott.

James had a sudden visual of Murphy's book cover.

"Did your proposal have anything to do with the mystery genre?" he asked woodenly.

"Nope! It's a game where you travel between fantasy worlds," Francis explained. "For example, you start as Alice and play in Wonderland, but as Alice advances in levels, she can travel to Tolkien's world."

"There, she can add an ally to her group, like Legolas, the elf, or a wizard like Gandalf," Scott continued.

"So with each new world, the group grows by another character," Francis finished.

James smiled at the twins. "It sounds brilliant and complex and really fun. I assume there would be a final battle scene once your group of characters has leveled out." When the brothers nodded, James asked, "In what setting would this epic fight occur?"

"Back in Wonderland," they answered together. "Against the Queen of Hearts, of course."

James praised the two young men until they blushed with embarrassment. "Don't you two quit on me! I still haven't found a replacement for Mrs. Waxman."

"Don't worry, Professor. The prize is that we're being hired as consultants during the two years it'll take to produce the game." Scott exchanged a look with Francis. "We'd never leave the library, but for once, we won't have to skimp on some of the things we've wanted to buy. Our bachelor pad is about to be totally transformed!"

"That should entertain your landlady," James remarked with a chuckle.

"Mrs. Lamb is a feisty lady," Francis said. "She said the first thing we should buy is a disco ball!"

The librarians laughed and went inside to begin their workday. All three of them had an industrious morning. Between the two book club meetings—James led the fiction club's discussion at ten while Scott led the biography club's discussion at eleven—lunchtime arrived quickly.

Watching Francis rush to the refrigerator with glee, James

realized that he had no lunch of his own. There'd been no time to stop on the drive from Jane's house to the library. He waited for the twins to finish their meals, and when he finally ventured into town, he was starving. Only Dolly's Diner would do. It was Tuesday and that meant Clint's perfect meat-loaf sandwich and a side of garlic mashed potatoes.

Dolly's was always packed on Tuesdays. The locals adored the meat-loaf special, and as summer approached, Dolly began serving her famous Blueberry Dream Pie. For a mere ninety-nine cents, her patrons could feast on a generous wedge of pie with the purchase of any entrée. Half of Quincy's Gap took advantage of this offer.

"Professor Henry!" Dolly shouted from behind the hostess station. "Such a pleasure to see you!"

Though this type of greeting was generally spoken out of politeness, Dolly meant every word. She'd known James and his family for years and was now as fond of Milla and Eliot as she was of her own kin. Dolly loved Clint, food, and gossip, and not always in that order. Somehow, her customers shared their problems with her despite knowing that their secrets would be circulated the minute they left the diner.

"Not even a seat at the counter," James mourned and his stomach rumbled in protest.

"Lemme see if anybody's about finished up. If they are, I'll give them a gentle shove out the door. I know you've got to get back to the library." Dolly hustled off, her sharp eyes searching for dawdlers.

As James waited, a pretty young woman with shoulder-length auburn hair, fair skin, and a dash of freckles got up from her chair at a table for two. She squinted in his direction and then slipped on a pair of tortoiseshell glasses. Leaving a paperback on her seat, she walked over to James.

"Did she say that you worked at the library?" she asked in a pleasant alto.

James nodded. "I'm the head librarian."

The woman gave him a bright smile. "I'm Fern Dickenson. I have an interview with you at two." She gestured toward her table. "I just ordered, and since there aren't any open seats, would you like to join me?"

"That would be great," James said, already feeling well disposed toward the thoughtful young woman.

Over lunch, James proceeded to ask Fern all the questions he'd been saving for the afternoon's interview. Fern told him that she'd been working as a freelance photographer for a dozen Virginia publications but was having a hard time making ends meet without a steady paycheck. She loved all areas of the humanities, was well read, and extremely personable. She'd had experience serving the public during her two years working part-time for the Virginia State Parks Department, and while she enjoyed the job, she was ready for a change.

From what James could tell, Fern had a great sense of humor, a solid work ethic, and a deep love of reading. She was perfect for the job.

When Dolly arrived to clear their lunch plates, Fern excused herself to use the restroom.

"Isn't she a little young for you, Professor?" Dolly wiggled her eyebrows and laughed, her whole body shaking with mirth.

James waved her off. "She's going to be my new part-time librarian. This meal became an impromptu interview."

Dolly was beside herself over being the first to hear such interesting news. "You need to celebrate. Be back in a flash!"

Before James could protest, she was gone. By the time Fern returned from the restroom, two dessert plates containing slices of Blueberry Dream Pie had been placed on the table.

"On the house!" Dolly told Fern. "And welcome to Quincy's Gap. We're mighty glad to have you. Are you movin' to our town? Are you on your own or do you have a *significant* other?"

Fern accepted Dolly's welcome and took her questions in stride. "Thank you. I'm glad to be here. As for my living situation . . . I'm apartment hunting and I'm single. I'm an only child and my astrological sign is Libra. Blood type is O Negative." She looked quizzically at James. "Wait, does this mean I got the job?"

"It's yours if you want it," James declared. When Fern enthusiastically said that she would very much like it, James gestured at his plate. "Shall we toast with a forkful of pie?"

Dolly hadn't budged during this exchange and James didn't dare offend her by turning down her gift of pie, so he loaded his fork, clinked it against Fern's, and popped the bite of pie in his mouth.

A blend of cream cheese, fresh blueberries, and sugar coated his tongue. Sighing as the fresh berries popped between his teeth, he waited for the feeling of intense pleasure to overpower him, to create that high he was accustomed to experiencing when eating a sweet food, but it didn't happen. He enjoyed the treat, but he wasn't so focused on it that he couldn't pause between bites to converse with his new employee.

"When should I start, Mr. Henry?" Fern asked when her pie was done. "I'm available whenever you need me."

James wiped a blueberry smear from his cheek. "How about tomorrow? I'll have Scott show you the ropes. I believe the two of you will get along very nicely."

Chapter Six

Cucumber & Feta Salad

After hiring Fern over lunch, James returned to the library with a light step. He hummed quietly all the way to his office, stopping only when he saw that he'd missed a call during lunch. Though he always muted his phone while eating at a public place, he was sorry that he hadn't realized Jane had left him a voice mail. In her message, Jane said that she'd filed a police report earlier that morning. The officer she'd spoken to promised to have a car patrol her neighborhood for the rest of the week. The helpful lawman had also removed the dead crow from her front door and buried the sad creature in the far reaches of the backyard.

"I feel so much better today," she said, and James could hear the relief in her voice. "And I want to thank you again for last night." She paused and he could easily picture the blood rushing to her cheeks as the double meaning of her words became apparent. "Um, about last night . . . I don't want to jump to any conclusions, but it felt really natural and, well, really wonderful! I've been acting like a preteen girl with a crush all day—wearing this goofy smile and writing your name all over my desk calendar . . ." She chuckled. "Okay, I'm not trying to make you blush or anything. I just wanted to say that you make me happy. Bye!"

James smiled. He felt buoyant, as if everything in his life was falling neatly into place. His reconnection with Jane had been a unique experience. After all, they *had* been married, but she'd been a self-centered lover back then and had seemed dissatisfied with their sex life. Last night, she was a different woman in bed. Playful and giving, she'd quickly put aside her shyness and allowed him to explore her voluptuous body. In return, she'd loved him with a mixture of tenderness and passion that she'd never shown during their marriage.

James could feel his pulse quicken as he replayed their nocturnal activities, but doubt began to worm its way into his mind, disturbing his reminiscences and causing him to question the wisdom of following his heart and not his head.

We can't mess around like teenagers, he thought. *No matter how good it feels. There's Eliot to consider. If Jane and I are going to be together, it must be for all the right reasons. I have to be one hundred percent sure she and I are the real deal this time.*

James knew that doubts would always assail him. After all, he thought they'd been the genuine article the first time around. He'd been so certain of their future the night he'd gotten down on one knee and proposed. Following his divorce, he thought Lucy might be the love he'd been waiting for. And then there was Murphy.

He'd been wrong about all of them.

"Let's face it," he remarked glumly to the photo of Jackson and Milla on his desk. "I don't have clear judgment when it comes to women. Yet you!" he pointed at his father. "You got it right—not once but *twice.* And you're a cantankerous old man! How'd you win the hearts of such wonderful women, Pop?"

"Talking to yourself again?" a teasing voice inquired.

James looked up to see Murphy Alistair standing in the doorway, her mouth upturned in amusement. If not for that expression, he might not have recognized her for several seconds, for she no longer looked like the small-town reporter he'd once dated. Her hair had been dyed to a glossy molasses brown, chic Chanel frames had replaced her academic-looking glasses, and she'd become shockingly thin. Her angular body was encased in a black sheath dress and she wore a multi-strand red coral necklace. To James, she resembled a younger version of Sarah Palin.

Out of politeness, he stood up. "You look very cosmopolitan."

Murphy laughed. "Everyone really *does* wear black in New York. I'd forgotten how all the Quincy's Gap ladies wear Pepto-Bismol suits and Beatrix Potter hats."

"Our whole valley is more colorful than your concrete jungle." James felt defensive of his beloved berg. "And there's a great pizza place in town now, so I don't think the Big Apple's got much on us."

"Right. Except Broadway, the Met, unparalleled architecture, hundreds of fabulous restaurants, and the latest trends in fashion, I guess Manhattan can't hold a candle to this place." She gestured out the window with a mocking smile.

James frowned. "If New York is such a utopia, why come back to the sticks?"

Murphy smoothed her sleek hair. "In all honesty, it wasn't easy to make friends in the city. I couldn't enjoy my success in a sea of anonymity. My family is in Shenandoah and I missed the hustle and bustle of putting out the *Star*. I now own the paper and a house that I always admired but couldn't afford."

"You have nerves of steel to move back after insulting half the town in your infamous *book*." He'd never infused such a beloved noun with that much spite. "How may a humble librarian be of service to you today?"

Crossing her arms over her chest, Murphy sighed in exasperation. "My novels are works of *fiction*. When are you ever going to accept that fact? And I'm here on a professional basis, especially if the rumor about your having a kid with your ex-wife is true."

"Your sources are correct. I have a son. His name is Eliot Henry." James felt a great deal of pleasure sharing this information with his former flame.

Murphy took a step deeper into his office, her posture like that of a stalking panther. "Are you all living together in your sweet yellow house on Hickory Hill Lane?"

There was no cynicism in her tone; she was genuinely interested in his current circumstances. It gave him a petty satisfaction to leave her thirst for information unquenched. Acting as if she hadn't spoken, he came around to the front of his desk and indicated that she should accompany him out of the library's inner sanctum. "How can I help you, Ms. Alistair?"

"I'd like to interview you for a piece I'm writing on Ned Woodman," she answered after studying him for a moment. Murphy had recognized that his formal tone meant that his personal life was not open for discussion.

James shrugged. "I can't help you there. I only knew that he was a councilman. His name and photo appeared in the paper a few times."

"But you found his body!" Murphy protested. "You must have *some* reaction. Do you think his death could be linked to the presence of the animal rights demonstrators?"

It wouldn't do for James to be misquoted regarding the protestors or the Wellness Village. "He had a heart attack. It's not like he was murdered. I don't see any connection."

"If he was murdered, we'll never know because his wife refused an autopsy," Murphy said. "He's had two previous surgeries for blocked arteries, so Donna Woodman wasn't surprised that he died from heart issues."

Studying her face and the glint in her eyes, James knew Murphy was chasing a tantalizing lead. "You don't think his death was an accident, do you?"

"He was a councilman, James. When guys like him die young, I always take a second look at their lives. According to my sources, Ned was acting strange the day he kicked the bucket." Her mouth curved in a predatory grin. "Those two facts are enough to make me want to dig deeper. Once you tell me how he looked when you found him, I plan to investigate his recent political activities."

Apparently, Murphy's success as a novelist hadn't cooled her interest in dragging skeletons out of the townsfolk's closets. James had no wish to fan that kind of fire.

"I have no comment," he said. "I don't want Ned's family to read a detailed report of the man they loved lying facedown in a bathroom stall."

"Even though you won't help me, I want to assure you that my article will be a tasteful memorial piece," Murphy promised and turned away. Over her shoulder she added, "Unless the councilman did something improper. If so, the community deserves to know the whole truth."

Again, he spotted that glimmer in her eye. It was a hunger, a lust for bringing secrets to light, and for the briefest of moments, he wondered how far Murphy Alistair would go to get what she wanted. What did she want, exactly? And why was she so interested in his living arrangements? Was she capable of nailing a dead crow to Jane's front door?

A patron requiring assistance in the audiobook section interrupted his unsettling musings. After discussing the merits of the new Baldacci release versus the latest offerings from coauthors Douglas Preston and Lincoln Child, the thriller fan checked out both titles and left the library with a jaunty stride. James envied the man an afternoon spent in a deck chair, listening to a book with his eyes closed and a cold drink in his hand.

"I see your old girlfriend's back, Professor," Scott whispered as both men completed organizational tasks behind the circulation desk. "She wouldn't listen when I asked her to wait out here so I could warn you she was on the prowl." The younger man ran his hands through his hair, his forehead creased in concern. "That's the perfect phrase for her, Professor. Especially now. She's got that look about her — like she's caught the scent of wounded prey."

Francis had appeared from the break room in time to hear his brother's metaphor. "Are you the prey?" he asked James.

"Lord, I hope not!" James cried.

• • •

When James left work at five, he looked up to see a blue sky filled with sunshine. Inhaling the scent of fresh-cut grass, he stretched out his arms as if he could embrace the beauty of the spring afternoon. Then and there, he decided that he would not allow Murphy's return to affect the good things happening in his life.

In the meantime, he had important issues to consider, such as what to bring to Gillian's house for dinner. It was her turn to host the supper club meeting and she'd sent a dictatorial email the day before announcing that dinner was to be comprised of all vegetarian dishes.

"And no pizza!" she'd written. "If Eliot Henry can eat balanced vegetarian meals at four years of age, then the rest of us can come up with something creative and colorful to grace our plates. I'll be preparing a sumptuous sushi platter."

James wasn't overly fond of sushi. He liked California or Philly rolls well enough, but in general he preferred not to eat uncooked fish. Bennett had replied to Gillian's email by informing her that there was an afternoon staff meeting at the post office, which meant he'd get to her place by six o'clock. With no time to cook, his contribution would be a bagged salad. Lucy had quickly volunteered to bring a sugar-free dessert from the town's bakery, the Sweet Tooth. Like James, she was a bona fide carnivore and probably didn't want the pressure of preparing a tasty vegetarian entrée. Luckily for the rest of them, Lindy offered to make a meatless moussaka casserole. This left James with the responsibility of preparing a healthy side dish.

Wanting his contribution to echo the Greek food theme of Lindy's dish, James checked out two cookbooks from the library. Sitting in the grocery store parking lot, he flipped through the books until he found a quick and easy recipe for cucumber and feta salad.

At home, he changed into shorts and a T-shirt, turned on his radio, and sang along to Brad Paisley's latest hit as he cut two cucumbers lengthwise and removed the seeds with a spoon. After chopping the cucumbers into cubes, he put them in a bowl, sprinkled them with salt, and added chopped green onions to the mixture. The next ingredient was a container of feta cheese—the brand that came packaged with a blend of black pepper, basil, oregano, garlic, and sun-dried tomato. Lastly, James drizzled lemon juice and olive oil onto the salad while pretending he was being filmed for the Food Network.

"Delicious and nutritious!" he declared to an imaginary cameraman.

Covering the bowl with plastic wrap, James grabbed the bouquet of sunflowers he'd purchased for the hostess and drove off. As he pulled up in front of the colorful Victorian, he saw Gillian and Bennett on the porch swing. Clearly, his friends hadn't heard the sound of his truck engine. In fact, he didn't think they were aware of much, being far too busy kissing. James smiled as he spotted Bennett's bagged salad on the welcome mat. It seemed that he'd arrived only a few minutes before James, dumped his salad, and dragged his girlfriend over to the porch swing where he could greet her properly.

James cleared his throat and dropped to one knee, feigning the need to tie his shoelace. Out of the corner of his eye, he saw his friends leap apart.

"The whole country knows you two are an item." James stood up and grinned at them. "Bennett, you declared your feelings on live television! A million people know your story. Why are you two keeping your relationship under wraps? It isn't because you're a mixed-race couple, is it? If people have a problem with that, it's their problem, not yours."

Gillian's face was nearly as red as her hair. Looping her arm through Bennett's, she said, "No, it's not that at all. We don't want our friendship with you and Lindy and Lucy to change. When the five of us are together, Bennett and I want to continue being our *individual* selves."

"So the moment we're not around, you turn all lovey-dovey?" James teased.

Bennett squirmed. "Look, my man. We live in a small town. Plenty of folks have a hard time accepting us as a couple. I figure it's best not to shove it in their faces, you know?"

He picked up his bagged salad and walked into the house, James following closely on his heels.

James placed his salad bowl on Gillian's wooden farm table and studied his friends. "You *can't* let those small-minded people get to you. You're in love. To hell with what those people think. Look how long it took you to find each other. Don't let any more time get away from you!"

Gillian paused in the act of setting the table and put a hand on James's forearm. "Are you sure you're still talking about us? I can sense a struggle going on within you. Has your relationship with Jane entered a *new* phase?"

Surprised by the accuracy of Gillian's statement, James was saved from having to answer by Lucy's arrival. The moment she stepped into the kitchen, Gillian's rotund tabby, the Dalai Lama, stopped bathing his hindquarters and growled. Lucy looked down at the bristling feline. "You've smelled my dogs for years now. Get over yourself, cat."

"You should try to approach the Dalai with respect and gentleness," Gillian suggested. "Animals know when a human dislikes them and it's hard to change their minds once they view you as a hostile invader."

"Hostile invader," Lucy grunted. "What am I, a video game from the eighties?"

Lindy appeared in time to elbow her friend in the side. "You sound cranky, Deputy." She bent down to scratch the Dalai on the neck. "What's up?"

"I am not cranky, I'm nervous," Lucy said. "Sullie starts tomorrow and we're going to be working a shift together. I don't want to act so into him that I forget to put the car in Park or walk out with my flashlight in my gun holster or —"

"Leave the bakery box open so the Dalai can lick the topping off the pie?" Lindy asked and pointed at the counter. The tabby's pink tongue was delicately scraping the whipped cream from the surface of the pie.

"Hey! I thought you were getting something without sugar!" Bennett protested as Lucy chased the Dalai off the counter.

Lindy slid her casserole into the oven and set the temperature. "That's right, *chica*. We're supposed to be giving up sugary treats." She pointed a finger at Lucy. "This guy is already making you crazy!"

Lucy scowled. "I bought one of the Sweet Tooth's new sugar-free desserts. This is a sugarless key lime pie. I figured a fruit pie would tie in nicely with our vegetarian theme."

James was delighted to hear about the bakery's new offerings. Though part of him felt the need to abstain from ingesting sugar whenever possible, the other part argued that if guilt-free treats were available, why shouldn't he enjoy them?

Gillian wasn't pleased. "Perhaps it's a sign that the Dalai tainted the pie. Without real sugar, it may be full of chemicals instead. Why don't we have a *naturally* sweet, organic dessert? I have local raspberries and boysenberries in the fridge."

Shrugging, Lucy took a seat at the table. "Whatever you all think is best. I can always take the pie to the station tomorrow. I'll cut off the piece your cat licked and give it to Donovan!"

The five friends laughed at this splendid idea.

"I have some news," Lindy said as she poured iced tea for the ladies and distributed bottles of cold beer to James and Bennett. "I don't have to fly down to Mexico to meet Luis's mama. Do you know why?" Without giving anyone a chance to guess, she cried, "Because she's coming *here*!"

Bennett snorted. "Why? To interview you for the position of future daughter-in-law? See what kind of cook and housekeeper you are?"

Lindy looked miserable. "Pretty much. She probably wants to get an eyeful of my breeding hips too."

"Don't worry, Lindy. We'll help you prep for the visit," Lucy assured her. "When does she arrive?"

"Sunday afternoon. And thank you, Lucy, but I can hardly ask my dearest friends to spend a precious Saturday cleaning my toilets." Lindy put on a brave smile, but they could all see the anxiety in her eyes.

Lindy desperately wanted to win the approval of Luis's mother, but she hoped Luis would propose regardless of what his dear mama thought.

Ruminating over parental blessings caused James to wonder if Jackson would ever be able to accept Jane back into their family. His father tended to hold grudges for eons, and though he was polite to Jane — probably because Milla forced him to be — he didn't speak to her unless it was necessary.

Relationships are never easy, he thought. Aloud he said, "If we have to scrub your toilets and dust the blades of your ceiling fans to impress this woman, we will. But she'll see what a treasure you are, Lindy. It won't matter if you serve her fried dog food, because she's going to love you."

Lindy sniffed back grateful tears. "Thank you, James. But I refuse to allow you to take part in the cleaning brigade. You need to spend time with your precious Eliot. I'm sure Bennett looks very sexy in rubber gloves and an apron!"

Bennett spluttered as his friends laughed.

The oven clock beeped and Gillian retrieved the moussaka and served steaming spoonfuls of it to the group. When it was cool enough to eat, they all devoured it, praising Lindy for her ingenuity in replacing the traditional ground beef with diced zucchini. The friends then compared notes on their hypnotherapy sessions and rehashed the events at the food festival. Naturally, this led to a conversation involving Ned Woodman's death.

"Rumor has it Ned may have been a bit crooked," Lucy said. She always enjoyed having insider information, and her friends could see that she was dying to tell them the latest bit of department gossip.

While everyone else waited patiently for her to continue, James said, "Let me guess. He was skimming from the town treasury."

Lucy trained her cornflower blue eyes on him. "How'd you know?"

Now it was James's turn to be surprised. "I was just joking!"

"Well, you're right on target. Not all of the evidence has been gathered yet, but it looks like Mr. Woodman overcharged the town for his landscaping services."

"Is that really serious?" Gillian asked. "Gas prices are so high these days. Maybe he needed to charge more because of increased costs."

Lucy finished chewing a mouthful of moussaka before answering. "We're not talking about the kind of money to buy oil for the weed whackers or a few tanks of lawn mower gas, Gillian. He took a ton of money! Not only was he billing three times the actual costs for his services, but apparently, whenever it was his turn to pay the town's bills, he'd pay himself for work his company didn't even perform!"

"What's the bottom line?" Bennett asked.

"I can't say anything in an official capacity," Lucy warned. "It's not my investigation, but we're talking somewhere in the neighborhood of thirty thousand dollars. His wife claims to know nothing about it."

"Whoa! Thirty grand for cutting lawns and trimming a few bushes!" Bennett shook his fork in indignation. "I'm in the wrong line of work!"

The friends ate silently for a moment. James became aware that he was picking at his entrée like a child forced to eat distasteful vegetables. The moussaka tasted fine, but he didn't care for the texture. The entire dish felt mushy in his mouth. Even chewing the crisp cucumbers of his own salad didn't quite match the satisfaction of grinding a nice piece of steak between his molars.

Don't be so close-minded! he scolded himself.

"I wonder what he did with that extra money?" Lindy mused aloud. "If his wife didn't know, where'd he hide it? In a safe-deposit box?"

"In his girlfriend's house?" Bennett quipped.

The supper club members exchanged inquisitive glances.

"Are you thinking what I'm thinking?" Gillian whispered theatrically and fixed her gaze on Lucy.

Lucy wiped her mouth with her napkin, folded her hands on the table, and nodded. "That someone else might know the location of Ned's money?"

"And has already helped themselves to it!" Lindy cried.

"Time out, folks." James rose and returned to the table with a bakery box from the Sweet Tooth. "The money could be buried under a tree for all we know, but if we're going to bat around wild theories for the rest of the evening, then we're going to need pie."

Chapter Seven

Bacon, Egg & Cheese Melt

By the time the weekend rolled around, Murphy had successfully ferreted out every detail of Ned Woodman's transgressions. The deceased councilman had overcharged the town for his services for years, but not by enough to draw attention. It was only within the last few months he'd turned truly greedy.

According to Murphy's explanation in the *Star*, council members took turns paying the town's bills. This rotation was put in place to protect the town's coffers, but it was effective only when each council member kept a close eye on the books. Because there hadn't been a penny unaccounted for in years, the council members didn't go over the numbers with a fine-tooth comb. Unfortunately, Ned took advantage of his trusting colleagues, and during his bill-paying rotation made large payments to his own company.

The bills included exorbitant fees for simple services such as pruning and laying mulch.

Eventually, someone else on the council would have noticed the depletion of town funds. It "seemed as though Woodman was attempting to stockpile ready cash in a big hurry," Murphy wrote in her column. "His widow claims to have no knowledge of her husband's illicit activities. Donna Woodman says that the stolen money wasn't deposited in their joint bank account and that her husband made no big-ticket purchases over the past few months. Authorities are currently investigating Mr. Woodman's finances, but it appears the councilman cashed a series of town checks over a twelve-week period. With no clues as to the whereabouts of the stolen money, the former councilman may have taken the cash, and his reasons for embezzling from his friends and neighbors, to the grave."

Next to Murphy's article on Ned Woodman's criminal acts was a shorter piece covering his memorial service. A large photo of Donna Woodman served as a divider between the two stories, and James found himself repeatedly staring at the black-and-white image.

Ned's widow was an athletic blond. Her sleeveless black tank dress showed off muscular arms and a stomach as flat as an ironing board. It was difficult to see her face as the photograph was a profile shot and a pair of enormous sunglasses obscured Donna's eyes. It was her lips, set in a thin line of grief, and the way she clutched a single rose in her hands that made the photo leap from the page. The emotion portrayed by those clenched hands looked like something Jackson would have captured in one of his paintings.

"Poor woman," James murmured and passed the paper to Jane. "I wish this stuff about Ned had come out after the funeral. That way, Donna Woodman could have buried her husband without the press circling the cemetery like hungry hawks."

Jane studied the photograph and made a sympathetic noise. "Can you imagine how she feels? She must wonder if she really knew her own husband. Why did he take the money? Did he have an addiction? A mistress? A desperate friend?" She shook her head. "His secrets will taint all of her good memories. She won't really be able to grieve until she knows the truth."

James tapped the photo. "Judging from this shot, I'd say she's begun the grieving process."

"That's not grief, it's anger," Jane answered with certainty. "Look at her mouth. Her hands. This woman is filled with rage and has no way to let it out. The source of her anger is dead, and she has to stand at the edge of his grave and stay composed in front of the cameras, when what she'd like to do is jump up and down on his coffin and scream." Seeing James's stunned expression, Jane gave a self-effacing shrug. "Maybe I'm reading too much into the photo."

"Let me look at that again." Scooting his chair closer to hers, James inhaled the clean scents of Jane's aloe body lotion and eucalyptus shampoo. As she leaned over to pour him more coffee, he caught a trace of lilac perfume and smiled.

Since his mother had also loved lilacs, he associated the scent with her warm embraces, easy laughter, and good-night kisses. He thought of all the evenings she'd snuggled with him on his twin bed, reading him story after story until he finally fell asleep. Every night of his boyhood, he'd drifted off to tales of bravery and adventure, dark plots and ruthless villains, enchantment and beauty. James's mother had gifted him with a love of books. It was a gift he wanted to pass on to his own son, and he was glad to know that Jane had been reading to Eliot since he was an infant.

"What are you thinking about?" Jane asked, nudging him with her elbow. "You have a very dreamy expression."

James gazed at his ex-wife, at how pretty she looked in her denim skirt and white blouse, her hair tucked into a headband and her face free of makeup. Had she known that lilac was his mother's trademark scent? Was she wearing it deliberately, to more easily win my affection? James folded the *Star* in half with a snap.

No, he thought. *Jane doesn't need to manipulate me. She has her own money, a successful career, and a supportive circle of family and friends. And I've seen the way men look at her. Jane could have her pick of guys. Stop second-guessing her,* his inner voice scolded.

"I was remembering how my mom loved the smell of lilacs," he replied to Jane after a long pause. "Your perfume reminds me of her. Actually, *you* remind me of her more and more now these days."

"What a lovely compliment!" Jane squeezed his hand. "Your mother was an incredible woman. Kind, generous, funny . . . and boy, did she know her way around the kitchen! I'll never be her equal when it comes to cooking. You know that, right?" She pretended to look alarmed. "You're not expecting me to start making soufflés and coq au vin, are you?"

"Forget haute cuisine, my dear. I'm very interested in your *other* assets." He leaned over to kiss her.

All too soon, Eliot's voice interrupted them. "Are you two going to make a baby?"

Jane's arms slid from James's shoulders, but her hand lingered over his. She laughed. "Where'd you get *that* idea?"

"Lesley-Anne. She said when grown-ups kiss, it makes a baby." Eliot was clearly pleased to be able to share this bit of knowledge with his parents.

James cocked his head. "What else does Lesley-Anne say?"

Eliot stirred his bowl of Honey Nut Cheerios before answering. "A stork brings the baby. The baby cries a lot because it has bad dreams about the stork." He looked at Jane. "Did I have bad dreams about storks?"

The mention of birds put a damper on Jane's lightheartedness. "No, darling. But your friend Lesley-Anne sounds like she has a good imagination."

Unsure of whether his friend had just been praised or slighted, Eliot shrugged. "She can be mean. She said Fay Sunray is for babies. She's not. She's pretty. I like her songs."

James carried his breakfast dishes to the sink.

Jane wiped off the counter and whispered to him over the sound of the running water, "Lesley-Anne is going to be *that* kid. You know, the one who ruins the Tooth Fairy, the Easter Bunny, and Santa Claus for the rest of the kids. Mark my words."

"Some mysteries were never meant to be solved—the locations of the North Pole or the pot of gold at the end of the rainbow, for example," James said wistfully. "And then there are the ones we'd love to unravel, like the reason Murphy Alistair moved back to Quincy's Gap, what prompted the vandalism cases against you, or what Ned did with the stolen money."

Jane paused in the act of loading the dishwasher. "Oh, you and your supper club will decipher all three of those riddles before the Fourth of July. I'm certain of that." Wiping her hands on a tea towel, she glanced around the tidy kitchen. "Let's get going. If we miss the Firefighters' Parade, Eliot will ask Miss Know-It-All Lesley-Anne how a kid can be granted a legal dispensation to live with his grandparents!"

• • •

Hours later, the Henry family was worn out from a memorable day of sunshine, music, and entertainment. At the annual Shenandoah Apple Blossom Festival, they'd listened to live bluegrass music, heard the energetic strains of marching bands, and watched a parade of fire department vehicles and floats bearing the Apple Blossom queen and her court. While Jane took Eliot to get a closer look at one of the rescue vehicles, James bought her an apple blossom necklace made of sterling silver from one of the many local craftsmen. After they'd dined on a meal of grilled cheese and tomato sandwiches, he slipped it around her neck.

"It's beautiful!" Jane exclaimed with delight. Observing her radiant face, James realized that he'd never surprised her with unexpected gifts when they were married. He couldn't even remember if he'd ever bought her a bouquet of flowers or a box of chocolates during their time together. Watching her examine the necklace resting against the soft skin of her chest using the compact from her purse, James made a silent vow to be more spontaneous with his displays of affection in the future.

After their picnic lunch, the Henrys lost a handful of dollar bills playing games on the midway, rode the tamer carnival rides, and then wove through the festival crowd toward the parking lot, content but thoroughly weary. Eliot was dragging his feet by the time they reached the outer rim of the festival, and James knelt down so the boy could climb on his back for the remainder of the trek. Eliot immediately placed his cheek against his father's shoulder and closed his eyes.

As they passed vendors selling funnel cakes, soft-serve ice cream, and hot dogs, James heard the sounds of raised voices ahead. Pausing, he listened to the shrill shouts and frowned. "It's those protestors again. The ones from the food festival last weekend. I recognize the shrieks of their ringleader."

"We'll just walk past as quickly as we can," Jane calmly responded.

Despite the increased noise level, Eliot didn't so much as lift his head. When James saw the graphic posters held by the demonstrators, he sincerely hoped his son would keep his eyes shut until they were safely away.

Unfortunately, the Henry family had chosen the worst moment to leave. The group's zealous leader, the young woman with the spiked hair and the rows of hoop earrings, nearly collided with James as she stepped forward to hurl a cute plush pig at the hot dog vendor.

"*Brute!*" she screamed at the middle-aged man in the green apron as James leapt backward. "You're serving ground-up pig! You're making money from bits and parts of an intelligent animal!"

The vendor stared at the place where the plush pig had landed and so did his line of customers. The man was obviously startled and more than a little intimidated by the group of protestors.

Seeking a quick escape, James tried to skirt around those

waiting for food and the encroaching throng of demonstrators, but the crowd bunched together, effectively cutting off the way through. James felt sorry for the hot dog vendor, for the young leader's eyes blazed with a righteous fury as she directed one of her companions to toss another pig at his booth. However, James's main concern was for his family's welfare, and the possibility of violence erupting seemed high. He looked around for help, but everyone seemed frozen by the unfolding scene.

"You're contributing to the *murder* of the *innocent!*" the spiky-haired leader yelled before pointing at the stunned customers. "And *you* people! You're about to pay four dollars for pulverized brains, bone, intestines, skin, and pink dye stuffed into a casing of edible *plastic!* How can you put that stuff into your body? Become vegetarian! Save animals from being bred to become *your* food! Preserve your body from ground-up refuse like this man's hot dogs!"

One of the male protestors handed her a sign. "Tia! *Now!*"

Together, Tia and her friend unrolled a large banner. Several members of the shell-shocked crowd gasped in horror. Under the text MEAT IS MURDER! were two pictures. The first showed a pig being shot in the head with some kind of gun. The second showed his body hovering over a stainless steel trough as blood poured from the slit in the creature's throat.

"This is how it happens, carnivores! The pig is stunned by a bolt pistol. Not killed, but *stunned.* It's *alive* when its throat is cut! *Alive!*" She pointed at a man in the crowd. "Think about that happening to your darling kitty." She directed her comment at a woman wearing a Crazy Cat Lady T-shirt.

A small girl in the funnel cake line began to cry. She was quickly joined by the sobs of several other children.

An angry mother stepped out of the line. "Shame on you for showin' stuff like this to a bunch of little kids!" The woman tried to tear the banner from Tia's hands. When that failed, she pushed by the other demonstrators with a snarl, her two tearful children in tow.

Her chastisement animated the crowd and there was a surge of hostility on both sides. Peering over Jane's shoulder, James saw a group of grim-faced security guards and burly firefighters moving in their direction.

"Help is on the way," he told her with relief as Eliot stirred on his back.

Tia saw the cavalry coming as well. After whispering something to the man holding the other end of the banner, she glanced in James's direction. Her expression abruptly changed. In one moment, the young woman's face had been aglow with passion and determination. Now, her jaw was slack and her eyes were wide with fear. Dropping her end of the banner, she turned and ran.

With their leader gone, the rest of the demonstrators rapidly dispersed. By the time the first security guard arrived, the commotion was over.

"I guess Tia didn't want to tangle with those firemen," Jane said as she pulled James to the far left, where they exited through the volunteer gate. "Can't say I blame her. Did you happen to notice that the hot dog vendor is wearing a Volunteer Firefighter T-shirt under his apron?"

Though James hadn't, he didn't want to linger another second to look. Eliot woke up for a few brief seconds while being strapped into his car seat, but the moment James started driving, the weary little boy fell right back to sleep.

"You know, I agree with the protestors about the majority of their platform," Jane whispered once they'd reached the highway. "But they take things too far."

"In these days of media sensationalism, they probably think that shock value is the only way to gain attention," James said. "I think it's awful to expose folks to those posters, but at the same time, I admire their passion. They weren't out there today or last week for personal gain, but to help creatures that have no voice. I respect them for that." He slowed down as the Bronco hugged a sharp curve in the road. "Perhaps there's a less-offensive method to get their point across."

Jane raised her eyebrows. "I recognize that look. You're hatching a plan."

He laughed. "I was just thinking that the new owner of the *Shenandoah Star Ledger* might enjoy interviewing Tia. If I mention what happened today, Murphy will be here before the sun goes down, sniffing around for traces of the Apple Blossom conflict."

"I can see the headline now: Firemen and Fugitives." Jane

chuckled. "Still, an article would grant the activists the exposure they're looking for." She reached over and squeezed James's arm. "You're a good man, Professor Henry."

"And you are the smartest, best-looking woman to have ever graced that passenger seat."

Jane ran her fingertips up his bicep and over the ridge of his shoulder so she could caress the back of his neck. He sighed in contentment as she worked the kinks from his muscles.

"Despite the theatrics back there, today was perfect," she said. "It was one of those days I wish I could pack away in a box—save it like a treasure and then take it out again whenever I need cheering." She blushed. "Am I a sap or what?"

"You don't sound like a sap, but a woman who knows exactly what she wants," James replied.

"That's true," Jane smiled. "And what makes me happiest in the world is here in this dear old truck. My two Henry men. What more could a girl ask for?"

An answer surfaced in James's mind and he was shocked to suddenly visualize an item that he never thought he'd think of in connection to his ex-wife ever again. But here he was, glancing at her left hand and wondering if the "more" Jane might secretly desire was a wedding ring.

• • •

Jane and Eliot left for their house in Harrisonburg after church on Sunday. Mother and son wanted to plant a small vegetable garden and surprise James with their efforts the following weekend.

"I'll see you on Saturday unless you need me to drive up during the week again," James said as he kissed Jane goodbye.

"Oh, I will *definitely* need you," she answered with a playful wink.

After Jane's car had disappeared from sight, James checked his watch. If he drove fast enough, he could reach his father's place in time for Milla's Sunday brunch. She often issued spontaneous invitations to her acquaintances from the First Baptist Church and prepared extra dishes ahead of time in the event her friends accepted. Luckily for James, the Methodist service ended thirty minutes before Milla's church let out, so he stood a fair chance of pulling into the driveway as his stepmother was serving her incredible food.

As the Bronco maneuvered the winding roads leading to his boyhood home, James visualized frying pans filled with bacon and sausage, a tray covered by buttery biscuits, and a platter of Milla's plump cinnamon buns, warm from the oven and covered with drizzles of sweet, buttery icing.

"Uh-oh," he spoke to his reflection in the rearview mirror. "With Jane sleeping over, I forgot to listen to my reinforcement CD. I've missed two nights in a row! No wonder I feel the old cravings stirring to life." He parked the truck next to Milla's lavender minivan, relieved that he'd be the only guest. "It's a good thing I'm seeing Harmony for another session tomorrow."

The renovated kitchen in his former home was filled with delicious aromas. Milla was just pulling a coffee cake from the oven when James tapped on the back door and let himself in.

"Oh! I'm *so* glad you showed up!" Milla placed the cake on the stovetop and gave James a hug. The warmth from her oven mitts seeped through his shirt, sending a soothing feeling across his back. "I asked Willow to join us this morning, but she couldn't make it. She and Francis are off to catch a matinee—some killer robot movie Francis has been waiting to see for months."

"Looks like you cooked enough to fill them to the point of exploding!" James exclaimed, eyeing a platter of crisp bacon and sausage links. "But I'd be delighted to eat Willow's share. In fact, I came over hoping you'd want to feed me."

Milla beamed. "Nothin' would please me more. And you know I have to make piles of bacon for your daddy. That man loves his meat!" She sprinkled pepper over a frying pan filled with scrambled eggs and gestured at the coffeemaker. "That's a fresh pot. Get yourself a cup and tell me how my grandson is doin' with his new diet."

James selected a mug from the cupboard, noting the chip on the rim. The majority of the coffee cups were damaged in some way and the dinner plates weren't much better. Jackson might have given the kitchen and upstairs bedrooms and baths a makeover, but those major cosmetic changes were enough to last him for decades.

Milla had brought her own cookware to the marriage, but she appeared to be perfectly content with the chipped crockery, the twenty-year-old curtains, and the ancient television in the den. She merely filled a closet with her clothes, added some pots and pans to the cabinets, and hung a few pictures on the wall. Most of these were of her beloved Corgi, Price Charles, who had passed away in his sleep shortly after Jackson and Milla were married. There were photographs from her childhood as well. The end result was a house simultaneously marked by both of Jackson's two wives, and no one entered the structure without feeling immediately at home.

"Eliot is still committed to being a vegetarian," James answered Milla's question as he fixed his coffee. "He complains about all the extra fruit and vegetables that show up in his lunchbox, but he eats them."

"Stickin' by his guns, just like his daddy and granddaddy." Milla used a spatula to lift a scalding bacon, egg, and cheese sandwich from her griddle onto a plate. James stopped her before she could add a piece of coffee cake, though the cinnamon crumble topping sorely tempted him. "You still trying to avoid sugar?" she asked.

"I am. I don't know that it's done any good, but I'll weigh myself tomorrow and hope for the best." James put his plate down on the kitchen table. "Where's Pop? Out in the shed?"

"Yes. He's doing a new series of paintings showing women at work." Milla set a loaded dish in front of Jackson's place. "'Course, he won't let me look at them until they're done, but will you go out there and tell him his lunch is ready and in danger of gettin' cold."

Jackson shouted his usual "Go away!" when James knocked on the shed door.

"Come on, Pop. Milla's made you a meal fit for a king!"

"I don't doubt that," Jackson mumbled, his voice betraying his anticipation. "I gotta finish this one thing, but it just ain't comin' out right." There was a pause and then Jackson shouted, "Damnation!"

James smiled. "Let me in, Pop. Or I'll huff and I'll puff . . ."

After a long hesitation, Jackson shuffled over to the door and slid a key into the padlock. His face appeared in the doorway, but he made no move to allow James inside. "That big bad wolf thing never gets any funnier, no matter how often you say it." He sighed and backed away, letting his son enter his private haven. "Go ahead. Never mind my food's gettin' cold as ice."

Jackson had begun his artistic career by painting birds. He then focused on the rendering of people's hands as they performed various tasks. After that, he produced a large number of paintings of little boys, all of which bore a close resemblance to Eliot, until the DC gallery owner—who also happened to be Lindy's mother—asked him to find a fresh subject.

Taking her advice, Jackson had worked feverishly for the past few months. He'd started at Dolly's Diner, watching the waitresses and of course Dolly herself. After painting a woman carrying a heavy serving tray, he'd selected a cashier at Food Lion, a female construction worker, and a mother balancing a toddler on one hip and a bag of dog kibble on the other. The women were shown concentrating on their tasks, their faces aglow with purpose. Every captured movement held a trace of strength, and the determination in each woman's plain face transformed them into radiant beauties.

"You've done it again," James whispered in awe as he stared at the canvases. "These are magical."

Suddenly, he had an idea. "Pop? I'd like to talk to you about a commission."

Jackson snorted. "You can't afford me, my boy."

Knowing his father was just giving him a hard time, James slung an arm over the older man's bony shoulders and squeezed. "Come on, Pop. I know how much you want me to drive you to Home Depot this afternoon."

"All right, son. We'll talk in the kitchen. I'm a better listener when I'm near a big plate of bacon."

• • •

Later that afternoon, James returned home with the parts he needed to replace the leaking faucets in the master bath and the kitchen sink. He'd never had reason to perform home repairs before, as Jackson had handled all the maintenance around the

Henry home, but he was excited to learn. Armed with a Time Life book on basic plumbing, James felt confident that he possessed the smarts and the tools to complete the necessary repairs.

He began with the bathroom faucet. By the time he'd figured out how to turn off the water, replace the faucet, and clean the water spots from the countertop, mirror, and floor, the sky had begun turning the orchid-purple of twilight.

James decided to repair the kitchen sink before heating up a dinner of roast chicken marinated in white wine and rosemary with a side of butter beans. It was only when he laid out his tools on a dishcloth next to the cutting board that he happened to glance out the window facing the backyard.

Something was hanging from the yellow birdhouse he'd placed in the center of a ring of Knock Out rosebushes behind the deck. The birdhouse stood on a tall wooden post and a light breeze was wafting through the yard, causing what appeared to be a piece of paper taped to the base of the birdhouse to flutter up and down.

Laying his wrench on the dish towel, James walked out to the garden bed. After pulling the letter off the birdhouse, he swiveled so the waning sun could illuminate the plain white sheet. He read the single sentence printed in plain block letters:

STAY AWAY FROM HER

Taped to the bottom of the paper was a single black feather.

Chapter Eight

Jalapeño Potato Chips

James stood rooted to the spot for several minutes, his eyes moving from the letter, to the deepening shadows in the trees, and back to the letter. His body became unnaturally still, as if a Gorgon had turned him into stone. When something flew past his face, startling him, he looked up and saw bats darting across the purplish sky. The rapid fluttering of their wings and their high-pitched squeaks broke the spell of immobility James had been under.

Rushing into the kitchen, he carefully slid the letter into a gallon-sized freezer bag, grabbed his car keys from the counter, and dashed out to the Bronco. A combination of anger and fear caused him to take the winding mountain roads at a risky pace, but his dependable old truck gripped the pavement as though sensing its driver's need.

Once, as James paused at a stop sign, he glanced at the bag on the passenger seat. The words of the letter seemed to be silently shouting at him, and the black feather looked like the curve of a malicious smile at the bottom of the paper.

He did not look at it again.

It took less than ten minutes to reach Lucy's house, which was on the outskirts of town. As James pulled into her dirt driveway, stirring up billows of dust as he rammed his gear stick into Park, her three German shepherds bounded from the open gate in the backyard and swarmed the Bronco. Though the dogs had known James for years and were intelligent enough to recognize his truck on sight, they enjoyed the idea of intimidating any intruder and began a chorus of snarling and barking raucous enough to wake the entire valley.

James rolled his window down an inch. "Bono! Bon Jovi! Benatar! It's me!"

The canines were not swayed by the voice of their mistress's ex-boyfriend. In fact, they curled their lips, revealing more of their threatening fangs. Their dark eyes glimmered with excitement.

"Come on, now." He pleaded with them through the window.

"I know this is all a front. A few Milkbones and you're putty in anyone's hands. Are you going to let me out or what?"

Apparently, they weren't. Tails swishing with glee, the dogs circled the Bronco and carried on with their howling until Lucy opened her front door. James saw her for only a second, but he could have sworn she was dressed in a slinky nightie. She vanished from view, returning less than a minute later.

Attired in sweatpants and a tank top, Lucy trotted down her front steps and walked toward the drive, shouting at the dogs to "stand down." James noticed that her feet were bare and she didn't seem too pleased to see him.

At this moment, James also noticed the vehicles parked along the fence line. There was Lucy's dirt-covered Jeep as well as a mud-splattered Camaro.

"I'm sorry," he said after she'd secured her dogs in the enclosed backyard. "If I'd known you had company . . ." he trailed off. "Actually, I would have come anyway. You're the first person I thought of to turn to . . ."

Lucy was immediately concerned. "What's wrong, James?"

He handed her the letter and explained about the dead birds left at Jane's house.

Lucy brought the plastic bag closer to her face. "Doesn't sound like a coincidence to me. A crow was nailed to her door and there's a crow's feather taped to this letter." She shook her head. "I don't like this. Someone trespassed on two properties and deliberately placed animal corpses or threatening letters in obvious locations. It's too invasive and sinister to be considered a prank."

"What should I do?" James hated the plaintive note in his voice, but he couldn't help it. "I'm not worried about me, but I feel like Jane and Eliot are vulnerable. The cops put her house on their drive-by list, but after receiving this, it's clear that the prankster followed her to my place. Jane has some kind of psycho stalker!"

Lucy studied the note a little longer. "You'd better come inside. I'd like to show this to Sullie and get his take."

So that's who owns the Camaro, James thought. He was surprised by how quickly Sullie and Lucy had become intimate.

Half expecting to see Sullie lounging on the sofa in silk boxer shorts while Barry White crooned from the stereo, James entered the house with trepidation. He found the hunky deputy seated at the kitchen table sipping a bottle of Budweiser. Like Lucy, he was clad in sweats and a T-shirt. Upon seeing James, he jumped up and smiled.

"Good to see you, man! You're looking well." He grasped James's hand and shook it heartily.

"You too," James replied, observing Sullie's flat belly, mammoth shoulders, and tree trunk legs. The man looked like he'd been carved from a block of limestone. Though he wasn't exactly Einstein, he was handsome and extremely friendly. James had done his best to cultivate a dislike for the man in the past but he now realized that he bore no ill will toward the amiable deputy.

"Welcome back to Quincy's Gap, Sullie. I apologize for disturbing your evening, but I'm feeling a little desperate." James gestured at Lucy. "She's always been the problem solver of our group and I have a major problem."

Lucy gave him a grateful smile and placed the note in the center of the table. When she spoke, it was as an officer of the law. She reviewed the pertinent details for Sullie and then awaited his assessment.

"Your ex-wife believes the perp could be one of her students?" Sullie asked.

James shrugged. "It seemed like the most logical conclusion at the time, but now that I've received this note, I'm not so sure. It's hard to imagine a disgruntled coed driving from Harrisonburg to here to leave me a creepy note because of an exam grade."

"Do you and Jane share any common enemies?" Lucy's fingertips hovered just above the crow's feather. "Someone who likes birds or spends lots of time outdoors?"

Sullie nodded, as though Lucy's question was a sound one. He then crossed the kitchen in three strides and retrieved two bottles of Bud from the refrigerator. Popping the caps off into the garbage can, he handed one to James and the second to Lucy. She declined, her attention fixed on the letter.

"Honestly, the only person who might have reason to dislike us both is Murphy." James felt his cheeks rush with heat. "I think she planned on rekindling our relationship after returning to Quincy's Gap and wasn't too thrilled to hear that I had a son and was on great terms with my ex-wife."

Lucy's expression was masked and James hoped he hadn't offended her. In describing Murphy's feelings, he'd described the way Lucy had felt about him until very recently. She remained silent, but Sullie took a swig from his beer and said, "Makes sense. If Murphy wants you to stay away from your ex and is angry about you two spending time together, she might have written this."

"Still, I can't see her driving to Harrisonburg and nailing a dead crow on Jane's front door," James protested. "You'd have to be pretty twisted to do that."

James had barely finished speaking when Lucy spread her hands. "May I remind you that this woman was secretly writing a book about you, about *us*, the whole time you were dating? Don't underestimate her ability to deceive!"

Chastised, James took a sip of beer.

Lucy touched him on the arm, as if to apologize for being too harsh. "The least I can do is try to find out what Murphy was up to this evening. I know she'll be at the Sweet Tooth tomorrow morning, picking up coffee and a croissant, and I can casually question her then." Lucy frowned. "That woman eats loads of carbs every day and is thinner than a tomato stake. It's not fair."

"Men don't like tomato stakes." Sullie put a proprietary hand on Lucy's hip. "We want soft curves with just the right amount of steel underneath. Like you, baby."

Seeming embarrassed but pleased, Lucy removed Sullie's hand from her hip and kissed him on the palm. James cleared his throat and said, "Well, I'd better be on my way. Thanks for hearing me out—both of you." He gestured at the letter. "Should I leave this with you?"

Lucy nodded and accompanied him to the door. "If I think Murphy is lying about her whereabouts this evening, I'll whip this out and see if it elicits a reaction." Her blue eyes flashed, reminding James of the aggressive glimmer he'd seen in her dogs' eyes.

"I know you'd like to bring Murphy down a peg," James said. "Lord knows she deserves some comeuppance instead of fame and fortune, but I can't imagine her doing something like this."

The pair stood on the stoop for a moment, watching the moths flutter around the lamppost guarding the entrance of Lucy's path. James glanced at her, trying to find the words to express how much he wanted their relationship to return to what it had been when they'd first formed the supper club.

"This is good," he finally said. "You and Sullie. I know it's still a new thing, but you seem perfect for each other. There's an easiness between you two." He looked out into the night and continued. "You're one of my best friends, Lucy. I want you to be happy. Thanks again for being so gracious tonight."

After flashing her a smile, he began to walk toward the Bronco.

"James!" Lucy called after him. "I'll also check in with the Harrisonburg police tomorrow. I want to let them know that the person bothering Jane is up to something down here too. That ought to ensure her house stays on their patrol list." She put her hands on her hips, doing her best to look fierce. "I'll be driving by *your* place myself. After all, nobody messes with one of *my* best friends and gets away with it."

And just like that, their friendship was restored.

James drove home beneath the white light of the full moon. Hung high in the sky among a cluster of stars and a brighter orb that was likely a planet, the moon seemed to grin down upon the round hills of the Shenandoah Valley.

At home, James took a beer out to the deck and settled into a plastic lounge chair. He listened to a chorus of crickets and the buzzing of other insects until his grumbling stomach reminded him that he'd forgotten about dinner. It was late and he was tired, so he settled for a generous snack of jalapeño-flavored Pringles. He sat outside for a long time, his anxiety ebbing as the night wore on. Sighing, he let his body sink into the chair. As his lids grew heavy, James realized that he'd eaten the entire tube of potato chips.

This does not bode well for tomorrow's weigh-in, he thought and sluggishly climbed into bed. Still, he decided that a threatening note could force even the most disciplined eater into a junk food binge. *It's not like I had a bunch of sugar,* he reasoned before drifting off to sleep.

• • •

The next morning, James shucked off his T-shirt and pajama bottoms and prepared to face the scale. It had nearly killed him to go through an entire week without weighing himself. He was a creature of habit, and it was his habit to wake up, shuffle into the bathroom, turn on the shower, and shed his clothes. He'd then put his hands on his belly in front of his bathroom mirror, pivoting this way and that while squeezing his flesh and trying to determine if his paunch felt bigger or smaller than the day before.

Pinching the flesh around his belly button, James's hand would then travel to his love handles. He'd grasp them between his hands, wiggling the flesh up and down. Finally, he'd suck in a deep breath and watch his stomach shrink by several inches.

Now, having gone through his usual routine, he murmured to the bathroom mirror, "Doesn't feel any different. Let's see what the numbers have to say."

As was customary, James inhaled a giant breath and then forcefully exhaled. When he believed every ounce of air had been expelled from his lungs, he stepped on the scale. Shifting until his feet were perfectly centered on the glass surface, he held himself as still as possible and waited for the digital numbers to surface in their silver window. He never breathed until they'd revealed themselves. Now, as his weight appeared, his inhalation was sharp with frustration and disappointment.

"I haven't lost a thing!" he shouted at the device. "Why give up sugar when my weight stays *exactly* the same!"

In the shower, he angrily massaged shampoo into his hair and roughly scrubbed his skin with a washcloth. It was as though he wanted to punish his body for a less-than-desirable result on the scale.

By the time James reached the library, his mood had improved slightly due to a large cup of creamy coffee and a breakfast of whole grain waffles and strawberries. When he saw Francis and Scott pedaling into the parking lot on their mountain bikes, racing to see who would reach the book drop first, he couldn't help but grin.

"Whoa!" Francis shouted. "You're like a lightning bolt today, bro! You must really want to get busy *training* Fern over in the Tech Corner, eh?"

Scott's cheeks burned red and he punched his twin in the arm. "Shut up, dude!" Next, he chained his bike to the rack and jogged up the stairs, saluting James when he reached the top. "We're all set for Mrs. Waxman's retirement party, Professor."

"Milla and Willow told us they'd handle the food, so all we have to do is make the punch and decorate," Francis chimed in as the three men entered the library. "Should one of the punch bowls be spiked, Professor?"

"Absolutely. And I have an amazing gift idea, assuming my father can paint as fast as you two can ride those bikes," James said. "Ah, here comes Fern for her final day of training. She's a quick study, isn't she?"

"Too quick," Scott muttered and then beamed at Fern as she breezed through the security gate, the full skirt of her rose-colored sundress billowing around her. Her eyes immediately sought Scott's and she gave him a special smile before greeting James and Francis.

The four librarians prepared for their first patrons of the day. When the clock struck nine, people trickled into the building, and the library hummed softly with activity all morning long. Just before lunch, James heard an inappropriately loud and combative voice from the direction of the circulation desk. He'd been busy helping Mrs. Withers navigate the computer. Having decided to sell her collection of Beanie Babies, she wanted to look up current market values on eBay. James had directed her to the online auction site and then paled when she produced a notebook filled with pages of Beanie Baby inventory.

"You'd like to check the value of each of these?" he asked, dreading her reply. "How many do you have, ma'am?"

"A thousand or so," Mrs. Withers replied merrily and patted the notebook. "I'm hopin' to raise enough money to take my daughter on a little trip. She hasn't been away since Roy Junior was born and *that* was five years ago. She won't leave the boy, but if I buy tickets, she'll feel like she has to go." She pursed her lips. "Parents hover too much nowadays. When I was a mother, I still had my own life. I played bridge and tennis and was president of the gardening club. My girl needs to cut the cord and I'm gonna help her do it!"

Using his concern over the raised voice at the circulation desk as an excuse to avoid a lengthy session of eBay tutelage, James hustled off.

He was most surprised to see Murphy and Tia in a standoff against Scott. Of course, Tia was the only one not speaking in hushed tones. Standing with one hand on her left hip, she gesticulated wildly with the other, clearly ignoring Scott's requests to lower her voice.

Murphy stood slightly apart from the younger woman, as if trying to distance herself. However, her face was alight with voyeuristic pleasure.

James stepped up to Tia and forced his lips into a tight smile. In an exaggerated whisper he asked, "How can I help you, ladies?"

Tia turned her dark eyes on him and then looked back at Murphy and hissed, "Forget about the library! Let's go to the grocery store!"

And with that, she walked out.

Murphy gazed at James with a mixture of wonder and befuddlement. "You sure have a way with women, Mr. Henry. She nearly lost a few piercings in her haste to get away from you. Why is that?"

James shrugged. "I have no idea." He glanced over at Scott, more interested in pacifying his distressed employee than satisfying Murphy's curiosity. "What did the young woman want?"

Scott pushed a small poster across the desk. "To hang *this* under the Community Happenings section of our bulletin board. I told her nicely that it was too scary for our younger patrons, but she wouldn't take no for an answer." His cheeks flushed. "I repeated myself several times and I tried to be polite, but when she called me a fascist and an accessory to murder I got a little mad." He raked his hands through his hair and sighed. "I shouldn't have mentioned that I was having a meatball sub for lunch."

James gave his employee a sympathetic pat on the shoulder before leaning over the counter to examine the poster. It portrayed the image of a cartoonish pig lying on its back with its legs sticking in the air. It had X's for eyes and a long tongue lolled from its mouth. Above the pig, a spider resembling Charlotte from the E. B. White novel had written the following words in her web: DON'T KILL WILBUR. BECOME A VEGETARIAN.

"Charlotte must have been worn out after spinning such a long slogan," James remarked. "You're right, Scott. I think it would definitely upset the kids and quite a few adult patrons as well."

Murphy, who had made no move to accompany Tia, crossed her arms and studied James. "Hasn't your own son recently become a vegetarian?"

"Yes, but . . ." James was about to say that Eliot hadn't been shocked or emotionally traumatized into the decision, but he knew that wasn't the absolute truth. After all, his son had been so influenced by Fay Sunray's words that he'd fled the dinner table after being faced with a slice of pepperoni pizza. Gesturing at the poster, he asked, "Is this your new method of conducting interviews, Murphy? I thought you preferred to gather material over one of Willie's frozen custards and a cappuccino?"

"I do," Murphy said. "But Tia is a sharp negotiator. She talked me into putting these posters all over town before she'd answer my more probing questions. I've been collecting background material on her as we work, but I'm her hired hand until the posters are all up." She glanced in the direction of the lobby doors and then reclaimed the poster. "She's not going anywhere without me because we took my car. And you can bet your Dewey decimal system that I'm going to find out why she looked at you like you were the Charles Manson of Quincy's Gap."

James scowled. "Perhaps she's read your *novel* too many times and thinks that hanging around me will spell certain death."

"You *do* have a certain magnetism when it comes to corpses." Murphy smiled and touched his cheek with an intimacy that made James uncomfortable. "I find that quality strangely sexy."

• • •

James didn't feel like skipping to A Better State of Mind as he had for his past two sessions. In fact, he'd been in a foul mood ever since Murphy's visit to the library, and he hadn't been able to shake it. Pulling into a parking space next to a shiny new SUV, James paused to admire the moss-green paint, the tidy tan leather interior, and the vanity plate reading VEG OUT.

"Hey, man!" Lennon called out as he headed in James's direction. "You like my ride? It's a Ford Escape Hybrid. Gets thirty miles to the gallon and has super clean emissions. *Totally* earth-friendly."

"It's a beaut." James glanced at the frayed ends of Lennon's jeans, his washed-out Bob Marley T-shirt, and his worn sandals. Leaving all tact aside he said, "That must have cost a pretty penny."

"Dude, like, a generous relative gave me some dough." Lennon smiled guilelessly. "I believe in living in the moment, ya know. I could totally get hit by a bus tomorrow, so why not live large today?" He gestured at the rack affixed to the back of the SUV. "Do you bike, man? I could show you some of the awesome local trails I've discovered. My all-time fav is the Brandywine Lake Trail. Fifty-two miles of rock 'n roll. Whenever I'm stressin', that place chills me right out. I have two bikes! I can put on the dual rack in a snap!" He gestured at the back of his truck. "Wanna let loose?"

James laughed at the image of himself barreling down a wooded path. "I think I'll stick to four wheels, but my coworkers, Scott and Francis, ride their bikes to work. You should drop by the library so I can introduce you. You guys are about the same age and I bet they'd love to check out a new trail." Looking at his watch, James saw that he still had a few minutes until his appointment. He wanted to linger with Lennon a little longer, as he enjoyed his buoyant personality. "Does Skye ride too?"

Lennon shook his head. "Nah, she's more into running. It's her time to center, ya know? Just her, an iPod, and a long stretch of road. That's cool, but sometimes a guy's gotta rip down a hill with the trees flying by like *whish*!" He gesticulated with his well-calloused hands. "Anyhow, the workday is done, my man, so I am outta here. Gonna go suck in some oxygen! Peace out!"

Feeling slightly silly, James returned the universal gesture for peace and walked through the Wellness Village to Harmony's office. Skye accepted his payment and offered him a glass of citrus-flavored water and a smile.

"Harmony is running a little late," she apologized on behalf of her employer. "Would you like to browse our newest magazines while you wait?"

James took a few from Skye's graceful hands. "Thank you." He placed the magazines on the sofa and watched Skye water a potted ficus tree in the corner of the reception room. "I ran into Lennon outside. He's such a friendly guy. I can see why you two make such a good couple. You both exude such a positive . . ." He trailed off, unsure of the correct wording.

"Aura?" Skye finished for him. "That's sweet of you to say. Lennon and I haven't been dating long, but I admire how he puts his entire being into everything he does The smallest details are important to him, from raking the rock garden to hosing out the trash cans to picking wildflowers for me." She colored prettily. "I've never known someone so gentle and yet so dedicated."

"Well, he's lucky to have captured your heart," James said as Harmony's door opened and Lindy walked slowly down the hall, still drowsy from her time of deep relaxation.

James was delighted to see his friend. "I didn't know you'd be here today."

"I *had* to get help!" Lindy whispered loudly. "I never thought the three hours I spent with Luis's mama would throw me into such a tailspin, but that woman is a Tasmanian devil—emphasis on 'devil'!"

Stifling a grin, James led Lindy to the sofa. "That bad, eh?"

"She ran her finger along the baseboard *underneath* my kitchen table and glanced at the dust like it might eat away her hand! She held up each piece of silverware to the light, looking for spots. And then she polished them on her *own* handkerchief. After eating three bites of the meal I'd slaved over all day, she had a sudden loss of appetite." Lindy rubbed her eyes. "She never spoke directly to me. If she wanted to know something about my house, my family, or my job, she'd ask Luis, as if I wasn't even there! It was awful!"

James gave his friend a hug. "Did Harmony make you feel better?"

Lindy nodded. "I asked her to help me keep a firm hold on my self-confidence, but this is going to be a mighty long week." She sighed lugubriously. "I'll be listening to my new reinforcement CD in all my spare time."

"Bring her along to Mrs. Waxman's retirement party," James suggested. "We'll pour champagne punch down her throat and stuff her full of Milla's cake."

"Can't I just drop her off at the local taxidermist instead? That would get her out of my hair forever," Lindy joked, and James was pleased to note that his friend's sense of humor was intact. "Are you going in for another sugar-busting session?"

"I don't know." It was James's turn to be downcast. "I haven't lost any weight and I feel like I'm at war with myself."

Harmony arrived at that moment and smiled at both of her clients. "Perhaps today's session should be about striking a balance between your mind and body," she gently advised. "Lindy, feel free to call me if you need to see me again this week. Just remember to listen to your CD and to believe in your value as a wonderful and unique individual."

Lindy nodded and shut her eyes for a moment. After opening them again, she said goodbye to James and reached for the front door, repeating Harmony's phrase like a mantra. "I am a unique and wonderful individual. I am a unique and wonderful individual."

Harmony didn't interrupt Lindy but softly directed Skye to catch up to their client outside, as Lindy had departed without her reinforcement CD. Skye neatly labeled the CD before heading for the exit.

"Won't she be too late to catch Lindy?" James asked as he followed Harmony into her office.

"Skye was a track star in college. She doesn't run like the wind, she *vanquishes* the wind." Harmony gestured at the recliner and James sank heavily into the chair. "Tell me what's going on."

"I haven't lost a single ounce and I'm angry," James answered. "Like Lindy, I've had a stressful few days and I feel like I'll never make any progress in the weight-loss department until I have more faith in myself. Right now, that's running a little low."

Harmony considered her client's problem for a moment and then wrote a few notes on a legal pad. "Considering these developments, let's change our direction slightly. Instead of focusing on sugar cravings, we're going to ask your mind and body to work together as a single unit—for your entire self to be one team, striving for health and a sense of well-being. How does that sound?"

"Can you throw in a dose of stress relief too?" James implored. "I feel like if I don't dial down that part of my brain I'll be hijacking Little Debbie trucks before long!"

The sound of Harmony's musical laughter filled the room.

When her expression of calm concern returned she asked, "In addition to your frustration over not losing weight, are other factors causing you anxiety?"

James issued an unattractive snort. "It'll take more time than we've got to cover them all! Let's just take care of my inner war today. We can tackle maniacal ex-girlfriends, psychotic letter writers, and zealous vegetarian activists next week." He cleared his throat. "No offense."

"None taken," Harmony replied and dimmed the lights.

Chapter Nine

Milla's Chocolate Mocha Cake

While running errands in preparation for Mrs. Waxman's surprise party, James and his coworkers encountered Tia's pig poster everywhere. Not only did it hang from the bulletin board at Food Lion, the YMCA, and the post office, but it had also been taped to the windows of dozens of small businesses, including the ABC store, Goodbee's Pharmacy, the Polar Pagoda, and the Yuppie Puppy. It seemed like Quincy's Whimsies and the Sweet Tooth were the only establishments in town that had refused to display the poster.

By the time Wednesday evening rolled around, the talk among the library staff revolved around Murphy's newspaper article on animal rights activist Katrina "Tia" Royale.

"Bro, she didn't act like someone whose parents were mega rich," Scott said to Francis. "When I think of a tycoon's daughter, I picture a mafia princess like Meadow Soprano or an airhead socialite like Paris Hilton."

His twin tied a knot in an orange balloon. "It's kinda cool that Tia isn't constantly taking selfies or carrying around a little dog in her purse. Maybe, to be her own person, she decided to put all her time and money into protecting animals. From what I read in the *Star*, she could spend every day shopping and still not put a dent in her trust fund, but she doesn't act like a spoiled brat."

Willow scowled and handed her boyfriend a yellow balloon. "Why don't you save your breath for the balloons, Francis?"

"What? Did I say something wrong?" Francis reached out to touch Willow's arm, but she swatted his hand away.

"*Some* of us don't have trust funds," she pointed out heatedly. "*Some* of us work at regular jobs *and* serve our causes in our spare time without making little kids cry!"

Scott passed Fern a roll of tape and a crepe paper streamer so she could affix the decoration to the exit sign. Peering down at Willow from the top of the small ladder, Fern said, "I haven't been your roommate for long, but *I'm* impressed by how many hours you volunteer at the animal shelter."

"I love being there," Willow replied, pleased to receive recognition for her efforts. "Don't get me wrong, I also love my work at Quincy's Whimsies, but it's *so* rewarding to watch a family adopt a dog or cat." Willow sighed happily. "Did you know that our shelter doesn't euthanize? It's wonderful, but it also means that our cages are always full." She pointed at James, who was busy pouring chilled champagne into one of the punch bowls. "I keep trying to persuade Mr. Henry to adopt a pet for Eliot. Every kid needs a furry friend. Especially an only child. It's nice for them to have someone to talk to. Can't you see Eliot and a frisky little puppy rolling around in that big backyard of Mr. Henry's?"

Fern smiled at Willow. "I'd like to volunteer at the shelter too, but I'm afraid I'd end up filling our apartment with animals. How do you keep from bringing them all home?"

"Easy—our landlord would toss us out on our butts!" Willow laughed. "Maybe when our lease runs out in the fall, we could rent a small house instead. That way, we can at least provide foster care for some of the shelter animals until they find permanent homes."

"I'd love that," Fern readily agreed. "And I'm one of those crazy people who actually enjoys yard work, so you'll never have to cut the grass."

As the two young women exchanged excited chatter, James finished arranging the plastic punch cups on a card table and placed a stack of napkins in the center. Standing back, he examined his handiwork with a frown.

"Doesn't look too good," he murmured.

"It was a nice try, dear, but this calls for a woman's touch." Milla gently pushed him aside. "Why don't you carry in the food from my van and leave the decorating to me? And keep your daddy away from the spiked punch," she ordered, her eyes twinkling. "He's been grumbling all day over having to attend and if he drinks too much on an empty stomach, he's gonna ride that wheeled book cart home before the party even gets started."

Laughing, James went out to Milla's lavender van and carried in trays of hors d'oeuvres, a platter of ham biscuits, and a stunning cake made to resemble a stack of library books. Easing the cake carefully onto a side table, James paused to admire Milla's artistry.

The frosted book on the top was entitled *Quincy's Gap Loves Mrs. Waxman.* Below that line was a chocolate fudge subtitle listing the years she'd worked at the library. In place of the author's name were the words *From Your Grateful Patrons.* James inhaled the delectable scents of chocolate and coffee and sighed.

"Chocolate mocha cake with coffee icing. It's Mrs. Waxman's favorite," Milla said as he admired the confection. "Why don't you take a picture of the food before the festivities start? Fern is going to make a scrapbook for our retiree." She glanced over at James's newest employee. "She's a lovely girl. I do believe she's sweet on our Scott, too. How do you feel about inter-office love affairs?"

James rubbed his chin. "Their shifts don't overlap much, so I'm not worried about things getting awkward if they start dating and find that they're not compatible. What perplexes me is Scott's reluctance to ask Fern out." He lowered his voice. "He's become close to someone online and feels that he can't pursue a relationship with Fern until he meets this other girl in the flesh."

Milla put her hands over her chest. "To see if sparks fly—how exciting! Where and when is this face-to-face going to happen?"

"It's hard to say." James removed the plastic wrap from a platter of sliced strawberries and baked Brie. "She canceled their original meeting time at the last minute, so Scott is now filled with doubts. Poor kid."

Clucking her tongue disapprovingly, Milla said, "Computer dating sounds awful sticky to me. Call me old-fashioned, but I don't think it's wise to fall in love with a person when you can't look into their eyes or listen to the sound of their laughter." She placed a silver ladle next to the punch bowl. "Folks just don't come off the same through a computer screen. You can make yourself into anybody you want by typing a few words and doctoring a few photos, but what's the good of someone falling in love with a 'you' who doesn't exist?"

"It's how our world works now, Milla. People communicate using their phones or the computer."

Puckering her lips, Milla waved her hand around the room. "A machine will never be able to replace *this!*"

James had been so busy placing the food trays where Milla instructed that he hadn't noticed the library's transformation.

Bright balloons and paper streamers hung from the ceiling and floral cloths covered the study tables in the main room. Fern and Willow were setting small vases filled with Gerbera daises in the center of each table, while Scott laid out a guest book for the partygoers to sign, and Francis programmed one of the computers to play three hours' worth of smooth jazz.

Several guests had shown up early to lend a hand. One placed garbage cans in strategic positions, another wheeled the cart of sale books in from the lobby, and a third helped Jackson lift his latest painting, covered by a white cloth, onto an easel on the counter of the Information Desk.

As the sound of saxophones, trumpets, and clarinets floated through the room, the supper club members began to trickle in as though lured by the enticing strains of music.

Gillian and Bennett entered first, and James was happy to see that they were holding hands. Lucy was the next to arrive. James had told her to bring Sullie along and she'd been pleased by the suggestion. Lucy introduced her handsome boyfriend to the other guests as a fellow deputy, but her face, glowing with happiness, betrayed her true feelings. Sullie kept glancing at her from the corner of his eye. Occasionally, he'd whisper to her, causing her to laugh or blush with delight. James had never seen Lucy look so beautiful.

When Lindy appeared, running ten minutes late, she sped right over to James and clutched his arm as if he could save her from slipping through a thin patch of ice. "Look out, James, she's here! The Dragon Lady of Mexico! Is there *anyone* you can find to entertain Luis's mama for five minutes?"

"Only five minutes?" James teased.

Lindy nodded. "That's all it'll take for me to chug down a cup of champagne punch. I don't want her to see me drinking or it'll be another strike against me. It's bad enough that I'm a 'half-blood.'"

"She called you that?" James frowned, but couldn't comment as Luis and a small, plump woman with wiry black hair and walnut-brown eyes entered the room. The woman surveyed the surroundings with a curled lip. Luis walked with rounded shoulders, darting apologetic glances in Lindy's direction as his mother pulled on his sleeve, forcing him to bend to her height so she might more easily release a stream of complaints—all in Spanish, of course—into his ear.

At that moment, Luigi joined the party. Mrs. Waxman had spent countless hours giving the restaurateur advice on the education of his six children and he'd become one of her adoring fans. He'd even offered to cater the event, but Milla and Willow wouldn't hear of it.

"Professor Henry!" he shouted from across the room. "The library—che bello!"

Waving Luigi closer, James offered him a glass of punch. The restaurateur accepted the beverage with a booming thank-you and then left James to mingle with the older widows and divorcées. By the time the other guests arrived, along with Mrs. Waxman and her closest family members, Luigi had made his way over to Luis's mother.

"Alma? Such a lovely name!" he bellowed. "You are thirsty? Come! Luigi will get you a drink!"

James held his breath, expecting Alma to reject Luigi's vociferous offer, but to his surprise, she smiled and took Luigi's proffered arm. Luis stared after them in amazement.

The noise level escalated as Mrs. Waxman made her rounds. James felt a pang of sadness as he watched his former middle school teacher and coworker accept handshakes and warm embraces from everyone in the room.

"I still don't think I should be here," Fern whispered to James. "It doesn't feel right."

"Mrs. Waxman specifically asked for you to attend," James reminded her. ",You're part of our team now *and* you're capturing the event on film." He pointed at her camera. "Whenever Mrs. Waxman misses us, she'll only need to open the scrapbook you're creating to feel like she's with her friends in Quincy's Gap again. See? You're already an asset."

"Your father's painting will help her remember too. I can't wait to see it." Fern glanced around the room. "Have you ever thought of using all that great wall space to display the work of local artists?"

James followed her gaze. The three walls surrounding the Tech Corner were well lit, yet rather bare. A few posters featuring celebrities holding their favorite books were the only adornment.

"That's a terrific idea, Fern. Maybe my father would let me hang his next series before the paintings are shipped off to DC."

As Fern navigated the room snapping candids, Scott acted as her assistant. He carried her punch glass, replenished her empty dinner plate, and directed the guests to stand this way and that so Fern could take their photographs.

The noise level rose as the punch bowls and platters of food grew empty. Francis had to turn up the music more than once in order for the guests to be able to hear the songs over Luigi's thunderous chatter.

Finally, it was time for Mrs. Waxman to cut the cake. She accepted a knife from Milla and then positioned herself behind the cake, dabbing under her glasses with a tissue. "Please don't force me to make a speech," she said and sniffed. "I know I've talked most of your ears off between my tenure as teacher and librarian, but there aren't enough words in the English language to express how grateful I am to have been a member of this wonderful community. To say that I will miss you all is the greatest understatement of my life. Thank you so much."

She slid the knife into the cake to a round of raucous applause. Afterward, she personally distributed a generous wedge to every person in the room. Even Alma's stony expression softened when Mrs. Waxman welcomed her to town and praised Luis for being the most progressive and talented principal she'd ever known.

"You are too kind," Alma responded, before turning to chat with Luigi again.

Once all the guests had eaten their cake, including each and every one of the supper club members, Scott and Francis directed everyone's attention to the Information Desk. Standing on either side of the shrouded easel, their boyish faces flushed with anticipation, the twins waited for James to say a few words about Mrs. Waxman's farewell gift.

"Thank you for coming tonight," James began. "I always suspected that Mrs. Waxman was friends with half of Quincy's Gap, but it wasn't until this evening that I realized it was true. We have all benefited from her wisdom, patience, and generosity. She's treated every student and every patron in this library with respect and dignity."

Mrs. Waxman honked into her tissue, and several members of the audience wiped their eyes and exchanged nods of agreement with their fellow townsfolk.

Turning to Mrs. Waxman, James concluded his brief speech. "Teacher. Librarian. Friend. You have left your mark on so many people. Now, thanks to my father, Jackson Henry, you can take a moment of your life in Quincy's Gap with you when you start your next chapter in sunny Arizona. Godspeed, dear Mrs. Waxman. You will be sorely missed."

The Fitzgerald twins reacted immediately to their boss's signal—a slight dip of the chin. In perfect synchronization, they whisked the white cloth off the surface of the painting, beaming as they witnessed Mrs. Waxman's reaction to her gift.

The guests broke into applause as they viewed the work of art. A portrait of Mrs. Waxman, the painting depicted her standing behind the information desk. For years she had reigned over that small territory, squared in by four equal countertops displaying the monthly staff picks and the latest book club reads.

Every evening, she'd put her dinner in the break room and then organize the stacks of bookmarks, recommended reading flyers, and piles of free magazines and community newsletters located on her countertops.

Jackson had included her regular workspace in his painting, but what he'd captured best was the joy Mrs. Waxman felt when helping another person. He'd positioned her standing at a slight angle and her face, gently etched with wrinkles and laugh lines, was focused on a young girl of about ten years of age. The girl had been painted in profile with her hands held out in order to receive the book Mrs. Waxman was presenting. Her young face was filled with gratitude, as if she understood that the librarian was offering so much more than a simple book. The painting showed Mrs. Waxman in her element—every fiber of her being was invested in opening up new worlds to her young patron. Passion shone from her eyes like a beacon.

"It's wonderful!" Mrs. Waxman cried, her lips trembling. James put an arm around her while she struggled to keep her emotions in check. "Your father is a maestro! How can I ever thank him?"

Knowing that Jackson was bound to be hiding, James promised

to take Mrs. Waxman to him before he made an escape. "Now that the food portion of the evening is done, there's a good chance he's out in the van, waiting to go home. He likes to sit in the den and watch game show reruns before he goes to bed. He says they settle his stomach."

Mrs. Waxman laughed. "His habits must have served him well. The man is fit as a fiddle. It must take a great deal of energy and concentration to produce paintings like his, so he's also strong." She patted James on the hand. "You have some good genes in you, my boy."

James tried not to frown. "I think I take after my mother. As you can see, the only thin part of my body is my hairline, and as far as possessing artistic ability, I can't even draw a stick figure." He smiled, not wanting to spoil a second of the guest of honor's special night. "There's just more of me to love," he joked and excused himself to go off in search of Jackson.

Tracking down his father took longer than expected. Everyone wanted to comment on how much they admired Jackson's work, and James found himself conversing with several guests about their own works of art. Before he knew it, he'd received commitments from three artists willing to display their water-colors, engravings, and textile pieces on the walls in the Tech Corner.

When he finally reached the circulation desk, he stopped to praise Fern for her wonderful idea. "Our library gallery is going to be a hit! Well done."

"I'd like to be included as a local artist too," added Fern with a trace of shyness. "I think I told you that I was a freelance photographer, but my passion is nature photography. I have a whole series of color photos that I took in the Great Smoky Mountains National Park. I framed them myself."

James put a hand on Fern's shoulder. "Your work will be displayed first. This was your idea and it would be a wonderful way to introduce you to our community. We could post a short bio and, if you have a website or an email where folks can buy prints from you, which might help with your long-term goal of renting a house."

"I don't have a website yet," Fern answered, her entire being sparkling with enthusiasm. "But maybe I could build a simple one over the weekend."

"If you need help, Scott's quite adept at that sort of thing," James suggested slyly and headed for his office. The moment he stepped inside, he knew something was wrong.

Jackson was seated in one of the office chairs facing the desk. His shoulders were slumped and he didn't look up when James approached. Milla was squatting on her heels, a hand on each of Jackson's knees as she spoke to her husband in a voice riddled with worry. When James entered the room, she shot him a fearful glance and then turned back to her husband.

"Your left side? Does it hurt?" she asked Jackson.

"What is it?" James's eyes darted from Milla to his father. "Pop?"

Jackson tried to wave him off. "It's nothin'. My leg's gone to sleep—probably from sittin' around this damned place all night."

James looked closely at this father's face. "But you're not experiencing any pain or discomfort?"

"Nah," Jackson answered, but his gaze seemed to be out of focus.

Brushing aside the apprehension blooming in his mind, James gently lifted his father's left hand. "Can you squeeze my fingers, Pop?"

"James!" Jackson's voice seemed to come from a long way off. He reached out with his right hand, clumsily feeling for his son's shoulder. "I can't see you!"

"Call 911!" James urged Milla before capturing his father's panicked hand in his own. "It'll be all right, Pop. Hold on. We're going to get you help."

James listened as Milla spoke to the emergency operator. He knew the call would be routed to the fire station across the street and that an EMT could be in the room in less than five minutes.

Those minutes were the longest of his life. As James held on to his father, trying not to concentrate on the frailty of his weathered hand, the left side of Jackson's face slowly drooped downward and a line of spittle leaked from his open mouth.

"Pop?" James tenderly shook his father. "*Pop!*"

A black pulse of fear throbbed in James's chest. Milla had left the room to wait for the paramedics in the lobby and, alone in his office with his unresponsive father, James struggled to keep his voice calm and even. "Don't leave me, Pop. Hang on. I'm right here with you. I won't let go." James had to stop speaking because his throat swelled tight with emotion. He refused to give way to despair, so he inhaled a deep breath, choked back the terror, and continued to repeat the words, "It's okay, I'm right here," over and over again.

He barely noticed when one of the EMTs placed a firm hand on his shoulder and eased him away from his father's unresponsive form. James stood to the side, listening to a blur of muted speech, a blood pressure cuff inflating, a stethoscope shimmering on the pale flesh of Jackson's chest, a light darting across a pair of unblinking blue eyes.

With infinite care, the paramedics lifted Jackson onto a stretcher. They placed an oxygen mask over his nose and mouth, and James couldn't tear his gaze from the device, for it seemed to foretell a future with limited independence.

James followed the EMTs as they wheeled his father through the lobby past rows of silent and sympathetic faces. When the Fitzgerald brothers detached themselves from the rest of the group to ask if they could help, James realized that he couldn't just race off after the ambulance. It was one of the hardest things he'd ever had to do, but he paused and took a moment to think.

"Francis, can you and Scott tidy up the library and handle all the opening duties in the morning?" He removed a set of keys from his key ring and handed them to Scott. The twin gazed at them wide-eyed and then closed his fist around the brass keys with reverence.

"Don't worry about the library, Professor. We'll run this place just like you would," Francis promised.

James clenched his lips together so they wouldn't tremble and gave each brother a pat on the arm. "Please ask Willow to do the same at Quincy's Whimsies. And give Mrs. Waxman a hand loading her painting into the car. Tell her I'm sorry I couldn't say goodbye," he added as he turned toward the doors leading outside.

Tormented by the unwelcome thought that the portrait of Mrs. Waxman might be Jackson's final painting, James jogged toward his truck. He tried to hide his misery beneath a façade of resolve as he opened the passenger door for his stepmother.

"He's strong," Milla said as James got in beside her and sped off behind the ambulance, the strobe of red lights bathing the white hood of his Bronco in an eerie glow.

They remained silent en route to the hospital. Milla's hands were clasped and her eyes were shut, and James suspected she was deep in prayer. He also made silent appeals to the Almighty until they reached the hospital complex.

In the emergency room waiting area, James completed the stacks of paperwork given him by the triage nurse, and asked Milla to buy two cups of coffee from the vending machine down the hall. He knew they were likely to spend most of the night in the waiting room and hoped the coffee could take an edge off the shock.

They hadn't spent long in the bucket-like chairs when another nurse asked them to follow her deeper inside the hospital. Within another smaller waiting area, this one offering padded chairs, an attractive female physician in royal blue scrubs met them with a kind smile. She introduced herself as Dr. Frey and, after shaking hands with James and Milla, gestured for them to take a seat.

"It appears that Mr. Henry has suffered a stroke," she said, and James appreciated her gentle directness. "He's been stabilized and we're sending him for an MRI. We should know more after those results come back." The doctor went on to ask Milla questions about Jackson's health history before leaving to check on Jackson and her other patients.

Time crawled. Doctors, nurses, and family members passed through the waiting room in an endless parade. James looked at every person dressed in blue scrubs with hopeful eyes, keenly watching their faces in case they had something to impart, but they all walked by, focused on other patients and tasks. It took over an hour for Dr. Frey to return with the MRI results.

She carefully reviewed what the test had shown and then advised them to go home and get some sleep and return during visiting hours in the morning.

When James started to protest, Dr. Frey touched his hand. "Your father is currently sedated. It would be best if he weren't stimulated. I know it's hard, but you'll do him the most good by being here fresh and bright-eyed first thing tomorrow."

The doctor's words were delivered with such sincerity and

kindness that James and Milla felt compelled to heed them. James led his weary stepmother back to the Bronco.

"I'm going to stay with you tonight," James told her as he pulled into his driveway. It felt like midnight, though it was only half past ten. "Just give me a minute to grab a few things."

Inside the house, the darkness seemed to close in on him. James turned on every light he passed, grabbing the portable phone off its cradle as he headed down the hall to his bedroom. As he shoved his toothbrush and some clothes into a duffle bag, he dialed his ex-wife's number.

"Jane," he croaked when she answered. "Oh, Jane."

He let the tears come.

Chapter Ten

Jane's Black Bean Chili

James made sure Milla was settled before trudging down the hall to his boyhood bedroom. Jackson had done little to change the small room since his son had moved to his own house on Hickory Hill Lane. The only alteration James noticed was that Milla was now using his aged kneehole desk to organize her business accounts. The corner of the desk once occupied by James's tin rocket-ship bank now featured a pair of framed photographs taken during Milla and Jackson's winter wedding. Another photo showed Eliot making a snowman in the backyard. Eliot had tried his best to create a snowman resembling his grandpa. To accomplish this, the little boy had taped a paintbrush to the end of one of the stick arms and wrapped Jackson's favorite plaid scarf around the snowman's wide neck. Milla had captured him planting a kiss on Snow Jackson's icy cheek.

Eliot's playful face was a balm to James. Cradling the photograph, he carried it to the nightstand and stared at his son while he wondered what news tomorrow would bring.

At first, James resisted sleep, feeling guilty that he'd be resting in comfort when his father was alone in a hospital bed miles away. As the night wore on, however, his tired body and weary mind were no longer able to dwell on the dozens of what-ifs that had been amassing inside his head. Eventually, he surrendered to slumber.

The next morning, he awoke to the pleasant sound of Milla moving about downstairs in the kitchen. These ordinary domestic noises—water whooshing through the pipes and the clanging of bowls and pans—allowed James to believe that life could return to normal. He jumped out of bed, showered, and dressed in record time, worried that his father was already awake and frightened.

"Don't fret," Milla said as he rushed into the kitchen. "I called and asked about your daddy. He's still resting quietly, so come fill your belly with a hearty breakfast. You know there won't be anything decent at that hospital. Lord knows I cannot take another swallow of the slop that vending machine calls coffee."

James accepted a plate of eggs and bacon but had to force down the food. For once in his life, he didn't feel like eating. He cleaned his plate because he knew it would please Milla, but it took every ounce of patience he possessed to watch her tidy the kitchen before finally turning toward the door.

"I know you want to race to his side, dear." Milla patted James on the cheek. "But we're still going to get there well before visiting hours start as it is."

James frowned. "I don't care about the rules. If they refuse to let us see him, the least I can do is track down Dr. Frey and get more details about Pop's condition. Why did he have a stroke in the first place? Is he going to need surgery? Rehab? Will he eventually be . . . okay?" The word came out sounding strangled.

Milla slid her arm around him and leaned her head against his shoulder. "We'll make it through, honey. And if I don't get a chance to tell you today, then let me say it now: I sure am grateful you're with me. I couldn't have asked for a better son had I raised you myself."

Hugging her tightly, James carried their travel coffee mugs to the Bronco and, after watching Milla load a basket of baked goods into the backseat, drove north toward the hospital.

"What time *did* you get up this morning?" he asked her, gesturing at the basket.

"About four," she said. "I figured it couldn't hurt to whip up some cinnamon scones for the nurses. Jackson isn't going to be the easiest patient they've ever had, so I'd better bribe them right off the bat."

James chuckled. "Nicely done."

The volunteer at the hospital's reception desk directed them to Jackson's room. As they approached the door, last night's knot of fear reformed in James's chest. Taking Milla's hand, he moved into the room and then stopped, inhaling sharply.

Jackson lay on the bed, attached to a multitude of tubes and wires. His arms and face were almost as white as the sheets covering his body and he looked shrunken, diminished. After all, to James, Jackson was the epitome of manliness. He was willful and fearless, his unapologetic personality rendering him taller and more powerful than his wiry physique suggested.

"Pop," he whispered.

A nurse bustled into the room and James turned to her in anxious appeal. "Miss? Can you tell us how he's doing?"

"He had a peaceful night," she replied brightly while checking Jackson's IV and making notes on a chart. "Woke up once during my shift and tried to talk, but he couldn't get the words out. I told him where he was and that his family would be here in the morning. He grunted and went right back to sleep." She glanced at her watch. "We change shifts at seven, so I'll introduce you to the nurse on duty before I leave."

"What about Dr. Frey?" James persisted. "Is she available?"

The nurse paused to think. "Dr. Frey was on call last night, so one of her partners will be seeing Mr. Henry today. His name is Dr. Scrimpshire. He's a neurologist. He's on rounds at the moment but should be swinging through here any second now." She gave them a comforting smile on the way out. "Your daddy's in good hands, I promise you."

Not knowing what else to do, James and Milla pulled chairs to the side of Jackson's bed and waited. They chatted to Jackson about last night's party in hopes that he could hear them, but he remained unresponsive. The only comfort his family could garner was the steady rise and fall of his chest.

Dr. Scrimpshire entered the room fifteen minutes later and James jumped to his feet. The physician placed a thin stack of folders on the nearest table and shook hands with Milla and James.

"Mr. Henry has suffered a cerebral embolism," he began in a deep, no-nonsense voice. "This occurs when a clot, usually originating from the heart, travels through the bloodstream and lodges in an artery in the brain. This blocks the blood flow to the brain."

Milla was wringing her hands. "That sounds pretty serious."

The doctor turned a pair of sympathetic eyes on her. "Your husband has sustained damage to his brain, Mrs. Henry. He will have to relearn many of the simple tasks we take for granted. But with the help of occupational therapy, there's no reason he can't live a long and fulfilling life."

Relief washed over James. "So he doesn't need surgery?"

"No." Dr. Scrimpshire shook his head and uncapped his pen.

He began to examine Jackson and made several notes in one of his files. James and Milla remained silent, watching the doctor with expressions of dread and awe. "We'll start him on blood thinners to prevent those clots from reforming, but he doesn't require surgery. That doesn't mean that his road to recovery is going to be quick or easy. Fortunately, patients with supportive families tend to show the most marked improvement in rehab."

"Is he going to wake up soon?" Milla ventured.

The doctor nodded. "It won't be long now. He may be disoriented at first, and I suspect he will have difficulty speaking. He may also express signs of fear, anger, or both. He's basically waking up to a body that won't do what he wants it to do." He capped his pen and closed the file. "Just so you're prepared . . ."

James glanced at his father. "Before the paramedics came, he seemed to have lost feeling in the left side of his face. Is there any way to tell the extent of the damage?"

"I have the results of Mr. Henry's initial imaging tests on my office computer. As soon as I've finished seeing the rest of my patients, I'll come get you and we'll look at them together. The nurse will page me once your father is awake." After giving them another compassionate smile, he gathered his paperwork and left the room.

James and Milla were silent for a moment.

"I'm not sure I understood all of that," Milla finally said, "but I'm holding fast to the part about Jackson living a long and full life."

Reaching out to cradle his father's limp hand in his own, James said, "Me too."

• • •

Less than an hour later, James noticed his father's eyelids fluttering and dashed from the room in search of a nurse. He knew he could have hit the call button on Jackson's bed frame, but he trusted his own actions more. As he rounded the corner of the hallway, he nearly knocked Jane right off her feet.

"I'm so glad to see you!" he cried. She gave him a fierce hug in return but James broke free and pulled her toward the nurses'

116

station. "Pop's waking up!" he simultaneously told Jane and the pair of nurses behind the counter.

By the time Jackson opened his eyes, a small crowd was gathered around his bed. A nurse bent over him, fussing with this and that while Milla squeezed Jackson's hand to alert him that she was near.

"Good morning, darlin'," Milla spoke tenderly, keeping her voice calm and even. Her husband looked in her direction and she exhaled loudly in relief. "You can see me, can't you?"

A strangled sound came from Jackson's mouth.

"Don't try to talk, sweetheart," Milla coaxed. "You're in the hospital. You had a stroke last night. Can you nod your head if you understand me?"

Jackson dipped his chin, his gaze never leaving Milla's face. Milla's and James's eyes met across the bed. The fact that Jackson could see, move, and respond to other people gave him a surge of hope.

From that point onward, the medical team took over. They ran tests and checked vital signs and machine readings and Jackson's fluid bag while James tried to find something useful to do. It was only later, when he met with Dr. Scrimpshire and stared at images of his father's brain on the computer screen, that he began to fully understand what had happened to Jackson.

The doctor swiveled his computer screen toward James and pointed out the shaded areas indicating damage. When James responded by blanching and gripping the arms of his chair, the neurologist put a hand on his shoulder. "The brain is a wonderful and mysterious organ, Mr. Henry. Damaged tissue does have the ability to recover."

"But not dead tissue?" James asked after he'd collected himself.

"No," the doctor admitted. "It will take more tests to see what kind of rehabilitation your father will need. The good news is that our rehab facility is one of the best in the state."

James looked away from the computer screen. "Sorry. I'm trying to digest everything. This hit us out of the blue. One moment he was my typical, cranky, feisty father and the next . . ." He stood and thanked the doctor. "Let me tell my stepmother about the results. I'd rather she didn't see this image unless it's absolutely necessary. She's already having a hard time taking all of this in, and I think it would be best if she and I focus on his recovery." His eyes strayed back to the color-coded screen. "That's the present. I'd now like to turn to the future."

Dr. Scrimpshire nodded in agreement. "That sounds like a very wise plan."

• • •

Later, after hospital visiting hours were over, Jane and James shared a quiet dinner at his house. Jane had arranged for Eliot to be picked up from preschool by his best friend's mother. To the little boy's delight, he was to experience his first sleepover that night.

"It's a good thing my parents were already planning a visit this month," Jane said as she dropped a dollop of sour cream followed by a sprinkle of Monterey-Jack cheese over a bowl of black bean chili. "I told them to fly in this weekend. As for me, I just need to turn in grades this week, tidy up the office, and then I'll be available."

James absently picked up the spoon she handed him. "Available?"

"To take care of you, silly." She smiled at him. "I know you, James. You'll work eight hours a day, help Jackson with his rehab, continue to be the World's Best Father, and go to church every Sunday." She sat across from him with her own bowl of chili. "That's too much for any mere mortal to handle. With that kind of schedule, you won't be able to do laundry or clean the house or stock your fridge. Whatever energy you have left will be spent driving up to see us, so I think Eliot and I should live here over the summer, if that's okay with you."

The fear and worry that had been holding James hostage for the last twenty-four hours eased their grip. He stared across the table at his ex-wife in wonder. "I thought you were teaching two courses this summer."

"They're online courses. My summer students are actually working adults, and with their busy schedules, courses via computer are what they want. This way, they can work toward their degrees without having to appear physically on a college campus." She took a bite of chili and gestured for James to do the same. "So all I need is my laptop and a few hours of quiet in order to post lectures and do my grading. It's perfect really. I get to spend more time with my favorite men. Three months of bliss."

James took a bite of his dinner and groaned. "This chili is bliss! No wonder Eliot has converted to vegetarianism so easily. Shoot, *I* could give up meat if you cooked for me like this." He spent a moment savoring the taste of black beans, garlic, onions, and fresh cilantro in a tomato base. Then, he scooted back his chair, walked around to Jane's side of the table, and leaned over to kiss her.

"I love you," he whispered into her hair. "For the chili, for being willing to upend your life to be near me, and for the way you make me believe everything will be okay."

Jane wrapped her arms around his neck and returned his kiss with passionate tenderness. "I love you too. So very much."

Later, after they'd cleaned up the kitchen, James took Jane's hand and led her down the hall to the master bedroom.

"I can rub your back until you fall asleep," Jane offered as she pulled back the covers. "You must be exhausted."

James flopped on the bed as though he was too weary to move, but at her words he sat up, grabbed her around the waist and pulled her on top of him. "I'd have to be half dead to fall right asleep with you here." He slid his palms over the soft curves of her hips and murmured, "Besides, I want to show you just how grateful I am to have you lying next to me."

"That sounds like a good deal to me." Jane stretched out her arm and switched off the lamp.

• • •

James went back to work the next day and did his best to concentrate on his usual tasks. He phoned Milla every few hours to ask after his father, but there hadn't been much of a change since the previous day. Jackson could barely speak and had lost the use of his left arm and leg. The medical staff told Milla that it was too early to tell how permanent his disabilities were, and added that they were unlikely to ever voluntarily discharge him if she continued to bring them such succulent baked goods.

"His vision is fine, so that's a blessing," she told him. "And we're able to talk in our own way. Your daddy's never really had a flapping tongue, so I blab away and he grunts and nods. It's not too different from our regular conversations," she added lightly.

Pleased that Milla sounded both rested and hopeful, James asked if she wanted him to check in on Willow.

"She can handle Quincy's Whimsies as well as I can," said Milla. "In fact, she'd been hinting for weeks that I should take a vacation, so now I'm taking one! I'm planning to read *The Jungle Book* to your father. He's never heard the story and it's been more years than I care to recall since I have, so we'll take a literary vacation. One of the nurses told me reading aloud is good for stroke patients."

"A well-written tale is as curative as homemade chicken soup," James agreed. "I'll be in after work to see Pop. And Milla, don't you worry about mowing the lawn or taking the trash to the street. I'll do all of that this weekend."

Milla clucked her tongue. "And *I* plan to stockpile your freezer, so don't you fret about your meals."

"Just keep on baking for the nurses. I have my own personal chef."

James told Milla about Jane and Eliot moving down for the summer, and Milla squealed in delight. "It'll do your daddy a world of good to have Eliot filling the house with energy and chatter. Jackson'll want to get better just so he can play with him again. Oh, I've gotta run. Dr. Scrimpshire's here to check on our favorite patient."

After hanging up, James spent the rest of his lunch hour helping Fern hang a collection of photographs on the walls surrounding the Tech Corner. Once the last framed print was in place, James stood back and admired the results.

"These are fantastic, Fern. You're really talented." He pointed at a photograph of a carpet of multicolored autumn leaves. "This one's my favorite." Turning to look at the four photos mounted on the wall behind him, he added, "But the close-up of the purple rhododendron, I must have that one for Jane. She'd love to hang it in her office."

Fern blushed. "Scott made me a website. It's beautiful. He used that photo as the frame for the home page. You were right when you said he was good with computers."

James studied Fern's bio, which had been fastened with thumbtacks alongside a series of photographs showing the Blue Ridge Mountains during each season. Taken from one of the scenic lookouts on the Blue Ridge Parkway, the photographs captured the beauty of the wilderness. The pine trees in the valley that were draped in capes of snow in the winter scene were just as lovely as the towers of dried brown needles serving as a contrast to the brilliant gold, orange, and crimson leaves of the hardwoods in the fall.

Casting a quick glance at the young woman, James said, "I think Scott has a bit of a crush on you."

Fern sighed. "I like him too. It's just, well, I have feelings for another guy. He's a fellow artist. Until I can sort out exactly what those feelings are, I'm trying to just be a friend and coworker to Scott. Still, the more time I spend with him . . ." Her expression was anguished.

"These things are rarely easy. Take it from me," James told her. "I've made two or three lifetimes' worth of romantic gaffes."

The relationship theme had him thinking of how wonderful it had been to wake up to the sound of his alarm that morning and to find Jane lying beside him, her hair fanned out over the pillow and her arm splayed over the edge of the bed. He'd stared at her lovely face as long as he could. He then showered as quietly as possible so as not to wake her. He hadn't succeeded, however, for when he stepped out of the bathroom to get dressed, her side of the bed was vacant. She was waiting for him in the kitchen with breakfast, a steaming cup of coffee, and a tender kiss.

"It's hard to imagine you making a serious mistake. You seem like someone who has it all figured out," Fern said.

James smiled. "Maybe I finally do. You see, I found out that I'm still in love with the first girl I ever loved. It's exhilarating, because she feels the same way, but it can be scary too. Once you've figured out what's important in life, you want to do anything in your power to hold on to those things." He glanced back at the seasonal photographs of the mountains. "But your work has given me a terrific idea. Go ahead and put me down for that entire series. Those photographs are going to help me secure my future."

"All four of them? Thanks!" Fern beamed. "I have to tell Scott I've made my first sale from this exhibit!"

Grabbing her gently by the elbow before she rushed off, James said, "If he's the one you run to when you have big news, then you really do care about him. Just don't leave him hanging too long, okay? He's not like one of these prints, Fern. That young man is an original."

At five o'clock, James trotted down the library steps, intending to hop in the Bronco and speed north to the hospital. Lucy was waiting for him by his truck, holding a cardboard box filled with food with one hand and her cell phone in the other. When she saw James, she pocketed the phone.

"Your fellow supper club members have made enough food to see you through at least six meals. We didn't know what else to do." She pushed her sunglasses onto the crown of her head and gazed at him with concern. "How is Jackson?"

James thanked her and gave an abbreviated version of his father's condition as he loaded the goodies into his truck.

"I haven't had a chance to tell you about my little chat with Murphy." Lucy rubbed at a grease spot on her uniform shirt and then gave James a crooked smile. "She was pretty cagey when we talked in the Sweet Tooth. Even Megan Flowers said she's never seen Murphy grab her croissant and run like she did when I asked her what she'd been up to Sunday evening."

Rubbing his temples, James frowned. "If Murphy is the note's author, what could she expect to gain? She's smart enough to know that I'd do anything to keep Jane and Eliot safe. This whole thing has only brought us closer."

Lucy looked thoughtful. "Maybe she wants to create stress between you and Jane. It's hard for you to protect your family when you live in separate towns, so Murphy might be using the fear and anxiety created by the threatening notes and creepy dead birds as a way to drive a wedge between you."

"Lord knows I'm stressed," James admitted. "But if she thought this crazy behavior would cause a rift between Jane and me, she's dead wrong. In fact, Jane and Eliot will be living with me this summer." An angry flare ignited in his brown eyes. "And no one will hurt my family. They'll have to get past me first!"

Lucy touched James on the arm. "Sullie and I will continue to do drive-bys until this weirdness is nothing but a distant memory. Let's just hope that when Murphy sees the three of you around town over the next few weeks, she'll realize there's nothing she can do to keep you apart."

She opened her mouth to say something else, but Francis came bounding down the library steps as if the building were on fire. Spotting James in the parking lot, he raised his hand. "Professor! Wait!"

James stiffened, bracing himself for bad news. Francis was rarely rattled, but now the young man's face was drawn and his pupils were tiny black dots of shock. "It's your wife . . . I mean, your ex-wife. It's Jane!" he blurted all in one breath. "She said something about the crazy note writer and that he went after Eliot. She's really upset and wants to speak to you right away!"

Francis hadn't even finished his sentence when James began to run. Lucy was only a second behind. "Where is Eliot?" she shouted.

"In Harrisonburg," James yelled, taking the stairs two at a time.

"Then it's not Murphy," Lucy said, holding open the lobby door. She raced behind James into his office. "I saw her a few minutes ago at the Wellness Village."

"Whoever it is—if they've hurt my son . . ." James grabbed the receiver and lifted it to his ear. He barely recognized his own voice; it sounded as though a stranger spoke Jane's name.

Chapter Eleven

Frozen Mac & Cheese

Lucy insisted on driving the Bronco.

"Your hands are shaking. You're a danger to yourself and to others," she pointed out as she accelerated around a tractor-trailer. "At a time like this you need a friend, especially one in uniform. Even if said uniform *is* a little wrinkled and there's a grease stain on the left pocket." Lucy smiled briefly. "When we get to Harrisonburg, I'll tell the local cops about the note you received. If we all put our heads together, we can figure out who's messing with your family. Tell me again exactly what happened today."

James was aware that Lucy was trying to distract him until they reached Jane's house, but he recounted the details for the second time. "Eliot was on the playground at school when a man wearing sunglasses tossed him a paper airplane. Eliot ran over to fetch it, and by the time he looked up again, the man was gone. Nothing about him was familiar. The plane had been made from one of those paper airplane books sold online and in lots of stores. A teacher in Eliot's school had bought a similar book for his son, so he recognized the World War Two bomber pattern, but not the black Sharpie writing on the sides of the plane."

Lucy frowned. "What bird did the man try to fashion the plane into?"

"I don't know." James clenched his fists. "A hawk? A vulture? I have no idea. He drew some feathers on the wings and made a sharp beak on the nose of the plane. It's the writing that makes me so damned angry. How dare this whacko call my son—"

"He called the *plane* 'the Little Bastard,' not your son," Lucy said in an attempt to mollify her friend, but her words had the opposite reaction.

"Come on, Lucy!" James shouted. "He was obviously referring to Eliot. My son was born out of wedlock. Even now, he has only a part-time father. I just wish . . . ." He trailed off, too upset to continue.

Lucy reached over and grabbed James by the hand. "Forget about how some lowlife defines him! You're a wonderful father, and he's a happy little boy. He doesn't know what these words mean. What he knows is that he has two parents who love him more than anything in the world."

James squeezed Lucy's hand in gratitude. "You're right. I need to get a grip before I see Eliot. I don't want him to be frightened, even though *I* am." He rubbed his temples and tried to focus on the scenery. "I hope he didn't get upset when the police questioned him."

"Jane may not have allowed them to talk to Eliot directly," Lucy said. "Cops can be pretty intimidating to little kids."

"Not to Eliot," James replied. "He thinks policemen are the coolest people ever."

"The kid has good taste." Lucy grinned.

Lucy had to park the Bronco in the street in front of Jane's house as a police car had already claimed the open space in the driveway. James ran across the grass and burst into the house, relieved to discover Jane and a female officer calmly sharing a cup of coffee in the kitchen. He kissed his ex-wife and whispered, "Where is he?"

"In his room listening to an audiobook," she said. James noted the red and blotched skin under her eyes and wished he'd been here to comfort her while she'd cried. "He has his headphones on and he's perfectly fine. He doesn't realize that anything out of the ordinary has happened. I think we should talk to Officer Beatty together before you see Eliot."

At that moment, Lucy entered the kitchen. "James was in no shape to drive," she explained to Jane before introducing herself to Officer Beatty. "I'm here to offer whatever help I can."

Jane gave her a warm smile. "Thank you so much. James told me you've been trying to find out who left that note on his birdhouse. I was freaked out by the bird carcass as it was, but now that this guy has targeted our son, I won't feel safe until he's been apprehended. Hopefully, he'll get thrown in a jail cell and end up with a serial killer as his roommate!"

"May I see the paper airplane?" James directed his question to Officer Beatty.

The young officer, who looked to be in her mid-twenties and had guileless blue eyes and ash-blond hair secured in a tidy bun, reached under her chair and retrieved the plane. Stored inside a plastic freezer bag, the object seemed innocuous at first glance, but as James examined the crudely drawn feathers and block lettering, a fresh wave of rage rolled over him. "No one at Eliot's school got a look at this guy?"

Jane shook her head. "The school's playground borders a fairly busy street. People walk by all the time."

"The only description we have is that he was an adult male wearing sunglasses?" Lucy asked Officer Beatty.

The pretty policewoman tapped on the open page of her pocket notebook. "Eliot also told his mom that the man wore a purple baseball cap. He said it looked like the purple shirt his mom wears when she works in the yard, so we're assuming he's referring to her JMU sweatshirt."

James groaned in frustration. "This is a college town. Those hats are for sale all over the place." He turned to Jane. "Did he notice hair color? Height? What clothes the guy wore?"

"Eliot's a little boy, honey," Jane answered in a soft voice. "He's not Poirot. He was following a trail of ants close to the fence and this guy in a purple hat and sunglasses tossed him the plane and then disappeared. End of story."

"I'm so glad that he can't read yet," James muttered.

Jane covered his hand with hers. "He's okay, James. Honestly. He thinks Officer Beatty is here because she's my new friend. Plus, he's so excited about moving to Quincy's Gap this summer that I don't think anything can bring him down."

The four adults exchanged ideas and theories, but since Murphy was no longer on the suspect list, no one could come up with a plausible substitute.

"Could it be another former romantic partner?" Officer Beatty asked, looking back and forth between James and Jane. Lucy shifted uncomfortably in her seat and asked the officer if she'd like a coffee refill.

"You're a guest, Lucy. Let me get it," Jane insisted. She set clean mugs on the table and collected the coffee carafe. "My list of ex-boyfriends isn't very long, and all of those relationships ended amicably. The only exception was Kenneth Cooper. He's a lawyer living in Williamsburg. He's also my most recent ex. He'd never do these crazy things though. He's too obsessed with his image."

Lucy eyed Jane with interest. "Then it must have been quite a blow to his ego when you left him."

Jane shrugged. "I doubt it. He was dating a Barbie look-alike behind my back months before we broke up, and he certainly wanted no part in raising Eliot. He—" She stopped suddenly and then picked up the bag containing the paper airplane. "Kenneth used that word once, in reference to Eliot." She gave James an apologetic glance. "I threw a vase at his head. It smashed inches away from his face and I'm still sorry that I missed. He packed his bags and moved out later that day."

"Have you seen Kenneth since?" Officer Beatty had her notebook out.

"No." Jane sank into a chair and wrapped her hands around her mug. "But why would he do this? He didn't want to be with me and he didn't want anything to do with Eliot. He was happy to be free of us."

Lucy and Officer Beatty exchanged a quick glance and then the younger woman closed her notebook and rose. "I'm going to make some inquiries about Mr. Cooper. Could you give me his date of birth, place of business, and last known address?"

After Jane supplied the necessary information, the two law enforcement officials went outside to converse in private. A few minutes later, Lucy announced that she planned to grab a bite to eat with her fellow officer.

"We'll leave for Quincy's Gap at seven thirty," James told her. "I want to give Jane time to pack what she and Eliot will need for the rest of the summer."

"Got it." With a wave, Lucy followed Officer Beatty to her squad car.

Back in the kitchen, Jane stood in front of the refrigerator, frowning as she peered inside.

"I didn't get a chance to shop for groceries today," she apologized. "I'm afraid we'll be dining on frozen mac and cheese and a side of canned green beans. I can melt fresh grated Parmesan over the noodles, but that's as close to gourmet as we're going to get."

"I've never met a bowl of macaroni and cheese I didn't like."

James pulled her to him and held her close. "Everything's going to be okay. I promise."

Jane wiped her face and smiled bravely at him. "Go ask your son which toys he can't live without this summer while I fire up the oven. I'll keep the wine corked until we get to your house. I'm already picturing myself drinking several glasses tonight."

"Me too," James answered as he headed out of the kitchen. Pausing, he added, "And it's not *my* house anymore, it's *ours*."

Night was falling in a curtain of deep blue by the time Officer Beatty dropped Lucy at the curb. James, who was loading two suitcases into the Bronco, swiveled around and searched her face. "Did you find out anything about Kenneth?"

"Other than he's got a squeaky clean record, no." She was clearly disappointed. "Not even a speeding ticket within the last three years."

James was deflated. "So that's it?"

"There's still the question of his whereabouts," Lucy said. "We called his office and were told by his secretary that he's on medical leave. She referred us to one of his partners, but that guy wasn't exactly forthcoming with information. Since we have no evidence against Kenneth, we had no choice but to back off when the partner refused to answer our questions." She tossed her purse into the backseat. "Don't worry, I'm not giving up. I have a feeling about this guy. I think he's our man."

"Thank you, Lucy." James hustled inside to collect the rest of Eliot's things. He finished loading the truck while Lucy and Jane spoke in hushed tones in the kitchen.

"We're all done, bud." James carried his son fireman-style and buckled him into his car seat. "Last call for Quincy's Gap!" he yelled in the direction of the house.

Jane shouldered her purse, turned off the lights, and locked the front door. "I can't begin to guess why Kenneth would be on medical leave," she whispered to Lucy as they walked across the lawn. "He didn't have any health issues when we were together. And I don't like the idea of him being off work for several days in a row. It means that he was free to drive here." Her voice was strained. "I can't understand why he'd want to scare me like this. Assuming he's the bad guy."

Lucy put an arm around Jane. "Don't let him get to you. He doesn't have the power to break the three of you apart, right?"

Anger flared in Jane's eyes. "No, of course not."

"Hold on to that truth and he loses, no matter how he tries to upset you." Lucy opened the back door and pretended to be nervous. "Oh! I don't know if it's safe to sit next to a T. rex," she said, referring to Eliot's plush dinosaur. "His teeth look *very* sharp."

Eliot laughed. "He's not a T. rex! He's an allosaurus. He only bites mean people."

"Then I might need to borrow him sometime," said Lucy. "We could make him an honorary deputy."

All the way back to Quincy's Gap, Eliot questioned Lucy about her job. He was especially interested in how she got assigned to work with the K-9 units and wanted to hear about Lucy's dogs.

When James pulled into his driveway, Lucy insisted on doing a sweep of the house before anyone else went inside. After receiving the all-clear, James carried Eliot to his room and tucked him in. He still had to run Lucy back to the library.

"I really think you should get a dog," Lucy said as they drove through their sleepy town. "Did you know that the sound of a barking dog is the number-one theft deterrent? A big canine with a mouthful of teeth and a deep growl is much better than an electronic alarm. No one's going to stick around long enough to tack notes to your birdhouse if they know there's a chance of being bitten."

James envisioned a wolfish-looking dog sinking a row of razor-sharp teeth into Kenneth's leg. It was a very satisfying image. Back when Jane had left him for Kenneth, James had looked up his rival on his law firm's website and had been sickened to see that not only was Kenneth the youngest partner in the firm's history, but he also looked like a Calvin Klein model.

"I'd want a kid-friendly dog breed, not Cujo," James said as he shook off the memory of Kenneth's headshot. "I know your German shepherds aren't child eaters, but they *are* enormous and intimidating." He grew thoughtful. "I could ask Willow. She volunteers at the local shelter, and I bet she could recommend the perfect pooch for our family."

The ringing of a cell phone interrupted Lucy's reply. "It's Sullie," she mouthed and then cooed, "Hey, Sugar," into the phone.

Whatever Sullie said in return wiped the smile from her face, replacing it with a tightening of the lips and a quick glance out the window. "We're coming up on the turnoff now," she told him, her voice tinged with urgency. "I'm with James. I'll explain later."

James wondered why Lucy was now sitting ramrod straight in her seat, every muscle tensed.

"Turn here!" Lucy directed before he had a chance to ask. The Bronco's tires screeched on the asphalt as James obeyed. He sped down a gently curved road leading to a thoroughbred farm and a development of upscale houses built at the feet of one of the Shenandoah Valley's beautiful blue hills. The residences of Bridle Path Road were some of the wealthiest in the county, and James couldn't imagine why Lucy suddenly needed to take a detour in this direction.

"Lucy?" he asked, slightly put out. "Where are we going?"

She was clearly trying to read the brass numbers secured to the mailbox posts. "Sorry. I don't want to blow by the house. It's number two-fourteen." She tapped on the window. "That was one-eighty, so we're getting close."

"To what? It's been a long day, and though I'm incredibly grateful to you for—"

"Sullie found a body!" Lucy interrupted. "He hasn't even had time to identify the victim, but there's been a struggle and he needs backup ASAP so he can secure the house." She took a shallow breath and continued. "He was responding to a neighbor's 911 call and has been inside for less than five minutes. The EMT guys are en route, but I couldn't drive right by without stopping to help. What if the perp is still around?" Even in the dark, James could see the glimmer of excitement in her eyes. "Here it is!"

James drove up a long driveway illuminated by solar lights. Sullie's cruiser was parked in front of a detached two-car garage. When James pulled in behind the brown sedan, Lucy said, "You'd better stay here."

Ignoring her, James followed her up a brick path lined with miniature boxwoods to the double entrance doors of a stately white

Colonial. A faint strip of light escaped from between the front doors, one of which was slightly ajar.

"Sullie?" Lucy shouted into the foyer.

James heard a heavy tread on the floorboards above their heads. "Upstairs!"

Lucy shot a warning glance at James. "Don't touch anything." Though he was tempted to remind her that this was hardly his first crime scene, James kept his mouth shut and followed her up the carpeted staircase. A strange odor hung in the air.

"Do you smell that?" he whispered. "It's familiar . . ."

Lucy sniffed. "Reminds me of that nasty incense Gillian likes to burn during her home meditation sessions."

"Yes, that patchouli stuff." He looked at the rich wood of the banister and the expensive chandelier hanging from the center of the ceiling. "Seems out of place in this environment."

By then, they'd reached the top of the stairs and James was glad to see that the hall lights were on. Sullie popped out from a room at the end of the corridor and glared at James. "What's he doing here?"

Lucy looked over her shoulder like she'd forgotten he was there. "I drove him up to Harrisonburg because the Birdman made contact with his son. He was driving me back to my Jeep when I got your call, so I had him make a detour."

Sullie stared at James for a moment longer as a range of emotions flitted over his face. Trust won out over suspicion, however, and he nodded at James in apology. "Is your kid okay?"

"He's fine, thanks." James gave the other man's hand a friendly shake. "My whole family will need your protection until this guy is caught."

"Don't worry, we've got your back." Sullie straightened his shoulders, looking like a linebacker prepared to drill an unsuspecting receiver deep into the turf. He then turned to Lucy. "E.T.A. for the paramedics is five minutes. The vic's in here." He handed her a pair of gloves.

As she put them on, she turned to James. "You need to stay in the hall. This is a crime scene now."

"How can you tell?" he asked, but as he moved to the threshold of the spacious bedroom, he realized that it was a dumb question.

The first thing he noticed was the pair of legs sticking out from behind the bed. It was hard not to fixate on them, for they were encased in a pair of purple and green striped socks. James had a flash of the Wicked Witch's feet protruding from Dorothy's farmhouse. The witch's corpse was pinned under a home, however, while this corpse was positioned between the wall and the bed.

James's gaze traveled around the room, taking in the rumpled bed, the overturned bedside table and the lamp lying askew on the carpet. The bare bulb threw circular shadows onto the back wall, creating the mirage of an eclipse on the floral wallpaper. Books and picture frames were scattered at the base of a cherry dresser, leaving only the incense holder containing a single stick of fragrance on its polished top. A poster tacked to the wall next to the dresser caught his attention. He recognized it as one of Tia Royale's animal rights posters. Looking around the room again, James counted ten different posters, some of which appeared much older than those he'd seen during Tia's recent demonstrations.

Lucy spent a moment absorbing the scene before she stepped carefully across the carpet to kneel down next to the body. James could only see the top of her head as the four-poster bed blocked his view. "Do you know her?"

"Yes. So do you." She peered at him over the coverlet. "It's Tia Royale."

James was flabbergasted. "Is this her house?" He'd pictured her living in a dimly lit apartment decorated with futons, beaded curtains, lava lamps, and shag rugs.

Sullie opened a door leading to the walk-in closet. "Lots of jeans and T-shirts in here. Some rolled-up banners with pictures of dead pigs and cows and chickens."

"This is her room, all right," Lucy said. "I know the girl rubbed folks the wrong way, but who would want to kill her?"

Standing anxiously in the doorway, James stuck his head into the room. "How did it happen?"

"She might have been strangled. There are bruises on her neck." Lucy suddenly seemed to realize that James was out of place at a crime scene. "You'd better go. Sheriff Huckabee won't be happy if he finds you here."

James wanted to be of assistance, but he knew he would only

impede both the paramedics and deputies if he stayed. Thanking Lucy again, he headed downstairs.

Just as he was about to leave, he heard a noise coming from one of the rooms at the back of the house. Fearing the killer might still be inside, James raced up the stairs two at a time and asked Lucy and Sullie to investigate the bottom floor.

"I did a preliminary sweep after I found the body," Sullie told Lucy as they responded to James's plea. "No sign of disturbance except in the victim's room."

Sullie took the lead, turning on lights with one hand while holding his gun out in front with the other. Lucy had also drawn her weapon and was walking slightly behind Sullie, training her gun to the side while also checking to make sure no one was sneaking up from behind. The couple's movements were so synchronized and graceful that they seemed more like dancers in a Russian ballet troupe than two sheriff's deputies on the hunt for a murderer. James followed in their wake, every muscle tensed as his blood surged through his body and his heart pumped at a frenzied pace.

Upon entering the kitchen Sullie immediately lowered his weapon. "Here are our intruders." He relaxed and pointed toward a side door facing the detached garage.

"Awww." Lucy holstered her gun and grinned.

James pushed past her and saw the pet flap built into the door. Alongside the door was a bowl of water and an empty ceramic dinner plate. Two animals gazed up at the three humans with hungry eyes. Lucy squatted down and stroked the head of a little schnauzer and then reached out to pet a tortoiseshell tabby. The animals responded eagerly to her attention, and soon a chorus of barks and meows echoed in the kitchen.

At that moment, a pair of male voices shouted, "EMTs!" and entered the house. Sullie dashed out of the kitchen, but as Lucy turned to go, James held her by the elbow. "What about these two? What will happen to them?"

"I'll call animal control in the morning." She glanced at the dog and cat and then jerked her eyes back to James's face. "Unless someone else takes them now."

James didn't even hesitate. "I'm bringing them home with me.

If I have to sign papers or something later on, I will. But I won't leave them here with their caregiver lying dead upstairs. They need food and a quiet place to sleep."

Lucy nodded and hustled out of the kitchen while James rummaged around in the cabinets until he found a stack of Alpo cans and another of Fancy Feast. He gave a can to each animal, surprised that they were so willing to share the same plate. By the time they finished, the noise level had increased within the house. James loaded a grocery bag with canned and dry food and was relieved to discover a pair of pet carriers in the far reaches of the pantry.

He placed the carriers on the floor, got down on his knees, and reached out to the animals. They both came right to him, snuggling against his leg.

"I'm James Henry," he told the friendly pair as he examined their collars. "Nice to meet you, Snickers," he said to the schnauzer. Smiling, he spoke to the cat. "And you too, Miss Pickles." He gently pushed each animal into a crate. "We're going home."

Chapter Twelve

Vegetarian Pizzadillas

When James returned home with two animal crates, a bagful of dog and cat food, and a litter box, Jane was speechless. As he quietly explained what happened on the way to drop Lucy off at the library, James unlatched the metal doors of the crates and coaxed Snickers and Miss Pickles out. Both animals took their time exiting their carriers. They each put their front paws on the floor and then paused, sniffing nervously. When James mentioned Tia's name, Snickers released a soft whine and James pulled the small dog against his chest.

Jane listened, horrified, as he described Tia's thin legs, clad in those silly striped socks, sticking out from behind the bed.

"I'm relieved I didn't see more than that," said James. He put out a water bowl and two dishes of kibble for the animals. "She was just a girl, really, and so infused with vitality. She had her whole life in front of her. I couldn't just leave her pets to be collected by animal control in the morning."

Nodding, Jane reached out and scratched Miss Pickles under the chin. "What if Tia's family wants to reclaim these guys? I know you were acting out of kindness, James, but Eliot is going to go berserk when he discovers these two tomorrow. He'll love them. How can we let him get attached to these sweet creatures when they might be taken away in a day or so?"

"I hadn't thought that far," James confessed. "When I saw her pets and thought of how passionately she fought for animals . . ." He broke off, smiling as Miss Pickles began to bat about a scrap of paper across the kitchen floor. "I'm sorry. I didn't mean to create any more drama for us."

Snickers licked Jane's hand and she giggled. "You did the right thing, honey. We'll simply explain to Eliot that we're acting as a foster family and that these animals might not be staying with us forever." She kissed the mini schnauzer on the crown of his head and smiled. "I always wanted a dog when I was a little girl, but my father was allergic to anything with fur. I had goldfish instead." Snickers rolled on his back, put his paws in the air, and gazed at

Jane with a look of pure adoration. "Oh, I hope we *can* keep you both! Come here, Miss Pickles. Let Mama get a look at you!"

Jane played with the animals for a little longer, but ultimately decided she was too exhausted to keep James company while he watched television. James was tired as well, but he found he couldn't go to sleep. He sat on the sofa while images flickered on the screen and blue light danced across the dark living room, but his mind refused to focus on a particular show. Instead, his thoughts kept returning to the events of the past week. He replayed the night of Jackson's stroke and called forth every physical detail of the sinister paper airplane delivered to Eliot. He then closed his eyes and traveled to Tia's room, seeing the overturned lamp, the posters on the wall, and the dead girl's legs.

As the hours passed, James was grateful to have the animals beside him. Both of them had explored their new environment. Now, as weary from the emotional evening as James, they curled up against his legs and placed their heads in his lap. He stroked each animal, feeling comforted by the warmth of their bodies and the soft sounds of their breathing. It was well past midnight when James finally drifted off to sleep.

He didn't recall waking during the small hours of the morning and making his way to the bedroom. When the alarm went off at a quarter to seven, Jane let out a groggy groan and Snickers jumped up from where he'd been sleeping between James's feet and began to yip in excitement.

Within seconds, Eliot was in the room. He climbed on the bed, squealing with happiness as he hugged Snickers, Jane, and James again and again until Miss Pickles meowed from the doorway.

"A cat too!" he cried in ecstasy. "This is the best day ever!"

Jane wasted no time explaining the situation to Eliot and the boy seemed satisfied to live in the moment. As James sat down for breakfast at the kitchen table, listening to the new range of noises filling his house, he felt a surge of renewed hope.

"Is the coffee really that good?" Jane glanced his way as she opened a can of Fancy Feast. Miss Pickles stood on her back feet and stretched out her front paws toward the cat food.

"I was just thinking that I am one lucky man to be able to wake up to this happy hubbub all summer long." He waved his hand around the room. "Our little nest—no one can touch us in here."

Jane pointed at her chest. "Or in here."

Later, she sent him out the door with a kiss and a brown bag lunch.

From that point on, James's day only grew brighter. The library was busy and almost every patron stopped by the reference desk to ask after Jackson's health. By midmorning, he was able to share the wonderful news that his father was being released from the hospital.

"I just got off the phone with Milla!" James shouted in the break room. "Pop's going home this evening!"

Francis, whose mouth was stuffed with an Italian hoagie, gave his boss a hearty thumbs-up.

"He'll still need to go to rehab every day, but I know he'll get better once he's sleeping in his own bed again." James spoke mostly to himself.

"And to eat Milla's cooking instead of hospital food." Francis grimaced at the thought. "But how is Mr. Henry going to handle the stairs? Didn't you tell me his left side is super weak?"

James hadn't considered the extent of his father's disability until that moment. He stood in the center of the room, awash with guilt. "There's been so much going on, I hadn't even thought about how different things will be for him now."

"Don't worry, Scott and I will meet you at their place after work." Francis gave him a reassuring smile. "We can just move his bed into the den."

"Brilliant!" James clapped Francis on the back so hard that the younger man nearly choked on an enormous bite of his salami, ham, and provolone hoagie.

After the twins were done with their break, James laid out the lunch Jane had prepared, noting that he was enjoying his vegetarian diet more and more. He gobbled up an egg-salad sandwich made with a hint of Dijon and lots of salt and pepper, and savored a bowl of fresh strawberries with a side of crème fraîche. When he unfolded a Post-it note from the bottom of his brown bag at the end of his meal, he smiled to see that Jane had drawn a heart with their initials inside with a purple crayon.

In the remaining minutes of his break, James called Milla to discuss the relocation of the master bedroom. Though she joked that Jackson would never go to therapy if he could spend all his time watching reruns of *The Price Is Right* instead, she was grateful to the Fitzgeralds for both the idea and the willingness to move furniture.

"James," she whispered conspiratorially. "If your daddy's singing catfish plaque happens to disappear during this little rearrangement, that would be perfectly fine with me."

Jackson voiced a garbled protest in the background and Milla laughed. "Just seeing if you were paying attention, darling!"

During the afternoon, Francis led a book club discussion while Scott assisted patrons in the Tech Corner and Fern manned the circulation desk. James offered recommendations to several mothers while their children played in the new and improved storybook area. Scott and Francis had recently built a small wooden puppet theater, and Fern, who was not only a talented photographer but a skilled seamstress as well, had sewn a dozen puppets. She made the Big Bad Wolf, the Three Little Pigs, Little Red Riding Hood, Peter Pan, Captain Hook, Tinkerbell, a crocodile, a prince, a princess, and a fire-breathing dragon. She'd also set up a special display of picture books containing the characters she'd turned into puppets.

As James carried a stack of strays back to the circulation desk, he smiled at his newest employee. "Everything going okay?" he asked. "Are you adjusting to your career as a librarian?"

Fern showed him a dazzling smile. "I love it! Other than my photography, this is the most rewarding job I've ever had. I feel like I was meant to be here."

"I was just thinking the same thing," he told her warmly.

She checked out a stack of romance books for a patron and then took a step closer to James. "I've been thinking about what we discussed the other day." She paused, gathering courage. "I do have feelings for Scott, so I'm going to meet with the other guy and tell him that I'm not interested in anything but friendship."

"Good for you, Fern. You and Scott seem to fit together. Like we all fit in this library. Sometimes, it takes a crazy chain of events to bring us where we are supposed to be."

"Waxing philosophical, Professor?" an elderly patron teased.

With a self-effacing grin, James wheeled the reshelving cart to the Fiction section. He'd barely placed the latest Lee Child novel on the shelf when someone tapped him on the elbow. It was Lucy. James took in his friend's glassy eyes and slumped shoulders. Abruptly, the memories of the previous night he'd been able to hold at bay by concentrating on routine tasks came rushing back.

"How are you?" he asked.

Lucy pushed some errant hairs away from her eyes. "It was a long and disappointing night. We found no clues. Not one!" Her mouth thinned into a line. "This job can be damned frustrating."

James had rarely seen Lucy so irritable, but he assumed that it was partially due to fatigue. "Was Tia strangled?" he whispered.

"Doesn't look like it. Someone pinned her down on the floor and held her by the neck, but that wasn't the cause of death. The ME's still working on that. With her parents being who they are, this case is a top priority." She ran her finger along the spines of the books on the shelf nearest her arm. "I heard Sheriff Huckabee break the news to them this morning. They couldn't be reached last night because they're on some exclusive Caribbean island where there's no cell phone service. They'll be here in a few hours though. Having a private plane comes in handy at times like this."

James guessed the reason behind Lucy's anger. "No suspects yet?"

Lucy shook her head. "None. The guy must have worn gloves. I'm assuming the killer is male because of the size of the bruises on Tia's neck. We've matched most of the prints in the room to Tia. Her mother thinks the other unknown set belongs to the cleaning woman. The parents haven't been upstairs since Tia moved in. I take it they weren't very close to their daughter. Can you imagine never having been in your daughter's room?"

"Does Tia have siblings?"

"Two brothers. Both work for Daddy, live in McMansions, and jet around the globe. They've never set foot in Tia's house." She glanced at her watch. "I need help with this case, James, and I don't have time to chase a bunch of dead ends. I'm going to call a supper club meeting so we can bat around a few theories. Plus, I want to ask Gillian to call Kenneth's office and pretend to be a client. If anyone can worm information out of a tight-lipped lawyer, it's Gillian."

James reached out and briefly squeezed Lucy's shoulder. "Let me make the arrangements. And don't even think about spending your last ounce of energy driving by my place. Go home and get some sleep."

"Sullie's going to do the drive-by on the way back from Luigi's. There's no way I'm cooking tonight, so we're having giant plates of pasta. I plan to fall into a food coma afterward." Suddenly, she brightened. "With all this drama going on, I forgot to tell you that Luigi and Luis's mama have been spending a ton of time together. He's even taught her how to toss pizza dough and shape it into a pie. Word is, she's a natural."

James was astonished. "They *like* each other? Romantically?"

Lucy laughed for the first time since she'd entered the library. "Stranger things have happened." She passed him a copy of Sue Monk Kidd's *Secret Life of Bees.* "Is this any good?"

"Very. Do you want to check it out?"

"No, thanks." Lucy took her keys out of her pocket. "My reading material is going to consist of the report from the medical examiner, Sullie's notes from the crime scene, and any background information I can find on Tia Royale."

"Some people have all the fun," James teased and walked his friend to the door.

• • •

After work, James, Scott, and Francis spent two hours at the Henry house moving furniture from the den to the dining room and from the master bedroom to the den. When they were done, Scott hobbled around the room on one leg, using a broom as a crutch.

"Dude, that is not cool," Francis scolded his brother.

Scott shoved his glasses up his nose and frowned. "I'm not making fun of Mr. Henry, bro. I just want to be sure he's got enough room to maneuver with his crutches." When Scott banged his knee sharply into the dresser, all three men winced.

"I'm glad you decided to put our arrangements to the test," James said as he and Francis moved the dresser to the far side of the room. Standing back, he surveyed their work and was pleased with the results. Jackson and Milla now had a convenient first-floor bedroom and Jackson's ugly and aged den furniture had been temporarily hidden under tablecloths.

Turning to the twins, James said, "We'd better get going. Pop won't want us to see him struggling inside. I'll need to give him at least one night to get used to all of this. I'd like to buy you both dinner." He reached for his wallet but Francis held out a hand to stop him.

"You're like family to us, Professor. And Milla cooks for us all the time, so we're totally square."

Scott nodded in agreement. "Yeah, we should be paying *you*. We're always getting free treats from Quincy's Whimsies too. We are so spoiled by your family that it's like Christmas all year long."

"Just remember who your friends are when you get that big paycheck from the software company," James teased and handed Francis a twenty. "I insist on a token of thanks. Go get one of Luigi's specialty pizzas."

"That's a deal!" Francis beamed and then turned thoughtful. "I kind of forgot about that monster check. We should be getting it any day now, right, Scott?" He elbowed his brother, who was staring off into space. "Right, Scott?"

The twin put a hand on his flat stomach. "You had me at 'pizza.' I'd trade our future computer monitor for a pineapple and ham, thin crust."

Francis's eyes lit up. "Let's go get one! We can eat it while watching season five of *Battlestar Galactica*. Again. G'night, Professor."

James waved at the twins and drove off, wishing that he too would be dining on something from Luigi's menu that evening. However, he forgot all about the pizza parlor the moment he stepped into his house.

"Hello?" he called and waited expectantly. Eliot always raced into his arms as soon as he heard the front door opening, but no footsteps sounded in the hall.

"Daddy! I'm cooking dinner!" Eliot shouted from the next room.

James walked into the kitchen to find his son dressed in a fire truck apron and matching chef's hat. He was standing on a stool, filling a bowl with grated cheese. Jane was setting the table.

The moment she set down the last fork and napkin she walked over and kissed James on the cheek.

"What are we having?" James asked his son, who waved at him with a spatula.

"Pizzadillas." His little chest puffed out with pride. "Mommy and I made it up."

James cocked an eyebrow at Jane. "Please elucidate."

Jane gestured at the buffet station she and Eliot had created on the counter. "Choose your toppings, just like you would at a pizza parlor, and then Eliot will arrange them on a tortilla. I will cook each pizzadilla in the skillet and you can create 'slices' using the pizza cutter."

"Wow," James said as he made a big deal over the display. "You two should have your own food show. You could call it *Vegetarian Creations.*"

The Henrys sprinkled cheese, black olives, mushrooms, and vegetarian sausage onto tortillas. As they ate, Miss Pickles amused herself by batting a grocery store receipt across the floor.

"That cat loves paper," Jane stated.

Eliot grinned. "Yeah, you should see what she did to the toilet paper in my bathroom!"

Jane formed her hands into claws. "Shredded the whole thing until it looked just like this bowl of mozzarella."

Snickers was laying half in the living room and half in the kitchen. When James asked Jane how the dog had fared that day, the little schnauzer lifted his head, wagged his tail, and then closed his eyes again.

"I'm a bit worried about him." Jane cast a concerned glance at Snickers. "He hasn't eaten much and he's been moping about. Do you think he's homesick?"

Eliot stopped chewing in order to listen to his father's answer. James shot Jane a warning look. "No. He's just a tired doggie." Later, as he and Jane loaded the dishwasher, he whispered, "Snickers might be sick. Not homesick, but physically ill. Is he drinking any water?"

Jane turned the dishwasher on and waited for the noise to overpower their hushed conversation. "He's lapped up a little, but not much. Also, he hasn't done his doggie business all day. I've already made an appointment with a vet Gillian recommended. I'm sure he'll be fine, but I wanted to play it safe." She slid an arm around James's waist. "How are you doing? After all that's happened lately ..."

"My supper club is going to meet tomorrow night to help Lucy with her case. She doesn't have a single lead in Tia's murder case. There's also the matter of our stalker. We're really going to have to think outside of the box if we want to flush Kenneth out of the bushes. If this whacko really is Kenneth." He smiled at her. "But all of these things—even Pop's stroke—are much easier to bear with you and Eliot here. You two chase away the shadows."

Jane squeezed him tightly and then snapped at his legs with the damp dishrag. "I'll finish in here. You go read to Iron Chef Junior. He's picked out *Green Eggs and Ham*, but I've been instructed to tell you that *ham* should be replaced by the words *yam* or *jam*."

"Green eggs and jam?" James grimaced. "Dr. Seuss is going vegetarian? Somebody had better warn the Grinch." He lowered his voice until it sounded like a radio announcer's. "This Christmas, he shall carve the roast beets!"

Groaning, Jane aimed the dishrag a little higher and shooed him from the room.

• • •

Lindy was in such high spirits over Alma's fascination with Luigi that she offered to make bean and cheese enchiladas for the supper club's gathering the following evening.

She entered Lucy's house humming a lively tune, her café au lait skin flushed with good humor. Popping the casserole dish containing the enchiladas into Lucy's oven, she performed a little twirl in the center of the floor, holding her flouncing black skirt out and clacking an imaginary pair of castanets.

"Alma's in love. Alma's in love," she sang.

"You hired a flamenco dancer for us, Lucy?" Bennett joked as he uncapped five bottles of cold beer.

"Better open the whole six-pack," Lucy instructed. "Sullie's coming over."

Bennett paused, the opener hovering over the last bottle. "For *our* meeting?"

James and Gillian exchanged glances. It had always been the five of them. Lindy had never thought to include Luis, just as James would never invite Jane. This was their time to celebrate their friendship and to tackle their eating issues. They were the Flab Five. The number five was sacred.

"It's *his* case," Lucy replied firmly. "And he knows how well we work as a team. I've told Sullie about every case we've cracked as a team. He'll just sit back and listen. You'll never know he's here."

Lucy's statement turned out to be false, because Sullie was a social creature. He small-talked with Gillian about her businesses, sympathized with Bennett over the subject of junk mail, told James he would come in to get a library card, and went out of his way to praise Lindy on her enchiladas—and James couldn't agree with the hunky deputy more.

"Have you transformed into a vegetarian too?" Gillian asked him, her face alight with pleasure.

James tried to ignore the thought that his friend resembled a bowl of tropical fruit with her papaya-colored hair, banana-hued blouse, and lime green skirt. She'd accessorized her vibrant ensemble with a pink belt and matching sandals. "I haven't officially converted," he said and carried his plate to the sink. "But I'm really enjoying the meals Jane's been making. She wasn't much of a cook before, but she's learned a ton for Eliot's sake, and I'm reaping the benefits too."

Bennett pointed at the fridge and made a drinking motion with his right hand, indicating that James should bring him another beer. "At least you're being healthy. I've slipped on the whole no-sugar thing," he said glumly. "Ate a bunch of donut holes during my route yesterday. I need to listen to those CDs more."

Gillian gazed at him fondly. "The problem is that you fall into a *deep* sleep the second the CD begins, and I don't think your subconscious can hear Harmony over your own snoring. I really think you should try an herbal remedy such as fresh ginger mixed with honey or some wild yam."

"Do I look like a man who wants to eat wild yam before I go to bed?" Bennett scowled.

Laughing, the friends worked together to clean up their meal. When the table was clear and the dishes were washed, Lucy produced a gallon of sugar-free frozen custard.

"Chilly Willie created a new flavor," she announced, brandishing an ice cream scoop. "I told him about our plan to kick our sugar addiction a few weeks ago and he's been experimenting with sugar-free flavors ever since. This is called Guiltless Grasshopper Parfait."

Lindy rubbed her hands together. "Mint and chocolate? Yummy!"

"I'll read you Willie's description." Lucy tilted the gallon sideways. "It says, 'Guiltless Grasshopper Parfait is a creamy blend of mint custard, ribbons of fudge, and chocolate mint cookie crumbles. You'll be hopping across town to get your feelers on this sugar-free treat!'"

Bennett accepted a bowl and took a bite of the custard. "Willie Lamont is an artist. This stuff is too good *not* to be bad for us."

No one answered, being too busy licking spoons clean.

Lucy finished her ice cream first, pushed her bowl aside, opened a file folder, and uncapped a pen. She placed a yellow legal pad at her right elbow and surveyed her friend's faces. "Okay, let's get to work. Tia Royale's death really bothers me. First of all, she was only twenty-six. Second, she was devoted to her cause. Third, her killer roughed her up, bruising her neck while he tried to pin her down to prevent her from fighting for her life."

"And that girl had plenty of fight in her," Bennett mumbled.

Ignoring him, Lucy continued. "Tia had no official job. Her parents bought the house where her body was found. They also gave her a monthly allowance. Though generous with money, they kept their distance. According to Tia's daddy, his daughter's image wasn't the kind he wanted 'associated with their company.' As her mother told me this morning, Tia was 'different' from the rest of the Royales."

Gillian sighed theatrically. "Poor little black sheep."

James smiled as Sullie gave Gillian a bewildered look. Turning his gaze to Lucy he asked, "Not to interrupt, but did you ask Mrs. Royale about Tia's pets?"

"Yes," Lucy said. "The Royales want nothing to do with them. Mr. Royale claimed that they travel too much to care for Tia's pets."

"It's destiny! Those animals were *meant* to be yours!" Gillian exclaimed. "Did Snickers go to the vet today?" She whispered the word *vet* as if her cat, the Dalai Lama, were present. Whenever her intelligent feline heard the threatening word, he took off for the hills, sometimes staying away for days.

"Turns out Snickers needed minor surgery. He'd stopped eating and drinking altogether. The vet said he had a blockage," James answered. "The procedure went smoothly and Jane should have picked him up by now." He looked at Gillian. "I'm glad he's mine, but I wish the Royales were footing the bill. I could have put on a new deck for the cost of that surgery. And if Miss Pickles doesn't stop shredding every object made out of paper—especially toilet paper—then I'm going to have to keep a basket of leaves in my bathroom!"

Once the laughter died away, Lucy finished relaying the case details. "Tia's assailant entered her bedroom and the two of them struggled, leaving her neck bruised. However, the cause of death was heart failure. Until the lab results come back, we won't know if she was drugged or not, but the ME says there are no obvious indicators of the presence of drugs or poison in her system."

Sullie stirred on the other side of the table. "The Royales are big supporters of the governor. Mark my words, those labs will be done in record time. It's our only break at this point."

Lindy was twirling a strand of black hair around her index finger, a sign that she was deep in thought. "The only evidence of struggle was in her bedroom. Ground or second floor?"

"Second," Lucy answered. Guessing what Lindy would ask next, she added, "There was no sign of forced entry around the windows. In fact, they were locked."

"So Tia knew her murderer. She let him inside," Lindy said with a shiver.

Sullie's eyes grew round and he stared at Lindy. "You all are sharp! Lucy and I came to that conclusion too. We believe she was expecting this guy and that she wasn't afraid of him. She also made a bunch of cash withdrawals over the last two weeks. Drained her account dry."

"Yeah, Sullie got a copy of her monthly statement right before the bank closed today," Lucy added. "Tia barely had enough to live on until her next allowance check came. Her balance was down to the minimum. We think she was being blackmailed."

James used the tip of his finger to capture the last drop of Guiltless Grasshopper Parfait from his bowl. "How much money are we talking about?"

Lucy consulted the case file. "Somewhere in the neighborhood of twenty-five thousand. She made five withdrawals of five thousand dollars each."

Bennett, who was pulling on his toothbrush mustache while Lucy talked, whistled. "Whoa! But why kill your own personal ATM?"

Gillian put her hands over her heart, her face forming an anguished expression. "How can you talk about that tragic young woman in such a callous manner?"

Ever the peacemaker, Lindy waved her hands to stave off Bennett's rejoinder. "Let's focus on the blackmail. What would someone have on Tia? Maybe she didn't always feel so passionate about her cause," she mused. "She might have eaten a double cheeseburger every night before she had some kind of life-changing experience."

"Her parents were of no help as to why Tia became so involved in animal rights," Lucy said, clearly disappointed. "Tia was never allowed to have pets, and she had no contact with farmers or livestock. Her brothers had nothing to add. According to them, she left for college a self-centered, fashion-conscious girl and came back a raving hippie activist."

"Were you able to make contact with any of her college friends?" James asked.

Sullie consulted his notes. "We talked to the girl she roomed with for two years. The roommate says Tia got involved with any group that would allow her to yell as loud as she wanted or march in demonstrations. Defending animal rights was one of a dozen causes. The lady said that Tia's family never paid her any mind, so she joined these movements as a way of getting attention and belonging to something. This girl was mighty surprised Tia didn't eventually grow tired of it all."

"She sure didn't! She poured all of her energy into protecting innocent animals!" Gillian shouted. "Maybe the murderer raises cattle or works for a big chicken company and wanted to shut her up." Knowing Gillian's unhappy history involving one of the region's chicken plants, the supper club members remained silent. That is, except for Bennett.

"Woman, not all the folks in this world who breed, slaughter, or eat meat are devils. Take yours truly, for instance. I don't lose any sleep thinking about where my bacon comes from. I'm going to buy it, eat it, and enjoy it. Does that make me *bad*?" He touched her hand. "The guy who killed Tia was after money. He might be a carnivore, but this isn't about the animals, it's about the twenty-five grand."

"I agree," said Lindy gently. "Now we need to figure out who uncovered a secret she'd pay to keep hidden."

"Knowing the secret would help too," James said. "If only the killer had left a single clue at the scene."

At that moment, his phone beeped and a text message appeared on the screen. James read the text and gasped.

His friends stared at him, concerned.

"What is it?" Gillian and Lindy spoke in unison.

"Jane sent a photo of the object obstructing Snickers's plumbing. According to the vet, he probably swallowed this the night Tia was murdered. Look!" He placed the phone in the center of the table and everyone leaned forward to examine the image.

Gillian squinted at the photo. "Is that a tree?"

"A gold fir tree pendant to be exact," James spoke quickly in his excitement. "We finally have a tangible clue." When his friends exchanged puzzled looks, he jabbed his finger at the screen. "You've all seen this tree before! This fir was on every landscaping T-shirt, baseball cap, and truck owned by the late Ned Woodman."

"So Tia's killer might also be Ned's killer?" Lindy seemed dubious. "But they were nothing alike. A young female activist and a middle-aged councilman?"

"There must be a common thread," Lucy said, pushing back her chair. "And starting tomorrow, we're going to find it."

Chapter Thirteen

White Cheddar Cheese Popcorn

When James got home after the supper club meeting, he found Jane riveted to the television, her eyes fixed on the foamy ocean waves surging across the screen and her hands curled around a bowl filled with popcorn. Miss Pickles and Snickers were asleep at her feet. They both opened their eyes when James entered the room, but seeing that he was neither a threat nor was he bearing food offerings, both animals immediately went back to sleep. James stooped down to pet their heads and was delighted that Snickers didn't appear any the worse for wear after his surgery that morning.

"It's Shark Week on the Discovery Channel," Jane whispered and passed the popcorn. "This episode is called 'Blood in the Water,' and it's deliciously scary!"

James glanced at an image of a Great White swimming through the water with its mouth hanging open, displaying rows of terrifying teeth. The camera zoomed in on the shark's jaw as the narrator described the damage these triangular, dagger-like weapons could inflict on fish, seals, and humans. Nearly forgetting what he was going to say, James tore his eyes from the King of the Deep and helped himself to the cheesy, salty popcorn.

"Where's the tree? The one the vet took out of Snickers?"

Jane didn't even blink. Hugging a throw pillow tightly against her chest, she gestured toward the kitchen. "In a cup next to the sink. And don't worry, it's been cleaned."

The gold fir tree didn't seem to have been damaged by Snickers's digestive system. In fact, it shone beneath the overhead lights as if it were brand new. James placed the pendant in his palm and turned it over. There were no markings on the reverse side other than the symbol denoting that it was made of fourteen-karat gold.

"Does this look like something a man would wear as a necklace?" James asked Jane during a commercial break. "Especially Ned Woodman, a middle-aged town councilman with a successful landscaping business?"

Jane's mouth dropped open. "The dead man you and Eliot discovered at the food festival? You think this was his?" James nodded and she took the golden tree from him and examined it in the light of the lamp. "After reading about him in the *Star*, I'd say he wasn't the jewelry-wearing type," she said. "I actually think it's a charm, like the ones you can attach to a woman's bracelet."

Frowning, James stared at a commercial for room freshener. He watched the woman gleefully spraying the curtains in her teenage son's room, her face lit with joy because the boy's room now smelled like oranges instead of dirty socks. "Could it belong to Ned's wife?"

"Maybe." Jane plucked the gold tree from his palm. "But how did it end up inside Snickers? That means Mrs. Woodman was in—"

"Tia's house." James completed the thought. "But why? What connection would Donna Woodman have to Tia? And how could we find out for certain? It's not like we can invite her for dinner and the third degree." He absently ate popcorn as he watched a shark swim toward a lone swimmer at the Jersey Shore. The moment he set the popcorn bowl aside, Miss Pickles jumped up onto his lap and began to knead his thighs.

The shark circled once, twice, and then sank its serrated teeth into the man's thigh. "Look at all the blood!" Jane cried. As the shark continued to attack his victim, she put her finger to her mouth and tapped her closed lips. "You know, there is a way to extract information from Donna. Remember the article the *Star* ran with all the funeral photos?"

Unable to look away from the carnage on the screen, James grunted.

"In that piece, Donna said that she met Ned as an undergrad at JMU. I could call her and ask for help in forming a Quincy's Gap alumni chapter."

James stared at her. "You would do that?"

"Of course. Lucy is trying her best to find who's been messing with our family, so I'd like to repay the favor." Jane hit the Mute button on the remote control. "I'll have to give Donna some notice, but I'll see if she's free for lunch this weekend. You can eavesdrop while you and Eliot construct the next phase of his LEGO city."

Gently removing Miss Pickles from his lap, James got down on one knee and grasped Jane's left hand. The light from the television painted her face with a soft white glow and James's heart swelled inside his chest as he looked at her. Words bubbled up in his throat, nearly catching there before launching themselves into the air.

"Will you marry me, Jane?" he asked. "Will you be my wife again?"

The remote slid from Jane's right hand and clattered onto the floor. "Goodness! What's brought this on?"

James turned off the television set. Reclaiming Jane's hand, he said, "It's been building up since the day I spotted you at that party celebrating Bennett's *Jeopardy!* appearance." He paused, forcing himself to slow down and speak clearly. "There was a time that I felt like I never wanted to see you again, but even when I was boiling over with hurt and anger, part of me longed for the chance to make things right. To go back in time and stop us from breaking apart."

Jane looked down in shame and James squeezed her hand until she met his gaze once more. "I'm not trying to open old wounds, sweetheart. I'm trying, in my own awkward way, to tell you that *you're the one* who made things right. You and I are better now than we ever were. We're a family. You, me, and Eliot. I want us to be like this from now on."

"He would love that," she whispered, her eyes shimmering.

He gripped her hand tightly. "But this isn't about our son or about the three of us living under one roof. I want *you*, Jane. Today and tomorrow and the day after that. Only you. Be my wife again, my girl. Grow old with me."

He waited while Jane sniffed back tears, too moved to speak. Finally, she slid her hand out of his, threw both arms around his neck, and cried, "Yes. A million times yes!"

Jane's tears of happiness moistened James's cheeks and her fervent whispers of assent were stilled by his hungry kisses. She pulled James down to her on the sofa, forcing Miss Pickles to relocate. The cat glared at the entangled pair and sauntered off to the kitchen.

Later, as Jane and James did their best to cover their bare flesh with throw blankets, the newly engaged couple sipped glasses of wine and discussed the future. Their faces were flushed from their lovemaking and they twined their hands together, sharing whispered laughter as they recalled some of the minor disasters from their first walk down the aisle.

"To this day, I believe that organist was drunk!" Jane giggled.

James recalled the wobbly notes and the congregation's startled looks. "And there's no doubt we had the world's feistiest flower girl. Remember how she kicked her brother as she passed his pew?"

"The highlight of the wedding video," Jane said with a smile. She sat up on one elbow. "We've had a big church wedding with the fancy reception and the four-tiered cake. Why don't we go the Town Hall route this time? Keep things simple. Just you and me. Quincy's Gap can marry us. The sooner the better."

James considered her suggestion in a state of drowsy contentment. "How soon?"

"We can get the ball rolling during your Friday lunch break. We need to drive down to the courthouse complex and apply for a marriage license."

He kissed her in reply. "We need a witness for that, if I recall. How do we choose just one person? Someone will end up feeling snubbed."

"I know just who to ask," Jane murmured sleepily. "Just meet me there at high noon, okay, cowboy?"

Sighing in happiness, James murmured, "I could get used to your calling me that."

He then stood, hastily tied the blanket around his waist and helped Jane up from the sofa. Wrapping a blanket around her shoulders, he pulled her close. The pair walked down the hall, heading for bed and a night filled with blissful dreams.

• • •

The supper club members had decided to meet at the library during their lunch breaks the next day to discuss the details of Gillian's telephone call to Kenneth Cooper's law firm. Even Lindy, who usually had to remain on school grounds until the bell clanged the official dismissal time, was able to attend. The student body had been given a half day to prepare for their final exams, and as soon as the hallways had emptied of teenagers, the teachers and staff had dashed out to their cars, as drunk on freedom and the invigorating spring air as their pupils.

"How's the hot love affair between your future mother-in-law and Luigi going?" James teased Lindy when she entered his office.

Lindy tried to smooth her windblown hair with her fingers, but her dark tangled locks refused to be tamed. Helping herself to a rubber band from his desk, she fastened the whole mess into a ponytail and smiled. "The good news is that he's mighty fond of her. The bad news is that she feels right at home behind the counter of his pizza parlor. She's bossing around his kids as if she's already their stepmama."

"Why is that the bad news?" Bennett asked as he walked into the room. He brushed a paper fragment from his postal uniform shirt and sat down in the chair closest to the window.

Lindy's smile shrank. "Because she's delayed her return ticket for another month. That woman is never going back to Mexico! And as long as she's here, Luis can't keep his mind on us!"

Lucy, who had been examining a bookmark listing bestselling crime novels, gave Lindy a sharp look. "Someone has to say this to you, so it might as well be me. Luis needs to pick you first and his mama second. What if she does move here? What'll happen to your relationship?"

Lindy paled. "I can't stomach that thought! Alma in Quincy's Gap? Twenty-four-seven?" She nudged Bennett roughly in the shoulder. "Gimme that chair. I feel faint!"

Bennett obliged, his dark eyes sparkling with amusement. He turned his gaze toward the door as the clink of Gillian's armloads of silver bangles preceded her into the room.

"Hello, friends!" she trilled merrily. "Oh, it is *so* good for my restless spirit to be working on a case with you all, to be truly *focused* on truth, justice, and the act of restoring balance!"

James indicated she should sit at his desk. "Review the plan for us, Gillian."

Settling into the comfortable chair, Gillian folded her hands and took a deep breath. "Bennett and I spent several hours reading up on Kenneth Cooper, Esquire. He's represented quite a few drug companies and other mega corporations in lawsuits against

individuals, but he's argued copyright infringement cases as well."
Here, she smiled smugly. "As though sown like a magical seed, the
idea bloomed in the deepest crevices of my mind to ask for Mr.
Cooper's help in suing someone who's stolen our Pet Palace plans.
I will *insist* that I only want Mr. Cooper to represent me, seeing as
he's won every single copyright or patent infringement case he's
argued."

Lucy gave Gillian an admiring nod. "That's good! But who will
you pretend to sue?"

"We called Beau Livingstone yesterday and told him about this
crazy plan," Bennett took up the thread. "He got right to work
setting up a website chock-full of the same Pet Palace designs
shown on the real site." He glanced at Gillian. "You struck it rich
the day you asked that man to be your business partner. For a
former roofer, that guy has almost as much computer savvy as
those Fitzgerald brainiacs."

James edged around his desk and pointed at his computer.
"We'd better take a look at the fake site."

"Surf away. You'd never know it wasn't as real as the touch of
my hand on your arm." Gillian typed in the URL and then
swiveled the screen so that everyone had a clear view.

"Very professional," Lindy said as James clicked links and
enlarged images of the Pet Palace designs.

"Who's this listed under the Contact Us link?" James pointed at
the monitor.

Gillian followed his finger with the cursor. "To order a Pet
Castle, an interested customer needs to email a Mr. Jerry Brickman.
Of course, Jerry doesn't exist. Beau set up a Gmail account using
Jerry Brickman's name, so he *looks* legit, but he's just a figment of
my colorful imagination. We used Williamsburg as the company
address because that's where Kenneth's law firm is located. It's
also why we didn't provide a street address."

"That's right," said Bennett. "We didn't want those pesky
lawyers to call a fake phone number or drive by some empty
warehouse and call our bluff."

"You two were very thorough." James looked at Gillian. "Are
your designs actually copyright protected?"

Gillian fluffed her hair. "Of course. Beau and I have put in hours upon hours dreaming up the Cockatiel Condo, the Pekinese Penthouse, the Siamese Suite, the—"

Lucy forced her friend to break off the list by thrusting the phone into her hand. "I recommend you speak to Kenneth's secretary first. We need someone who will feel sorry for you, so get a woman on the line and lay it on thick."

Inhaling deeply, Gillian closed her eyes and began chanting under her breath. James raised his brows and grinned at Bennett, and though his friend shrugged his shoulders in befuddlement, there was a glimmer of pride in his eyes.

The supper club members perched on the edge of their chairs and listened as Gillian successfully navigated an assortment of gatekeepers until she finally reached Kenneth Cooper's personal assistant. Her friends knew she was speaking to the right person because she gave them a quick thumbs-up before spinning her chair around to face the room's only window.

"Mr. Cooper's not there? Are you expecting him back soon?" Gillian already sounded as if she were on the verge of tears. "A *leave of absence*! Oh, what am I going to do?" She hesitated. "Miss?" Another pause. "It's Katherine? Thank you, it's so much easier to speak informally. Would you be willing to give some advice to a lady sitting in a pot of boiling water?"

This question was followed by a long and pregnant pause, but the answer must have been positive, for Gillian's fingers, which had been curled around the telephone cord, suddenly relaxed and she began her tale. The fabrication began with Gillian running away from an abusive boyfriend and finding a safe haven in Quincy's Gap and ended with her feelings of peace and fulfillment working with animals.

"Do you have a pet, Katherine?"

The response led to a lengthy sidebar about the merits of the Boston terrier. Eventually, Gillian was able to share her good fortune in being able to open her own pet-grooming shop and after many years of loving toil, launching her second business, Pet Palaces.

"Can you imagine what it's like to have this *man* stealing my ideas? He's making money from *my* designs and I *hate* how powerless it makes me feel." Here, Gillian's voice trembled. "I searched for lawyers in the Williamsburg area because that's where this *thief* lives—probably high on the hog off of *my* hard work too!" She paused and made a great show of trying to rein herself in. "Mr. Cooper's name stood out from all the other attorneys because he's *never* lost a copyright infringement case. Without his help, what will I do?"

James winked at Gillian. It was a smart move to end with a question, leaving the decision with the other woman, whom they all hoped sympathized enough with Gillian's plight to supply her with information.

They held their collective breath as Gillian waited for an answer, exhaling in relieved unison as she scribbled something on James's desk calendar.

"Oh, I see," said Gillian in a solemn tone. "That's quite a burden for you to shoulder, but Mr. Cooper is very brave to confront his demons. You'd like to introduce me to one of his partners?" She glanced up at her friends in a panic. "Um, I'll call you back! One of the dogs has hopped off the groomer's table and is shaking soap all over the mayor's wife. Bye!" She abruptly ended the call.

Leaning back in his chair, Bennett began to clap. Soon, all the supper club members were laughing and applauding, but their raucousness died away when Gillian pointed at the note she'd written on the calendar.

"Kenneth Cooper is *not* in Williamsburg. His medical leave really means that he's receiving help for his substance abuse problem in Culpepper." She turned to the computer on the desktop and typed rapidly. "There is a treatment center in that town. It would be easy for Kenneth to drive from there to Harrisonburg or Quincy's Gap."

Lindy looked confused. "Don't you have to stay inside once you're checked into one of those places? Could he just walk out whenever he wanted to write notes and kill a bird or two?"

"I wouldn't think so," Lucy answered and placed her hands on her gun belt. "Leave it to me. I will find out exactly why Kenneth needed treatment and whether he stepped foot off the property for more than a millisecond." She moved toward the door.

Gillian also rose. "How will you do that, Lucy? Those places are designed to protect a person's privacy. It wouldn't be right for the facility to share confidential information with you!"

"If this guy were the pope, I'd still beat down the doors to discover what he's been doing!" Lucy snapped. "By threatening my friend, Kenneth has lost his right to keep his secrets." Passing a hand over her face as though to wipe away the anger and frustration, she hastily apologized. "However, I'm open to other ideas."

Gillian waved her off. "You need to do this your way. I shouldn't feel sympathy for this man, but I can't keep myself from thinking that perhaps the drugs have turned him into a monster. Maybe, underneath it all, he's a decent man."

"Maybe," Bennett said as he glanced at his watch. "But it's still no excuse to set about ruining James's life or scaring his family right out of their skins." He turned to Lucy. "How will you get those folks to volunteer info on Kenneth? The man's a lawyer, Ms. Deputy. He's *not* going to stand around while you and his doctors have a nice chat about his medical file."

"That's true," Lucy agreed. "And I could lose my badge, so I'm going to assign this job to someone else. Someone who's dying to get back into our good graces."

Having made her mysterious announcement, Lucy told her friends that she'd be in touch and walked out of the office.

"Okay, that's one item to check off the list. What about Tia's case?" Lindy asked.

He shared Jane's idea about inviting Ned Woodman's widow over for lunch.

"Clever!" Gillian exclaimed. "We may have to make her an honorary supper club member!"

Thinking of last night's marriage proposal, James smiled. "Yes, we just might."

• • •

On Friday, James met Jane at the Town Hall to present their forms of identification to the Clerk of Courts.

As she signed one of the documents, Jane looked over at James and whispered, "I feel like I'm twenty years old again. I have butterflies in my stomach!"

"You are *so* much better at forty. Smarter, sexier—a woman of the world." Ignoring the clerk's impatient frown, James kissed Jane before she could finish writing her name.

Someone cleared their throat behind them and James looked over his shoulder to see Scott and Francis Fitzgerald gazing at the floor, their hands stuffed in their pockets.

"Our witnesses are here!" Jane hugged each brother while they blushed furiously.

"We are totally honored to be signing these papers," said Francis sincerely. "This is a big secret, right? We're the only ones who know you two are getting hitched again?"

"Yes," James answered. "We'll tell our families and friends when it's a done deal." He smiled at the twins and then grabbed Scott by the arm, suddenly alarmed. "Wait a minute. If we're all here, who is running the library?"

Scott's eyes darted to the wall clock. "Fern's manning the helm. We figured we'd scratch out a John Hancock and dash right back. She should only be alone for fifteen minutes."

On the other side of the counter, the clerk scowled. "I only need *one* witness."

Francis and Scott exchanged looks of dismay. "Paper, rock, scissors!" they shouted and commenced with a series of frenzied hand motions.

"Two out of three," Francis said as the clerk rolled her eyes.

In the end, the paperwork was completed, witnessed, and notarized.

"You should have your license in the next two weeks," the clerk said after James paid the required fee.

The twins shook hands with their boss, hugged Jane once more, and rushed out of the building.

"Do you need to get back or do we have time for lunch?" Jane asked, linking her arm in James's.

"Forget about lunch. Let's go shopping!" James led her to the passenger side of the Bronco and gallantly opened the door.

Jane laughed. "Stranger words have never come from your lips. You hate shopping."

"Not in this case," he said with a smile. "It's not every day that I get to buy a pair of wedding bands."

Chapter Fourteen

Chocolate Chunk Peanut Butter Cookies

James knew that he should be focusing more of his energies on unraveling the mysteries of Tia Royale's death and Kenneth Cooper's whereabouts, but he couldn't stop thinking about Jane. He walked around the library with his mouth turned upward in a goofy smile. He greeted each patron like they were his favorite person on the earth, and several older women felt inclined to pinch his cheek and tease him for being hit by Cupid's arrow.

When Willie Lamont came in to pick up a fresh stack of presidential biographies, he shook his head and made a clicking noise with his tongue. "You got it bad, my man. You're gonna break out in zip-a-dee-doo-dahs any minute."

"Stranger things have happened," James said as he checked out the frozen custard shop owner's books with a flourish. "Summer's right around the corner. The song might make a good name for your next flavor."

Willie raised his brows. "Little wordy, don't ya think?"

"How about Second Time's a Charm?" James slid the books and the checkout receipt across the counter.

Laughing, Willie gathered up the thick tomes. "I might just have to do some experimentin' this afternoon. Maybe I'll create somethin' like Wedding Bell Buttercream."

"Sounds perfect. Especially if you make it guilt-free like that Grasshopper Parfait flavor."

Willie shook his head. "No way, man. We're talkin' about eternal love here. You gotta have sugar and cream and pure vanilla! I can practically hear the church bells a-ringin'!"

James found it hard to bite back his secret at the mention of wedding bells, but he wished Willie a good day and said nothing more. The twins knew about James and Jane's upcoming nuptials of course, and having them in on the secret helped James keep from letting the cat out of the bag. The toughest part of remaining mum until their vows were exchanged would be keeping the engagement from Jackson and Milla.

Though part of James wanted the ceremony to be private,

another part wanted to share the good news with his parents. Milla would be delighted, and even though it would take Jackson time to come around, James knew that his father would approve of the family becoming a bona fide unit. What James really wanted to do was to rush to his father's side and tell him that Eliot would not be going back to Harrisonburg in the fall. Or ever, for that matter. James would love to see how such an announcement would bring joy to Jackson.

James and Jane had arrived at several decisions about the future the day after their engagement. Jane had immediately called the head of her department and asked to continue teaching courses online. Because these kinds of courses were growing in popularity, she would be able to retain her position. She'd have to appear on campus to attend faculty meetings and other business, but there was no longer any reason for her to live near the university.

"As soon as we're married, I'll put my house on the market," she assured James. "Thanks to my parents, there's no mortgage. We'll put every cent of that money in savings and live happily ever after at 27 Hickory Hill Lane."

The arrangement suited James perfectly. He didn't want to give up the library or his little yellow house for Jane, but he would have done so in a New York minute. Instead, everything he loved would be in Quincy's Gap. It was no wonder he felt like the luckiest man in the world.

In fact, James felt so blessed that he did his best to tone down the joy radiating from his face when he took Eliot to visit his grandparents on Saturday morning. Jane wanted father and son out of the house so she could clean before Donna Woodman's visit, so the Henry boys ate a hasty breakfast and knocked on the back door of James's childhood home at a quarter past nine.

Naturally, Milla was cooking up a storm in the kitchen. She'd made breakfast for Jackson and was now baking a chicken casserole and a peach pie for a woman from church who'd fallen and bruised her hip. She also had a mixing bowl filled with cookie dough on the cluttered counter.

"I smell peanut butter," Eliot said after returning Milla's warm hug.

She wrinkled her nose. "That's because I'm making *you* a special batch of chocolate-chunk peanut butter cookies." Lowering her voice to a whisper, she led her grandson to the mixing bowl. "Do you think it's too early in the morning to lick a beater?"

"Nope," Eliot said, his eyes shining at the thought.

"Me either." Milla smiled at James over Eliot's head. "I have a beater for you too, if you'd like one."

James grinned as Eliot poked his tongue through the tines of the metal beater. "I'll wait for a cookie when it's hot from the oven instead. How's Pop?"

"Already painting," Milla answered proudly. "Some top-secret project."

Gesturing toward the shed behind the house, James asked, "Is he out there now?"

She nodded. "He won't use the walker, so he hobbles around with his crutches. He also leans on one while he paints. It seems to be doing him a world of good—to be working again so soon after the stroke—but he gets real tired. Can you remind him to stop and rest? Trick him into coming in for coffee and cookies."

"I'll try," James answered.

As usual, James had to knock on the shed door and wait for admittance. It took Jackson several minutes to put down his paintbrush and palette and shuffle to the door. Poking his head out through the crack like a suspicious turtle, Jackson looked at his son. Though his mouth remained an immovable line, his eyes smiled.

James had been calling his father every day since he'd come home from the hospital, but Jackson was even more reluctant than usual to talk on the phone. His speech was still slurred and the already taciturn man had grown even quieter. Milla served as Jackson's communicator, giving James updates on his father's physical therapy and general well-being, but none of the details regarding his slow and steady recovery were as rewarding as seeing that unique glimmer return to Jackson's eyes.

"I'm glad you're back at work, Pop. Can I come in? Or would you rather take a break and have some coffee and cookies in the house?"

Jackson hesitated, clearly wondering if he wanted James to see his unfinished painting. Finally, he stretched his lips into a lopsided grin and waved his son inside.

The finished paintings were on large horizontal canvases. Jackson had always painted on vertical canvases before and never on such a large scale. The painted shapes were difficult to distinguish at first, but as James stepped closer, he saw that his father's new pieces were actually made up of dozens of small paintings, similar to a collage.

"The amount of detail," James breathed in awe. He leaned closer, noting the familiar features of his childhood self. There he was in his high school marching band uniform, as an infant in his mother's arms, as a seven-year-old scarecrow at Halloween. In another square, as precise as a photograph, he was raking leaves with his father. In another, Jackson was laughing as he carved the Thanksgiving turkey. These were pictures of a happy life, but there were representations of pain and loss too. There was his mother's casket, strewn with white lilies, and a portrait of Jackson sitting on the bed with her wedding ring in his hand, his face crumpled in grief.

"Your memories, Pop." James felt a tightening in his throat. "This painting shows glimpses of your life."

Jackson reached out to James. "It's been a good one, my boy. I need you to know that."

James turned to his father fearfully, but Jackson shook his head. "I ain't gonna drop dead. I just wanted you to know. You're a fine son and a damned good daddy to Eliot."

The two men embraced, and for once, Jackson was in no rush to pull away.

• • •

After a second breakfast of cookies and milk, Eliot joined his grandfather in the shed and spent the rest of the morning painting his own masterpiece. By the time he'd placed the final brushstroke and named his work *Melted Popsicles*, it was lunchtime. Knowing Jane would soon be entertaining Donna Woodman, James decided it would be wiser to spend another hour with Milla and Jackson. After all, he didn't want to arrive home just as Donna was on the brink of revealing something important.

However, as soon as Eliot had finished eating a grilled cheese sandwich and a ripe nectarine, he suddenly ran out of steam. It was time to take the little boy home.

"Let's go work on your LEGO fire station, okay, buddy?" James wiped Eliot's sticky chin, clapped his father affectionately on his good shoulder, and gave Milla a kiss on the cheek.

In return, she handed him a baggie filled with cookies.

"These are for Jane. Tell her we're sorry we missed her and hope to see her soon." Milla squeezed Eliot and beamed as he broke free, only to wrap his arms around Jackson's neck. He whispered something into his grandfather's ear and Jackson's entire face crinkled in delight. As Eliot darted out the door, Jackson gazed after him in wonder.

"I'll be damned." Jackson chuckled and looked at James. "I never thought I'd say this but hell, I wish you'd had more kids. That one there just . . ." He couldn't find the right words, but the light in his eyes spoke volumes.

On the drive home, James considered what his father had said. Would he have another child? Were he and Jane too old? Did they have enough money or enough room in the yellow house for more children? Suddenly, the idea of a helpless infant shrieking out its wordless demands in the middle of the night filled James with anxiety. He knew nothing about babies. Eliot had come into his life eating solid foods, speaking in sentences, and totally toilet trained. But a baby! Now *there* was a mystery.

"What did you whisper to Grandpa back there?" James asked his son at the next red light.

Eliot shrugged. "I said he was my favorite playdate friend." He colored. "'Cept you, Dad."

"That was a nice thing to say," James told his son. "To both of us."

Minutes later, the two Henrys stepped through the front door of their house to the sound of a woman sniffling.

"We're home!" James called out and hurriedly followed his greeting with, "I'm taking Eliot to his room for some quiet time."

He winked at Eliot, signaling that what he really meant by "quiet time" was an hour of design and construction using LEGO blocks.

Eliot shouted, "Hi, Mom! Bye, Mom!" and dashed down the hall.

Jane didn't answer, but as James tiptoed after Eliot he heard her gently murmuring to the other woman. Donna sounded as if she was crying.

Nice sense of timing, James ruefully thought. He lingered in the hallway for another moment but was unable to hear distinct words, only the rise and fall of exchanged voices, soft and melodic, like two instruments playing a lullaby in *pianissimo.*

James soon forgot about the women as he became engrossed in building a version of the Empire State Building. When he heard the front door close and a car engine start, he told Eliot that it was time to rest and handed him a portable CD player and an audio CD of Curious George stories. Eliot snuggled under his covers, put on his headphones, and loaded the CD player. James was amazed at the technical savvy of today's kids and knew it wouldn't be long before Eliot ran circles around him when it came to technology.

He found Jane standing in front of the kitchen sink, staring out the window into the backyard.

"How'd it go?" he asked.

"You can cross Donna Woodman off your suspect list. She really loved her husband and is genuinely grieving." She pointed at the gold fir tree on the counter. "That belonged to Ned, but it wasn't a charm for a necklace or a bracelet. Donna had it made for his key chain."

"So the two deaths must be connected! When Ned's killer came after Tia he must have dropped the charm. It was pretty dumb of him to have kept it in the first place." James picked up the shiny tree. "Did Donna mention the Wellness Village at all?"

Jane looked surprised. "Funny you should say that. When I asked her about the masseuse she visits there, Donna started crying. She thinks Ned was having an affair with someone who worked in the Village. She was going to confront him about it the day of the food festival, but Ned was killed before she had the chance."

James blinked. "An affair?" He recalled how anxious Ned had seemed before his death. "How did Donna come to that conclusion?"

"His landscaping company took care of the mowing and fertilizing for the complex—apparently, they're the only organic landscaping company in the area—but Donna said Ned went there way too often. She'd drive by and see his truck parked in the Village's lot during odd hours."

"Couldn't Ned have been a client? Maybe he was seeing Harmony or Roslyn or even the acupuncturist, but wanted to keep it a secret?" James didn't know why he was playing devil's advocate, but he felt compelled to do so.

Jane frowned. "I said 'odd hours.' After closing time. If he was the acupuncturist's client, for example, then he was getting X-rated services after she put away her hot needles!"

"Oh, I see." James fell silent. Mechanically, he loaded the lunch plates into the dishwasher. He then opened a liter of Coke Zero and poured a glass over crushed ice. "Could Donna be the killer? After all, she's a woman scorned."

Jane shook her head emphatically. "No way. She was angry, but she wanted to fight for her marriage. She and Ned had a child together. That kid is now fatherless. Donna is embarrassed about the missing money and she is really, really hurt, but she would give anything to have Ned back. She truly loved him."

"I trust your judgment," James said, brushing a strand of hair from Jane's cheek. "So could the other woman be the killer?"

"That's what I've been turning over in my mind. Maybe Ned's lover wasn't as keen on him as he was on her," Jane said. "Perhaps her feelings were never genuine and she was using him as a source of easy money."

James took a sip of soda. "And then she disposed of him because she'd gotten all the ready cash she was going to get? That's pretty ruthless." He considered the theory. "It also means she'd have to be strong enough to strangle Tia until she lost consciousness."

"Or she had a partner."

It was James's turn to be surprised. "No one's considered that possibility." He rubbed his eyes. "Boy, this is getting complicated."

"Looks like you need to book another appointment with Harmony," Jane said, handing James the phone. "And you'll have to give yourself enough time beforehand to check out the other women working in the Wellness Village."

Putting down his sweating glass, James dialed Harmony's number. When the office voice mail came on, he left a message saying that he was having difficulty keeping a secret from his family and friends.

"It's a good secret," he added and smiled at Jane. "Still, I'd like to make peace with myself about the whole thing. I haven't quite resolved my sugar issues either." He sighed, recalling the number of chocolate-chunk peanut butter cookies he'd eaten that morning. "Honestly, life has gotten in the way of my being healthy again. I just cannot seem to stay focused on my physical fitness goals."

Jane was studying him. "Is that true? That you feel guilty about keeping our upcoming nuptials from your family and friends?"

He reached for her hand. "Guilty, no. It's difficult because I'm having a hard time hiding how happy I am. I want to climb on top of the town's water tower and shout our news to the world." He jerked his thumb at the phone. "But I had to tell her something."

Relaxing, Jane closed the distance between them. "As far as your second reason for seeing Harmony goes, I want you to know that I wouldn't change a thing about your looks. If you want to be healthier, that's great. Eliot and I want you around for a long, long time." She wound her arms around him. "But I do like a man who can push me around in bed. I don't want some bag of bones lying next to me."

"You don't, huh?" James grinned. "Say, how long do you think Eliot will listen to his Curious George CD?"

Before Jane could answer, the doorbell rang.

"Lucy!" James greeted his friend loudly. Even though she couldn't possibly have heard his exchange with Jane, he felt slightly embarrassed. "What brings you by?"

She put her hands on her gun belt and rocked back on her heels looking extremely pleased. "News! Good news. Can I come in?"

Jane gave James a playful push. "Please do. I was just about to brew some coffee. Can I offer you a cup?"

"Yes, thanks." Lucy settled down at the kitchen table. "In all the crime books I read, the authors always talk about how foul the coffee is in every law enforcement agency across the country. It may be a cliché, but it's totally the truth. Ours is mixed with jet fuel, I swear it."

Laughing, Jane filled the coffeepot and got a pint of half-and-half out of the refrigerator. While Lucy talked, Jane placed a sugar bowl, a small pitcher of cream, and an assortment of Pepperidge Farm cookies on a tray.

"Kenneth Cooper checked into the rehab facility under a false name. Most people can't get away with that, but since he paid in cash, he didn't need to show them an insurance card." Lucy helped herself to a Milano as soon as Jane set the tray on the table. James raised his brows at his fiancée, perplexed that she was making an effort to impress Lucy. "Yum. I love these." Lucy saluted Jane with her cookie. "Anyone can get their hands on a fake driver's license, and if pressed, I'm sure Kenneth would claim that he only lied because he wanted to protect his reputation as a top-notch attorney."

"You don't believe that's the reason he used a fictitious name though," James guessed.

Lucy took another cookie. "No. I think he wanted to hide his identity so he could freely terrorize you three. We have a record of every single second he left the clinic grounds." She paused dramatically, picking off crumbs from her lap. "Each time he left, one of *you* received a little love note."

Jane's hand shook as she poured coffee into mugs. Seeing her agitation, James took over the serving. "But can you prove anything? Is this going to stop now?"

"We don't have any hard evidence, but my assistant on this project has obtained permission to write an article on the clinic. She'll be sure to find Kenneth and ask him a few pointed questions." Lucy clenched her jaw in determination. "Because this is an emotional issue for him, we need to stir up those emotions and get him to confess."

James paused in the act of shaking a sugar packet into his coffee. "An article? Lucy, please tell me you haven't recruited—"

"Murphy's been searching for a way to make peace with us," Lucy interrupted. "I needed her help on this and she was more than willing to give it. As far as I'm concerned, if she ends up getting me what I need to keep Kenneth Cooper from ever stepping foot in Quincy's Gap again, then she's forgiven." She hesitated. "At least until her next book comes out."

Breaking a shortbread cookie in half, Jane stared at the pieces. "I realize that Murphy Alistair is known for her doggedness, but how will she get him to confess? He's not a dumb man. Kenneth's going to see her coming from a mile away, even if his emotions *are* boiling over."

Lucy grinned. "That's why I'm here. I'd like your blessing to let Murphy tell Kenneth a few tall tales to get a rise out of him. For example, I thought she could mention that you two are getting married in an intimate service next week. Then, after dropping Eliot off with his grandparents in Nashville, you're jetting to Paris for a second honeymoon."

"That sounds lovely!" Jane exclaimed with a laugh. "Are we flying first class?"

James avoided looking at her, fearing his face would give their secret away. "Sounds great. Except for the Paris part. I like the food in Italy better." Remembering that he wanted to tell Lucy what Jane had discovered about the golden charm found in Snickers's stomach, he retrieved the fir tree from the soap dish and handed it to his friend. Her cornflower-blue eyes grew wider and wider as he told her about Donna Woodman's visit and his plans to snoop around the Wellness Village.

"Let's have another supper club meeting after your hypnotherapy session," Lucy said, holding the charm up to the light. "Sullie and I received an interesting update from the medical examiner today that may help us link Tia's murder with Ned's seemingly accidental death. Tia died from heart failure and her tox screen was totally clean. However, the ME found some burns on her chest. The kind you can get if someone uses defibrillator paddles on your bare skin."

Picturing an ugly red welt on Tia's youthful and unblemished skin, James grimaced. "Is that what happened to her?"

"We're not sure yet, but it's a strong possibility. The ME told me that the use of a defibrillator on a healthy person throws the heart's rhythm out of whack and can often stop it beating altogether," Lucy explained.

"We have one of those A.E.D. machines hanging in the hall right near my office." Jane sounded shocked. "I didn't realize they could be used to kill people as well as revive them!"

"Apparently, the new models don't work that way," Lucy assured her. "Those machines test for a rhythm first so that a layperson can operate them without making a serious mistake. The one used on Tia must be an older machine or one used by professionals, like EMTs or hospital personnel. Sullie and I have been running in circles looking for the machine, but so far not one paramedic in the county has a connection to Ned or Tia." She examined the gold charm again. "But I think we need to start knocking on the office doors at the Wellness Village. Ned was killed there, and if someone was dumb enough to stash their defibrillator in the back of a broom closet, we're going to find it."

"Was his chest burned too?" James asked.

Lucy shook her head. "The coroner said it wasn't, and the folks at the funeral home didn't remember seeing any marks on his chest either. Still, the ME's report on Ned is identical to Tia's. Without the bruises on the neck, that is. But we have a pair of healthy adults dropping dead of heart failure and now we know how. We just don't know why." She took another hasty sip of coffee. "I need to get back to the station and print out a list of all the Wellness Village employees. Maybe one of them used to work around defibrillators."

"Thanks for coming over and please tell Murphy that we're grateful for her help," said Jane.

The sheriff's deputy pushed back her chair and rose while eyeing the fresh smear of chocolate on her uniform shirt with annoyance. "You two need to have a baby. That way I can borrow its bib. Look at me! I'm a mess."

She didn't notice Jane's subtle blush, or that James suddenly reached across the table for his ex-wife's hand, but even if she had, it wouldn't have bothered Lucy. She had found her soul mate and he was waiting for her at the station, poring over the case file for the millionth time in hopes of picking out an essential detail—something they'd missed that could turn the tide in their favor.

"I have what you need, Sullie." Lucy whistled as she hustled outside to her brown sheriff's department cruiser. "We are going to have a hell of a night."

Chapter Fifteen

Iced White Chocolate Mocha Latte

James was just shutting down his computer when Fern floated into his office. At least that's how it appeared, since she danced into the room on nimble feet, which were completely hidden by a long, gauzy skirt made of crinkled white cotton.

"Guess what, Professor?" she asked, her eyes shimmering with excitement. "Some guy from the Wellness Village just paid me for *ten* of my prints! He emailed me over the weekend and asked me to bring them to work today. Look!" She waved a fan of twenty-dollar bills in front of her.

"That's great," he said, noting that Fern had begun calling him "Professor" in lieu of "Mr. Henry." James snapped his briefcase closed and wiped a fingerprint smear off the brass lock. "A guy? I've seen very few men around the Village. The workforce and clientele seem to be predominantly female."

"His name is Lennon, like the Beatles' singer," Fern went on. "He was *so* complimentary about my photographs. He wants to give them to his girlfriend as a surprise birthday gift. Isn't that sweet?"

James nodded. "I know his girlfriend. Her name is Skye, and I think she will absolutely love your work." He picked up his briefcase and walked around the desk to where Fern stood. "I've chatted with Lennon a time or two as well. He's a nice young man."

"I have to tell you something else!" Fern's smile grew even wider. "Do you remember how I mentioned that I needed to give another guy a gentle brush-off before I could get involved with Scott?"

Wondering why Fern suddenly felt the need to discuss this now, when he was clearly anxious to be on his way, James kept his impatience in check. She didn't know that he had to get going to make it to the Wellness Village before his appointment with Harmony. Besides, it was difficult not to fall under the spell of his winsome employee. However, just as Fern opened her mouth to continue, someone at the circulation desk caught her attention.

"Oh, there's Mrs. Honeycutt and her daughter. I promised to talk to them about my favorite Newbery Medal winners. I'll let Scott tell you the rest of my story." And with that, she practically danced out of his office.

Scott intercepted him in the lobby. "You can't go yet! I've been dying to tell you this story all day, but I promised to wait for Fern's shift to start. Now, she's too busy to act as my co-narrator. The Honeycutt girl might only be in the sixth grade, but she reads five books a week. Mrs. Honeycutt wants books that are sophisticated and deep, but without too many adult themes. Fern told me she used to be the same kind of reader in middle school. She typed up a whole list to show mother and daughter."

"We aim to please here at the Shenandoah County Library," James said, proud of the excellent service Fern was providing. Scott was gazing at Fern like he'd never tire of looking at her. "Scott, if you're going to tell me a tale, you'd better get started. I need to be at the Wellness Village in fifteen minutes."

Scott rubbed his hands together, clearly eager to be able to share his news with his boss. "Before Fern was hired, I told you how I really liked this person I met online. I'd never met her in person, though, so I tried to make that happen. However, our meetings kept getting postponed."

"I remember," James said.

"Well, her gamer ID was CAPTRDMMT. Here. It's easier to understand if I write it down." He scribbled the capital letters on the back of a bookmark announcing Harlequin's new releases. "What do you think this stands for? Just take a wild guess."

James loved word riddles of all kinds, so he was happy to oblige. "Capture the moment?"

Scott's mouth fell open. "Whoa! You are *totally* correct! Guess I'm not as sharp as you are, Professor, because I was so caught up in gamer mode that I figured it was an acronym for Capture Dragons, Mages, Men, and Trolls. I assumed she was an evil sorceress."

"What happened? She turned out to be a fairy godmother instead?" James couldn't help teasing Scott a little. The young man took his computer games very seriously.

"Magical, yes! Evil, *no.* And she turned out to be a professional photographer. *Our* photographer! Someone who captures the moment." He beamed. "This person, this cyber goddess, was Fern! She and I have had this online connection for the past six months! And then, she ended up working here. With me!"

James was stunned by the coincidence. Forgetting about his time constraints, he leaned against the circulation desk and stared at Scott. "*Fern* was the woman you kept trying to meet face-to-face?"

"Yessir!" he whispered exuberantly. "She got cold feet the first time. The second time I canceled because Jane asked Francis and me to swing by the courthouse and watch you sign some seriously important paperwork." He looked around wildly, as if the closest library patrons might be listening in on their conversation. "But last night, when Francis went over to Willow's place and I tagged along because . . ." He blushed.

"Because you like Fern," James finished for him.

Scott grinned again. "Yes! But anyway, I saw the screensaver on her computer, and when I asked her about it, she started talking about her character in our game. I just *knew*! There, right in front of me, was my beautiful druid priestess. A fantasy made flesh! How cool is that?"

James smiled and clapped Scott on the back. "It's very cool. Am I to assume that you two are dating now?"

"That would be correct." Scott's eyes grew dreamy. "As of ten thirteen Sunday night. That's the exact moment I kissed my Druid slash photographer slash librarian. I've had an online crush on her for over six months and then I thought I had a new crush on the girl who walked through that door two weeks ago." He pointed toward the lobby. "I had no idea I'd fallen for the same girl twice over."

"Scott, that is the best story I've heard in a long time. Congratulations, son." He pumped the younger man's hand and darted out into the afternoon sunshine.

Weightier knots of air, hinting at summer's impending humidity, had snuffed out the spring breeze. Still, as James drove through town, he detected an atmosphere of anticipation. From the teenagers driving by with their arms hanging out of car windows to the appearance of sun-loving petunias in the sidewalk planters on Main Street, the seasons were gearing up for a change.

To the teens, summer meant freedom. To James, the vibe created a feeling of urgency. He put aside thoughts of Scott's newfound happiness and the details of his own imminent vows and concentrated on a plan to coax information from the Wellness Village's business owners. However, by the time he stood in front of the Village's map, he realized it would be impossible to canvass each and every cottage and make it to his appointment on time.

"What's with the glum look?" Lindy asked, appearing on the sidewalk beside him.

James was thrilled to see her. He needed help. "What are you doing here?"

"Did you really think Lucy was going to sit around twiddling her thumbs while you traipsed in and out of all these Health Houses?" Lindy rolled her eyes. "She's given each of us an assignment. I'm in charge of investigating the Soothing Touch. I even booked a hot stone massage, which means I'll have *plenty* of time to grill the masseuse. Lord, I hope she's some kind of miracle worker. My back is so tight you could bounce a quarter off it!"

"Is Alma still giving you grief?"

Lindy sighed. "No, not really. She spends most of her time with Luigi. It's Luis I'm worried about right now. I've hardly seen him over the past few days. I'm really worried that he's viewing me through his mama's eyes and I'm just not measuring up."

"Don't think that way, Lindy. Isn't this a crazy time of year for everyone in the educational field? Grading final papers and projects, having those last-minute conferences, and seeing who's going to summer school while you're lazing about on a beach somewhere?" James gave his friend a sideways glance, hoping his words would prod her out of her depression.

Her dark eyes flashed. "You know I teach over the summer! We don't get paid enough to spend twelve weeks working on our tans!" She swatted him on the arm. "Ha! You're just messing with me. And yes, the *teachers* are super busy, but what can be taking up so much of Luis's time?"

"The *Star* ran an article about a county-wide plan to prevent the spread of the flu in our schools. It sounded like all the area principals have been attending scores of meetings to figure out a way to implement the new system come autumn."

James knew he was grasping, but he continued. "I bet half his life is comprised of those kinds of bureaucratic headaches."

"Our faculty meetings aren't exactly Mardi Gras either," Lindy scoffed, but her mood had brightened. "Here come the rest of our troops."

James swiveled to see Bennett and Gillian making their way over from the parking lot.

"I never thought I'd see the day," Bennett grumbled. "I'm going to talk to some twisty pretzel yoga lady. Pretend to be all kinds of interested in bending my body in ways an animal made of two hundred and six bones is *not* meant to bend."

Gillian was unfazed by Bennett's sour mood. "I have the honor of speaking to the acupuncturist. I'd love to explore the idea of setting up services for some of my Yuppie Puppy clients."

Seeing that James and Lindy looked perplexed, she elaborated. "Acupuncture can be a *wonderful* alternative to traditional medicine. Instead of taking drugs to relieve joint pain, a person can turn to acupuncture for relief. Avoiding prescription medicine can also mean avoiding harmful side effects." She took a quick breath and then continued. "There are a number of progressive veterinarians who believe that animals can be treated using holistic methods."

"So a dog with an arthritic hip is gonna sit still while some fool human sticks a hot needle in his side?" Bennett shook his head in disbelief. "I'd like to see that!"

The friends laughed and decided to move ahead with their search. James had only to interview the natural healer, Roslyn Rhodes, before asking Skye and Harmony if they happened to own a defibrillator. Of course, he felt silly questioning any of the even-tempered ladies. It wasn't as if they exhibited the slightest inclination toward violence or villainy, but he had to be thorough.

Roslyn was in the middle of a consultation when he dropped by her office. James noted that she had no assistant but simply hung a plaque on her door entreating visitors to make themselves comfortable and that most consultations lasted between fifteen and thirty minutes.

Hoping she'd be finished before his own appointment with Harmony, James sat down to wait. After ten minutes of trying to concentrate on a magazine entirely about herb gardens, James grew restless. He decided to take a risk and peek behind some of Roslyn's closed doors.

The first place he checked was the bathroom where he and Eliot had found Ned Woodman's body. He hadn't really taken a close look at the room at the time, but his secondary inspection revealed nothing. The room had two stalls, two sinks, a garbage pail, and a paper towel dispenser.

James darted a glance at Roslyn's closed door and then tried the handle of the door next to the bathroom. The door was locked.

There was one more door at the far end of the hall on the same side as Roslyn's office, so James moved as quietly as he could and was gratified that the handle moved easily in his hand. After hitting the light switch, he looked into a large walk-in supply closet filled with dozens of boxes, glass jars, and tiny vials containing herbs and holistic medicine. He had time to read label names like Licorice Root, Milk Thistle, Bilberry, Grape Seed Extract, Fenugreek, and Thunder God Vine before he heard movement from inside Roslyn's office.

Shutting the door, James sprinted back to the waiting room and picked up a random magazine. He then felt a stab of panic. Had he remembered to turn off the lights? However, he relaxed again, recalling how Roslyn had previously mentioned that she was chronically absentminded.

"Thank you. I have as much energy as a teenager these days," a woman said with a laugh as she and Roslyn walked toward the waiting room. "After twenty-two years of marriage things can get mighty dull in the bed—" She stopped short upon seeing James. Her cheeks flamed red and she shouldered her purse and hurried toward the exit. "See you soon!" she called back over her shoulder and left.

"Enjoy!" Roslyn shouted cheerfully and then smiled at James. "How nice to see you. How is your son doing?"

"Fine, thanks," James answered. "Eliot's adjusted to vegetarianism with relative ease. As a matter of fact, the whole family has been following his lead. I still eat meat, but I have it for lunch when he's not around."

Roslyn nodded. "In the beginning, I had those cravings too. But

I wanted to commit to veganism for a lifetime, so I wanted to be absolutely sure about my decision. Eventually, I got over the taste of meat and have felt much healthier and happier ever since."

"Eliot's conversion to vegetarianism prompted me to seek you out." James indicated the framed posters showing the human digestive, circulatory, and nervous systems. "Now that the three of us are eating natural foods, I'm realizing how good they make us feel. So when Eliot started getting a little cold, probably because we wore him out at the Apple Blossom Festival, I wanted to find a natural remedy for him. Any suggestions?"

"Absolutely!" Roslyn waved him into her office. "I'd definitely recommend echinacea. It will decrease his symptoms and the length of his cold. I also have some wonderful dissolvable vitamins that include Ester-C and elderberry. They're a wonderful source of vitamins. Would you care for a sample?"

"Yes, please." James followed her into the hall. "Do you mind if I check out your stores? I've never really laid eyes on these types of medicines and I'm pretty interested in how they're packaged." Roslyn led him into the hall and pointed at the door James had unsuccessfully tried to open earlier. "Some have to be kept cold, so I have a small fridge in that closet, but most of my products are in here." She opened the supply room door and frowned. "Did I leave this light on?"

James did his best not to fidget and to maintain a blank expression. "Wow, look at all of this stuff! I haven't heard of half of these plants. These products are all natural?"

"Plants in their purest forms," Roslyn proudly replied.

"Were you always a holistic healer or did you start off learning traditional medicine first?" he asked, even though he knew Sullie and Lucy had spent the day running background checks on everyone in the Village. James was certain that not everything made it onto a person's official profile and it wouldn't hurt to dig a little deeper.

Roslyn pulled her long graying braid over her shoulder and twirled the end around her index finger. "Yes. In fact, I graduated from pharmacy school. It was there that I began to see that the major drug companies were really complicating plant character-istics to make cheaper products. I began researching on my own and realized that the more concentrated the plant part is, the more effective it is. For those giant pharmaceutical companies, it all comes down to dollars and cents. For me, it's always been about finding the purest product, so I started practicing holistic medicine."

"That means you have twice the knowledge of most pharmacists. You know the traditional drugs and the natural ones. Look out, Mr. Goodbee!" James referred to the town's senior pharmacist. "But there are hundreds of plants, and I'd guess that most have more than one use." He pointed at a box of thunder god vine tea. "What does that one do, for example?"

The question was meant to distract Roslyn from focusing on the lights. It worked. "Extracts from the thunder god vine root can be used to treat inflammatory conditions such as rheumatoid arthritis. A study is currently being conducted to see whether it can be used on lupus patients." She handed James a brown box covered with a print of green stalks from which dozens of tiny white flowers burst. In the center of each delicate bloom was a canary-yellow center. "Like many herbs, this one can be harmful. In ancient China, farmers used it as an insecticide and it was believed to be quite an effective murder weapon as well."

"Do not add thunder god vine to my spaghetti sauce," James joked. "But seriously, this is fascinating. And I honestly think death by thunder god vine sounds more dignified than death by defibrillator."

Roslyn leaned forward and replaced the tea box on the shelf. Because her raised arm obscured her face, James was unable to see her reaction. When she turned to him again, she looked bewildered. "I'm not sure I understand."

"I don't think I was supposed to say anything about Ned Woodman's case. That just slipped out." He put on his best expression of chagrin. "I'm not very good at keeping secrets. But neither was Ned, I guess. The authorities believe he had a girlfriend and that she's sitting pretty with all that money Ned stole from the town."

Something flashed in Roslyn's eyes, but it happened so swiftly that James wasn't certain he'd seen anything after all. He blinked and Roslyn was now shaking her head, her face full of sympathy. "His poor wife. It's bad enough that she lost her husband, but she now has to endure public humiliation too. I feel terrible for her."

The words sounded genuine and James decided that he'd grilled the friendly holistic healer enough. He purchased the products Roslyn had recommended, though he doubted he would ever use them. James didn't plan on giving anything to his son that wasn't approved by the FDA.

When he stepped outside into the warm evening, he found Bennett lounging on a nearby bench, engrossed in the latest edition of the World Almanac.

"Planning another *Jeopardy!* appearance?" James quipped.

"Nope, but I never get tired of learning new facts." Bennett folded down a page corner and closed the book. Seeing the look of horror on his friend's face, he quickly smoothed the page flat again. "Jeez, man! It's not like I killed somebody!" he protested, thumping on the fat paperback. "And neither did the yoga lady. That woman's one of those happy-all-the-time types. Not a mean word to say about anybody. She was a stay-at-home mama until her hubby gave her the money to open her own studio. Says all her dreams have come true. We can cross her off the list. What about the medicine woman?"

James shook his head. "Roslyn Rhodes doesn't seem like she has anything to hide. Like your yoga lady, she's found her place in life." He hesitated. "It's just that when I mentioned Ned's having a girlfriend, I thought her eyes turned strange. But it happened so quickly that I'm not sure I really saw anything."

"Go with your gut, man. She could be sneaking that heart-shocking machine out the back door as we speak."

Though Bennett was partially jesting, a wave of doubt assailed James. "Can you stick around to see if she comes out of the office looking worried or, like you said, carrying a large box? I have to meet with Harmony."

"Will do," his friend agreed. "Gillian's gonna be jibber-jabbin' with the needle lady all evening long anyhow. Why do you think I brought this book?"

Inside A Better State of Mind, Skye was humming as she watered the houseplants. She welcomed James with her customary grace and warmth, and then apologized, saying that Harmony's current appointment was running a little late.

"No problem." James settled into the chair nearest her desk and began chatting with Skye about Lennon, her passion for running, and how she had ended up working for Harmony. They were interrupted once by a customer looking to purchase a gift certificate for his wife.

"She wants to quit smoking. Let me tell you—after living with that smell for eleven years, I'd do anything to help her stop!" he exclaimed, passing Skye a credit card.

After the satisfied customer had gone, James used the subject of gift certificates as a transition to the subject of birthday presents. He told Skye about the mailbox shaped like a stack of books that Scott and Francis had carved for him. He really wanted to find out if she'd received Fern's lovely photographs so he could tell his new employee that Skye had been delighted with her work. "How about you? Do you have a birthday coming up soon?"

Skye shook her head. "Mine was last month. Lennon got me a fantastic pair of running shoes. They're so light that I barely feel them on my feet."

"Cool." James moved off to pour himself a glass of water, but his mind was spinning. If the prints weren't for Skye, who were they for?

He didn't have the opportunity to ponder the question any further because Harmony and a pretty female client entered the reception area. The hypnotherapist bid her previous client goodbye and then smiled at James. "Come on back," she said.

Before he could settle into the recliner, his phone chirped, signaling the receipt of a text message.

"This is from Lucy," he explained to Harmony. "I don't think we should start the session as it's bound to be interrupted."

Harmony gazed at him quizzically. "Oh?"

"She and her fellow officers are on the way here. Apparently, they have a search warrant for every cottage in the Village."

"Does this have something to do with Mr. Woodman's death?" Harmony asked, the picture of calm.

James nodded. "And possibly Tia Royale's as well." If he'd expected to provoke a dramatic reaction by bringing up the dead woman's name, he was to be disappointed. Harmony simply gazed at him with concern .

"I'm afraid I don't understand," she confessed.

It was time to pull out all the stops. "Ned Woodman and Tia Royale were probably killed by the same person. The investigating deputies believe this individual may have some connection to the Wellness Village. I can't say anything else. All I know is they're on the hunt for a very specific object."

Again, Harmony appeared unfazed by the knowledge that her office was about to be invaded by members of the Shenandoah County Sheriff's Department. Extending her hand, she indicated James should follow her to the reception room. "We'll have to reschedule your appointment, and I guess I should have Skye cancel the rest of tonight's clients. This way we can be available to assist the deputies in whatever manner possible."

If that woman's hiding something, then she's a master of concealment, James thought. In truth, he was relieved that Harmony seemed above suspicion.

• • •

After a pair of brown Sheriff's Department cruisers had disgorged six deputies with search warrants, Lucy met with the rest of the supper club members to get their take on the Wellness Village employees and business owners.

"The background checks were useless," she told her friends. "Some moving violations, a shoplifting charge that was later dropped, and a few people who were late paying taxes here and there. That's it. Not a single red flag on our end."

The supper club members gave Lucy summaries of their casual interrogations. After James shared his experience questioning Roslyn, Bennett added that no one had entered or exited her cottage since he'd been watching her front door.

"Each house has a back door," Sullie pointed out, having just returned from examining the perimeter of the complex. "It's where the dumpsters are located and probably where they get their deliveries. The trash has already been picked up. If there was any evidence in those things, it's sittin' in a heap at the landfill now."

Lucy scowled. "Seems like Roslyn would be more likely to kill someone with one of her thousand herbs than with a defibrillator, but we'll search her cottage first. I want to see what's behind that locked door James mentioned. Thanks for doing your best to flush out the perp, everyone. I'll let you know if we find anything."

She and Sullie hustled off. James noticed a sulky Deputy Donovan waiting for instructions and couldn't help but smile. The combative redhead didn't dare start trading insults with Lucy when Sullie was around. Donovan might look like a bulldog, but Sullie towered over his fellow officer and was a solid mass of muscle. James cast an envious glance at the snug fit of Sullie's uniform shirt before hurrying out to the parking lot. He still had one more errand to complete before heading home.

A half hour later, James left the local jewelry shop with a small bag containing a pair of gold wedding bands nestled inside red velvet boxes. As he waited for the clerk to polish the bands, he strolled over to the coffee shop next door and ordered an iced white chocolate mocha latte. The jolt of sugar flowing over his tongue and his teeth was a shock to his system. It was, amazingly, too sweet.

James knew that he should stop sipping the cold coffee drink then and there, but he'd paid four dollars for the thing and couldn't make himself throw it out. Slowly, as he became distracted examining and paying for the rings, he grew accustomed to the taste. By the time he crossed the street and headed in the direction of the public parking lot, the plastic cup was empty.

Irritated with himself, James chucked the cup into a nearby garbage can from several feet away and was surprised when someone applauded his successful shot.

"He shoots and he scores! Would you like to coach our JV basketball team next year?" James turned to see Luis Chavez grinning widely at him. "They didn't exactly have a winning record this past season."

James shook the principal's hand. Lindy's boyfriend was good-looking and charismatic, with dark intelligent eyes and a ready smile. James hid the bag from the jewelry store behind his back and fell into stride next to Luis. Together, the two public servants headed toward the parking lot.

"School's almost out for the summer," James said as they walked. "Any big plans?"

"Besides shipping my mama back to Mexico?" Luis laughed

loudly. "Always. I'm a man filled with big plans." And before James could ask him to elaborate, Luis dug around in his pocket and pulled out a handful of tickets. "I was going to drop these by the library, but now that I've bumped into you there's no need. These are tickets for our musical this Friday night. I'm asking you, as a special favor, to come to our play with your family, the library staff, and all of Lindy's supper club friends. Can you do that for me?"

His curiosity piqued to its highest level, James accepted the tickets. "Is this some kind of special performance?"

"Absolutely!" Luis clapped James heartily on the back. "It's at *my* school, after all! And it's Shakespeare. A musical version of *Much Ado About Nothing*. I promise that it will be the most memorable dramatic performance this town has ever seen."

James raised his brows. "In that case, I wouldn't dream of missing it."

Luis waved and took off in the opposite direction. Even though his pace was brisk, the light timbre of the song he started to sing drifted through the warm air. James smiled. He couldn't hear any of the song's words, but he recognized the emotion underlying the tone: Luis Chavez was singing about love.

Chapter Sixteen

Wedding Cupcake

The official search of the Wellness Village proved fruitless. Lucy found Roslyn quietly filling out paperwork in her office and, after taking a cursory glance at the proffered search warrant, the holistic healer was more than happy to unlock the supply closet where she kept organic medicines in a small refrigerator.

"I've never met a bunch of people so eager to help after being told that we plan to rifle through their stuff," Lucy said to James as he shelved books in the New Releases section. She pointed at a James Patterson hardcover. "Does this guy ever sleep? Seems like he churns a book out every three months."

"Some critics would agree with your choice of verb, but I think the man has too many ideas and not enough time." James handed Lucy two tickets to the Blue Ridge High production of *Much Ado About Nothing*. "I've been told by Principal Chavez that attendance is mandatory. Are you bringing Sullie?"

Lucy shrugged. "Plays aren't his thing, but he has another reason to be there."

Perplexed, James was about to ask Lucy to clarify her statement when Fern finished assisting a patron and joined them in front of the display. "You wanted to ask me something, Professor?"

"Actually, I did," Lucy answered with a friendly smile. "Don't mind the uniform. This isn't official. I'm just trying to satisfy my own curiosity."

Fern visibly relaxed. "For a second there I thought you were here to scold me for parking in the loading zone in front of Quincy's Whimsies, but I was helping Willow with a delivery."

Lucy laughed. "I try to leave the dispensing of parking tickets to Deputy Donovan. Nothing perks him up like a row of cars with tickets stuck under their wiper blades. No, I wanted to ask you about the photographs Lennon purchased. Can you describe the prints and repeat the conversation for me?"

Fern pointed at the computer behind the reference desk. "It's easier for me to show you the photos online. My boyfriend created a gorgeous website for me."

Curious, James followed the two women behind the counter, leaving Francis to man the circulation desk. Scott was busy in the Tech Corner and was likely to be there for some time, considering Mrs. Withers was back with a tote bag full of Beanie Babies and a digital camera.

"I'm ready to sell these on eBay!" she'd announced upon entering the library and grabbed James by the elbow.

Scott had witnessed the encounter and had quickly intervened. "I can show her the ropes, Professor. Francis and I have been on eBay since the dawn of online trading. I know a trick or two to get Mrs. Withers the best price possible."

As the pair sat down in front of a computer, Mrs. Withers ruffled Scott's hair. "You're such a nice boy. I'm glad I baked up a batch of my homemade peanut butter brownies for you and your sweet brother. You two go outta your way to help us old coots and we sure do appreciate it. Besides, someone needs to put a bit of meat on your bones! When are you gonna find a good girl to cook for you?"

"Oh, I've found the girl, Mrs. Withers," Scott happily declared. "And she might not be a whiz in the kitchen, but she is a shining star in every other way!"

Returning his focus to the present, James turned away from the Tech Corner and peered over Lucy's shoulder just as Fern was pointing at some images on the computer screen. Fern's website was beautiful. The background was a soft moss green and framed her photograph of a purple rhododendron flower. Fern clicked on the thumbnails showing more close-ups of plant parts.

"I took these shots when I was working as a part-time park ranger," Fern explained. "All of these plants grow wild in Virginia."

"How many photos did Lennon buy?" Lucy inquired.

"Ten," Fern said. "They were all framed prints costing one fifty apiece. It was the biggest paycheck I've ever gotten for my photographs. Actually, it wasn't a check. Lennon paid me in cash."

Lucy drew back. "That's fifteen hundred dollars—a big chunk of change for the Wellness Village maintenance man. And he said the photographs were a gift for his girlfriend?"

"Yes. He was really excited about giving them to her." Fern

searched Lucy's face. "Why would he pretend to be buying the prints for her birthday when he really wasn't? Unless"—her lips scrunched up in thought—"he has more than one girlfriend."

"Unfortunately, two-timing's not against the law." Lucy thanked Fern and pulled James to the side. "I think I need to look a little closer at Lennon's spending habits. See you at the play." She moved a few steps away and then paused. Walking back to the desk she added, "We haven't stopped driving by your house. I may be nose-deep in this case, but I haven't forgotten about Kenneth."

Neither had James. In fact, his dreams the previous night had been tormented by hundreds of sinister crows. Reminiscent of Alfred Hitchcock's *The Birds*, the feathered assailants gathered on tree branches, telephone wires, and on the roof of Eliot's tree house. They squawked and ruffled their black feathers but never took their dark eyes off James's bedroom window. He knew they were waiting for a signal, but from what or whom he couldn't tell. It was as if their master remained hidden in the shadows of the distant trees, waiting and watching.

"James!" Jane had finally shaken him awake. "If you don't stop thrashing around. I'll be black and blue by dawn!"

Despite his anxiety, the workweek passed without incident. No one in the Henry household received strange letters and no dead birds were left on the property. By the time Friday rolled around, James was immersed in thoughts of his upcoming marriage ceremony. It was to be performed by the justice of the peace that very afternoon. Their marriage license had arrived by mail on Wednesday and Jane had wasted no time in securing the last available spot in the JP's schedule.

"It'll be tight," she told James Wednesday evening. "We need to be ready by five thirty. Our marriage officiate, whose name is Frank Love, if you can believe that, says we'll be man and wife by six o'clock. After that, we need to eat dinner and hightail it to the school by seven."

"Our first appearance wearing our wedding rings," James mused and then asked, "What are your thoughts about our vows?"

Jane, who had been stirring spaghetti sauce at the time, stood still. "I think we should write our own. We went by the book last time. Let's make this ceremony really personal. Oh, and I forgot to tell you. We're getting married right here, in our house."

"That's wonderful! You, me, Eliot, Snickers, and Miss Pickles. We could tie the rings onto Snickers's collar."

"And put a basket of tissue paper flowers on the floor. Miss Pickles would scatter those in a heartbeat!" They'd chuckled at the idea. After passing James the wooden spoon so he might taste the sauce, Jane said, "The more I think about it, the more I believe your parents should be here too."

"But won't your folks be hurt when they find out they weren't included?"

She'd shaken her head. "They'll just be happy we made things official. Besides, we're not taking pictures or having a cake or anything like that, so there really won't be any details for them to hear about later on. I'm wearing a blue and white sundress and sandals and you can be just as casual." She'd put an arm around his waist. "We're stripping away all the trimmings this time around. On Friday, it's all about the promises we make to each other. Nothing else matters."

By the time the Fitzgerald brothers finished with their lunch breaks that Friday, James had already thrown out page after page of rejected wedding vows. He spent his entire break surfing wedding websites and flipping through books stuffed with sample vows. None of them felt right.

By the afternoon coffee break, James was nearing a state of panic. The twins knew something was amiss with their boss, so when James ducked into the kitchen to start the coffee machine, Francis trailed after him.

"Professor?" the younger man said. "Do you need a hand? An ear? A shoulder to cry on? A punching bag? Scott and I have watched the clouds gathering over your head all day long."

James, who had been staring at the tin of coffee grounds as though he might see his future written there, jumped at the sound of Francis's voice. The scoop in his right hand jerked sideways and grounds went everywhere. "Blast!" He dampened a paper towel and waved at Francis to stay back. "It's not your fault. My mind is a tangled knot today." He glanced at the younger man. "Jane and I are getting married in two hours and I haven't written my vows yet!"

"Ohhhh," Francis whispered and squatted down to push the grounds on the floor into a tidy pile. "But you're good with words, Professor. Can't you just tell her you love her and that you'll cherish her for the rest of your life?"

Shaking his head, James dumped the paper towel in the trash can. "I need to promise more than that. I need to make her realize that she is the only one in the world for me, that she makes my dreams come true, and that she's given me a second chance at happiness." His eyes grew distant as he thought about Jane. "I want her to know that her love is a gift to me and that my love for her is, and always will be, the forever kind. She's my friend and my partner and my soul mate, and together we can make all the days of our lives whatever we want them to be. As long as she's with me, I will face each new day with gratitude and joy in my heart."

Francis had stopped cleaning. Sitting back on his heels, he stared at his boss open-mouthed. "Wow, Professor. *I* would totally want to marry you if you said that to me!"

"That was okay? It wasn't formal or grammatically incorrect or—"

"It was awesome!" Francis leapt up, dashed from the room, and returned with a pen and scrap paper. "Write it down. Quickly! And then post a copy on YouTube for the rest of us hopeless guys."

James sat at the table and wrote his vows, smiling all the while. As soon as he was done, he wolfed down a peanut butter and jelly sandwich and then called his parents. He would later swear that Milla squealed in delight for a full thirty seconds.

He failed to accomplish even the most menial tasks that afternoon. It wasn't nerves. James wanted nothing more than to recite his vows and slide a ring onto Jane's finger. Now that the ceremony was almost upon him, he found he couldn't concentrate on books. When a female patron asked for a light beach read, James handed her *The Color Purple*. Right after that, he gave Dan Brown's *The Lost Symbol* to a patron who despised books having anything to do with conspiracy theory. Fortunately, Scott remedied both blunders as soon as James turned away to collect the wrong amount of money for an overdue fine.

At four thirty, Francis tapped James on the shoulder. "Scott and I think you should go home, Professor. You have a big evening ahead. We'll see you at the play tonight. If anything work-related comes up, we can always fill you in then."

James gave his employee a crooked smile. "You're right. I've never bumbled about the library as much as I have this afternoon. If I stay here any longer, I'm going to let some seven-year-old check out a Laurel Hamilton novel."

Scott walked over and, one at a time, the twins embraced their boss. "Congrats, Professor. Now go get married."

When he got home he found Jane in the backyard, weaving a daisy chain. She'd already made several for Eliot and wore one around her head like a crown. When she saw James, she finished the chain in her hands and placed it around his neck. He closed his arms around her back and planted a soft kiss on her mouth. She smelled like grass and sunshine. As he released her, Eliot bellowed a pirate's "Arggh!" from his tree house and waved at James with a plastic sword.

"You go in and change," James told Jane. "Or stay like this. I think you look like a queen in your tank top and bare feet. And the crown of daisies is very bridal."

Jane laughed. "I'd keep it on, but then I'd look like an aging hippie. Perhaps a single bloom tucked behind the ear is more fitting. See you at 'the altar.'"

"I'll be there!" James waited for her to go inside before scooping Eliot up in his arms. "Now, you're mine! Consider yourself pirate-napped!"

For the next thirty minutes, James and Eliot raced around the yard, alternating between warring pirates and co-conspirators in search of buried treasure.

"Arggh, I wish I could remember where we left our booty!" James growled out of the side of his mouth while squinting one eye shut.

Eliot poked at the base of the birdhouse pole with a sharp stick. "It was the robbers! They stole our treasure!"

James stood as tall as he could and put his hands on his hips, surveying the yard with a fierce glower. "Let's make 'em walk the plank!"

Together, he and Eliot prodded a plastic velociraptor and a wind-up robot to the end of a narrow wood board jutting out over the deck railing. On the ground below, they'd placed a rubber crocodile and a pair of Halloween vampire teeth on a blue towel.

"You must pay for your treachery!" James snarled.

"Yeah!" Eliot echoed with glee.

Once the sea monster had finished devouring the toys, the Henry men went inside and clinked glasses of ice water, signifying their victory over the forces of evil. By the time James showered and changed into fresh khakis and a light blue polo shirt, the wedding officiate had arrived. James welcomed him and introduced Eliot. Milla and Jackson weren't far behind the officiate. James was unsurprised to see Milla carrying a large cardboard box into the kitchen.

"I didn't think you'd have enough time to bake anything," James complained. "You were supposed to just show up and enjoy yourselves. No gifts, no food, just a simple champagne toast."

"Fiddlesticks!" Milla exclaimed. "I was *not* going to let this occasion pass without contributing in some way. You were so wonderful to Jackson and me when we got married. How could I sit around and twiddle my thumbs when I knew I had the chance to whip up something for you and Jane. Believe me, with only two hours I was forced to make a simple dessert."

Jackson snorted. "You should see what she's callin' simple."

"Hold the box for me, dear." Milla smiled at her husband. Placing his good arm around the base of the box, Jackson looked on with pride as Milla lifted out a small tower of cupcakes. The cupcakes were vanilla frosted and rimmed with white sugar crystals. In the center of each cupcake, Milla had drawn a heart using silver icing. The top cupcake featured the bride and groom's initials, *J & J*, in elegant silver script.

"How lovely!" Jane cried upon entering the kitchen. "Thank you, Milla!"

Milla embraced her future daughter-in-law and elbowed Jackson in the ribs. "Go on, dear. Tell Jane what you wanted to say."

Jackson spoke slowly, making a powerful effort to form his words clearly. "I'm right glad you and my son are puttin' your lives together." He glanced at James. "It's a real gift to this old fool to have you all livin' close by. You three and Milla give me reason to get this bag of bones outta bed in the mornin'." He hesitated, gathering the needed strength to finish his speech. "Guess what I'm tryin' to say is I'm right honored to be here today."

Jane threw her arms around Jackson and kissed him on the cheek. As she led him into the living room, James turned to Milla and whispered, "He's walking much better this week."

Milla nodded. "Your daddy's been working real hard in therapy. He wants nothing more than to get on his hands and knees and play with his grandson. The nurses say they've never seen someone Jackson's age make such speedy progress."

Indeed, Jackson barely limped as he walked into the living room to shake hands with Mr. Love. Snickers had made himself at home on Eliot's lap, while Miss Pickles perched like a gargoyle behind his shoulder on the sofa back. James had to laugh when he noticed that the animals' collars had been replaced by daisy chains.

"All set?" asked Mr. Love.

James and Jane smiled at one another.

"We've never been more ready," James answered and took hold of his bride's hand.

• • •

Sitting in the auditorium of Blue Ridge High School, James kept touching the gold band encircling his left ring finger. Even though it had been years since James last wore a wedding ring, he was surprised at how wonderful it was to feel the warm metal against his skin and to be able to display his status as a married man to the entire world.

Next to him, Jane glowed. James had never seen her looking more beautiful and he couldn't stop leaning over and whispering in her ear or kissing her on the cheek.

"Ease up on the PDA, kids!" Lucy teased as she took the reserved chair next to James.

With flushed cheeks, James craned his neck toward the back of the room. Nearly every available seat had been taken and the noise level was rising exponentially. "Is Sullie here?"

"He wants to hang out in the parking lot for a bit," Lucy answered cryptically. "Where's Eliot?"

"With his grandparents," James said. "We're having a date night."

Bennett and Gillian walked briskly down the carpeted aisle and settled in the two seats next to Jane. The two women immediately fell into conversation about what they planned to purchase at the farmer's market the next morning while Bennett frowned over the paper program in his hands. "I could be watchin' baseball!" he moaned and James chuckled.

"Luis promised us a night we'll never forget," James reminded his friend.

"He did?" Lindy asked as she took the last open seat in the row. She reached across Lucy to poke James in the leg. "When did you run into him and what *exactly* did he mean by that?" Her eyes darted around the room as she waited for his answer. "Where's his mama? She could be up to no good."

"I saw her sitting right in the middle." Lucy pointed at the opposite side of the room. "With Luigi and his brood." She shook her head. "Call me crazy, but she seemed to be thoroughly enjoying his kids."

Lindy brightened. "Those darlings might just save me! If Alma gets wrapped up in *their* lives, she won't have enough spare time to meddle in mine."

Suddenly, the lights blinked and the clamor from the audience died down. A teacher walked up to the piano positioned offstage and began to hammer out a lively melody. The heavy red curtain parted and a pretty young girl dressed in contemporary clothes began to sing. Soon, the crowd was completely absorbed in the blossoming romance between Claudio and Hero and the antics of Beatrice and Benedick. Just when things seemed to be going smoothly for both couples, the treacherous Don John appeared at the back of the auditorium, singing in a bold bass voice about his plans to ruin Claudio and Hero's wedding. As the spotlight followed the teenage thespian down the aisle, Jane suddenly gasped and jabbed her fingertips into the flesh of James's arm.

"It's Kenneth!" she hissed fearfully. "I saw him when the light shone on the section near the fire door!"

James tried to scan the shadowy faces in the far back rows, but they'd been pitched into darkness now that the spotlight had passed. He leaned over to Lucy. "Jane says she saw Kenneth! Sitting near the fire door. What should we do?"

Lucy's shoulders stiffened. "Sullie was right. He had a hunch Kenneth might come around tonight—said he was due for another appearance. You stay here. I'll handle this jerk."

When Lucy left, Lindy slid into her vacant chair. "What is going on?" she asked James and was angrily shushed by the older woman seated behind her. Onstage, the girl playing Hero sang a duet with the boy cast as her father, Leonato. As their voices intertwined, the pair walked with extreme slowness down a red velvet aisle, the train of Hero's wedding gown being carried by her maid, Margaret. Suddenly, it became painfully apparent from his balled fists and hostile glare that the groom was waiting in a state of extreme anger, and the joyful melody abruptly morphed into a song filled with discord and strife.

The disharmony of the music spurred James into action. "Come on!" he whispered urgently to Jane. "What if Kenneth goes to the house . . . ?"

"Eliot!" Jane's eyes flashed with fear. Ignoring the rumblings of the woman behind them, James told Gillian and Bennett what was happening and then jogged up the aisle.

"His chair is empty now," Jane said as soon as all five of them were gathered in the school hall.

Lindy's face was stormy. "This creep is going down! No one runs around *my* school bullying people without getting in trouble. Kenneth Cooper is about to serve the longest detention of his life!"

Minutes later, armed with aluminum baseball bats taken from the school's P.E. supply closet, they moved down the empty halls rattling each and every classroom door, but all were locked.

Outside, the night sky blazed with brilliant stars and a luminescent half moon. The parking lot, which formed an L shape around the building, was eerily quiet. James looked around, trying to discern the shape of a man's body in the darkness surrounding the parked vehicles. The glow from the parking lot lights added to the confusion, refracting off hundreds of windshields like mirror images of the stars above. More than once, James was certain he'd seen movement in the periphery of his vision, but it turned out to be merely a wink of light bouncing off a car window.

Deciding that subtlety was not necessary, James shouted, "Lucy! Where are you?"

"At your truck!" Lucy's voice rang out across the parking lot.

James broke into a run, Jane and the rest of the supper club members close on his heels. He'd parked near the football field, and as he approached the Bronco he could see the beam of a flashlight playing over his truck. Sullie was barking terse orders into his cell phone while Lucy examined the Bronco's hood.

"What the—!" Bennett began and then stopped.

Kenneth had formed a heart made of black feathers on the hood of James's Bronco. But what made the women gasp in horror and rendered James and Bennett speechless was the blood splattered over the feathers and in wild zigzags across the windshield.

"There's more." Lucy gestured at the back of the truck. There, tethered to the bumper, were three dead birds. Ropes were tied around the crows' necks and they dangled midair, heads lolling and dark eyes set in fixed stares.

James put a protective arm around his wife.

"It's like a twisted version of the tin cans people put on a newlywed's car," Lindy murmured in repulsion.

James and Jane exchanged fearful looks. "Do you think he knows?" Jane gulped. "Could he have *been* there?"

Lucy was observing Jane closely. "Been where?" she demanded.

"This isn't how I wanted to tell you." James held out his arms to indicate that he was addressing everyone. "Jane and I were married by the justice of the peace earlier this evening." Taking Jane's hand in his, he showed his friends their rings. "We didn't want it to be a big deal. We just wanted to quietly make things official."

"Second time's the charm," Jane added with a nervous smile.

For a moment, his announcement hung in the air, but as the supper club members wrapped their minds around the news, their grim and anxious expressions were transformed into smiles. "Mazel tov!" Gillian shouted and embraced the couple.

Lindy congratulated them next. "You really *are* meant to spend your lives together!"

"Way to go, man." Bennett clapped James on the shoulder and then kissed Jane on the cheek.

Lucy touched each of them on the arm and said, "I'm happy for you both," while Sullie beamed at them briefly before turning businesslike again. "Okay, so this event must have prompted Kenneth into action. And he hasn't gone anywhere. He's hiding." He crossed his arms, making his biceps appear even bigger than before. "No vehicles have entered or exited this lot since the play started. Our guy went in with the rest of the crowd, and since I didn't see him come out, I bet he plans to wait and leave when everyone else does."

"But we're not going to let that happen," Lucy stated with authority. "This nonsense stops right here, right now." She turned to Jane. "I have to be blunt: this is all about you. For some reason or another, your ex is going crazy because you've moved on. To draw him out of hiding, I need to use you as bait."

"No!" James protested, but Lucy held out her hand. "I'll be with her. It'll seem like we're two vulnerable women alone in the parking lot, but I can handle anything this guy dishes out. Sullie, you take Lindy and Gillian and do a sweep of the area near the bus drop-off. James and Bennett, you guys check every row of this lot." She handed James a flashlight. "Don't forget to sweep under the cars too. A grown man can hide under a jacked-up truck or some SUVs."

"If we find him, how will we signal you?" Bennett asked. Lindy dug around in her purse and came up with a whistle. "Here. I always have one with me."

Before the groups moved off, James touched Lucy's holster. She apparently kept a weapon stashed in her Jeep. "Do you think Kenneth is armed?"

She shook her head. "I don't, but be ready to swing those baseball bats just in case. Let's go, people, I don't know much about Shakespeare, but it seems like the play is nearing the final act."

Lucy was correct. As the two deputies and the supper club members spread out across the parking lot wielding flashlights and baseballs bats, a double wedding was taking place onstage. Before the cast raised their voices to belt out the final number, Luis Chavez jogged up to center stage, his hand gripping a cordless microphone.

"Sorry to interrupt, folks, but the students have graciously allowed me a minor speaking part in the wonderful conclusion of this year's stellar musical. Like Claudio and Benedick, I too need a partner to complete my scene." He smiled at the crowd, unable to see clearly with the spotlight bathing his face. "Lindy Perez, would you join me onstage?"

The student actors cast knowing glances at one another and an air of strident expectation filled the room. When Lindy didn't appear, Luis shielded his eyes against the light and stared at the section where she'd been sitting minutes before. "Don't be shy, Lindy. I have a quick question to ask you."

"She's gone!" Luigi's voice boomed out from the middle of the auditorium.

Luis sagged, his buoyant face deflating, the sparkle in his eyes extinguished. Glancing at the diamond ring in his palm, he waved at the students to continue and managed to slink off stage right. He kept walking, numbly, past pieces of scenery and members of the chorus waiting for their moment to dance onstage. Music exploded around him and his precious students sang their hearts out, as though trying to erase their principal's awkward moment.

On any other night, Luis would have savored the experience, his chest swelling with pride. On any other night, he would have presented the pianist and the drama teacher with a bouquet of roses. Even now, the flowers were carefully tucked beneath his auditorium seat. On any other night, he would have shaken hands with every audience member and would have stayed until every last person had left the building. But tonight, the night he'd planned on proposing marriage, he could no longer be himself. He hadn't realized until that long minute onstage that he'd waited far too long to ask for Lindy's hand; that his mother's approval wasn't as significant as he'd thought; and that nothing mattered until he found the woman he'd taken for granted for years and dropped to his knees before her.

With renewed purpose, Luis burst from the emergency exit at the back of the building, flinging open the heavy metal door with the passionate impatience of a man consumed with the desire to gaze upon the face of his lover. Unbeknownst to Luis, a stranger had chosen that unfortunate moment to try to gain access to the building. The door hit this man like a sledgehammer and he crumpled in a heap to the ground.

"*Dios Mio!*" Luis shouted and sprang to the aid of the unconscious man. He reached into the man's pockets in search of a cell phone in order to call for help, but found nothing but a handful of sticky black feathers.

Chapter Seventeen

Granola Bar

Luis dropped the feathers on the ground and stared at the blood on his fingers. Believing that the impact from the door had injured the man, Luis yelled "Help!" at the top of his lungs.

He was relieved to hear footsteps approaching. A woman with a camera slung over her shoulder dashed around the corner of the building and came to a sudden stop when she saw the body on the ground.

"Do you have a phone on you?" Luis asked Murphy Alistair. "I smacked him with the door when I was coming out. I think I knocked him unconscious."

Murphy pulled out her phone and called the emergency operator. After calmly requesting an ambulance to meet them at the back of Blue Ridge High, she scuttled around the man's body to get a closer look at his face.

"Kenneth Cooper! I'll be damned." She raised her camera and immediately began to take pictures of the unresponsive man. After that, she took several close-ups of the black feathers scattered on the ground.

Luis was initially shocked into paralysis by her actions, but when the light of the camera flash continued, he leapt forward and put a hand in front of the lens. "What's wrong with you? This man is injured!"

Murphy lowered the camera. "Before you get too judgmental, allow me to introduce you to the person who's been terrorizing James Henry and his family for the past month."

Stunned, Luis took a step away from Kenneth Cooper.

"And that blood on your fingers?" Murphy continued. "That's from the dead birds he killed and hung on James's truck. I have some beautiful photos of that artistic display. This guy is truly imbalanced. It's a good thing you took him out."

Luis gaped at the inert form on the ground, but it wasn't long before the sound of more footfalls caught his attention. Two groups converged on the scene. First came James and Bennett, panting from exertion, followed by Lucy and Jane. Jane looked frightened, but Lucy's eyes glimmered as they fell on Kenneth.

"Nice work, Principal," she told Luis after he explained what had happened. She then called Sullie, who appeared shortly afterward with Lindy in tow. Lindy lagged behind to flag down the ambulance, and before Luis could even speak to her, the sound of boisterous applause echoing from inside the building signaled the end of the play. Knowing that it was his duty to direct the flow of traffic away from the ambulance, Luis asked Sullie for help and the two men hustled off, flashlights in hand.

"I like a man with leadership qualities," Murphy murmured to James as she stared after the two men. "Dark, handsome, and authoritative. I might have to schedule an exclusive interview with the charming Principal Chavez."

James scowled. "He's spoken for. He and Lindy—"

"There's no ring on *his* finger," Murphy said with a sly smile as she stepped aside to give the paramedics room. Turning to Lucy, she pointed at her camera. "Do you want a ride to the hospital? I'm going to try to get a comment from Kenneth as soon as he wakes up."

"Only after I'm done with him," Lucy declared with a firm glare.

Murphy gave a little bow. "Naturally. On the way over, I thought we could discuss our strategy."

Lucy's expression was inscrutable. "Our strategy?"

"Yes. Kenneth and his lawyer buddies are going to argue that the evidence in this case is too circumstantial for a conviction. If you and Sullie can't coerce him into making a confession, then I have another idea of how to rid ourselves of this menace."

"I'm all ears," Lucy said.

Bennett watched the women walk away. "I wouldn't trust that woman for all the donut holes in the bakery."

Gillian took his arm. "I believe Murphy is trying to make amends. Did you hear how she said 'our' town? I think we need to open our hearts to the possibility that she is capable of selfless acts of kindness."

"We'll see when her next book comes out," Bennett muttered. "Come on, woman. The long arm of the law has nabbed the bad guy and I'm right sure our newlyweds wanna get on home." He pointed at James. "And don't think you've wormed your way out of having some kind of party. No friend of mine ties the knot without booze and a speech or two."

Gillian beamed at Bennett. "You are *so* right! Let us throw you a little dinner party. Nothing fancy—just the supper club, the library staff, your parents, and Eliot. A nice vegetarian reception!"

"That would be lovely, thank you." Jane accepted and then sagged against James's chest. "This has been quite an evening. Let's go back to the house, relieve your folks, and spend the rest of the night watching TV in our pajamas."

Holding hands, the newly married couple navigated the busy parking lot. They were both glad to be among the animated crowd, to have to maneuver around bumper-to-bumper traffic, and listen to half the town shout greetings to James or wave to him out of car windows.

"I feel like the wife of a movie star," Jane teased when they finally reached the Bronco.

James sighed happily. "Thank goodness I'm just a small-town librarian. I'm so exhausted after all this drama that I can only hope to have enough strength to carry you over the threshold."

"I'll settle for a piggyback ride," Jane replied before leaning back against the headrest and closing her eyes. "Do you think we'll live peacefully ever after now that Kenneth's been caught?"

Easing the truck into the stream of blazing red taillights, James shook his head. "There's still a murderer at large in Quincy's Gap." Stalled in the knot of traffic, he gazed out the windshield, lifting his eyes to the dark shape of the mountains looming above. "We have miles to go before we sleep."

The house was quiet when Jane and James tiptoed inside. Jackson was watching a television program on the most destructive car chases ever filmed while Milla embroidered Eliot's Christmas stocking. She'd been working on the stocking since February and had already warned Jane that it would be a miracle if she had it ready for Christmas Eve. When James saw the tiny stitches and the intricate pattern of Santa Claus removing toys from his sack, he marveled at Milla's skill.

"How was the play?" she asked James, easing a piece of silky thread from beneath one of Miss Pickles's paws.

James smirked. "Dramatic." He told his parents every exciting detail while Jane went down the hall to peek in on Eliot. When he was finished, Jackson turned off the television and struggled to his feet.

"If this Kenneth fellow comes 'round here again, you need to scare the tar outta him." Jackson's brows furrowed in anger. "I'd best loan you my shotgun."

James shook his head. He had no intention of keeping a gun in the house. "Thanks for the offer, Pop, but Lucy will deal with him."

"That is a comforting thought," Milla said and patted James on the back. "You can have a nice, carefree summer now." Gathering her things together, she paused at the front door. "Oh, I almost forgot! A lovely woman stopped by with some herbal iced tea. She said it would help with Eliot's cold, but that you might want to taste it first to see if he'd find it too bitter."

"Roslyn Rhodes was here?"

Milla nodded. "Yes, that was her name. I told her Eliot seemed right as rain and she said you'd probably given him some of her products already and that the tea would be good for you too. She said you must come in contact with all sorts of germs handling those library books and this tea would help rev up your defenses."

Slightly bewildered by the healer's house call, James wished Jackson and Milla good night and crawled into bed, too tired to open the fridge and investigate Roslyn's gift.

The next morning was Saturday. That meant cartoons, pajamas, coffee, and James's famous pancake faces. He got up before the rest of the family and set about brewing coffee and making Eliot fresh-squeezed orange juice. He was just folding blueberries into the pancake batter when Eliot shuffled into the kitchen. The little boy rubbed sleep from his eyes and hugged his father. He then pulled a stool over to the counter and watched as James used a ladle to spoon the batter onto the hot skillet.

"Can we have alien pancakes today?" Eliot asked.

"Aliens with blue spots," James agreed. He cooked one oval-shaped pancake and two silver-dollar-sized pancakes. The bigger pancake made up the alien's face while the smaller ones served as his eyes. Strawberries cut into triangles formed a sinister mouth while half a banana cut lengthwise became the nose. James added two chocolate chip pupils and presented the plate to his son with a flourish.

"Earth has been invaded by aliens with blue spots." James spoke in a robotic monotone. "Only one boy can save the day. Eliot Henry, will you rescue our planet by destroying the mean, spotty-faced aliens?"

"Yes!" Eliot shouted and stabbed the banana nose with his fork. James howled as though wounded and then they both laughed. Jane entered the kitchen and headed straight for the coffeepot. James knew better than to start a conversation with her until she'd had at least three sips, so he merely smiled at her and continued making pancakes.

"I have the best husband in the world," Jane declared. "Makes his pancakes light and his coffee strong."

Kissing Eliot on the top of his head, she took her cup out to the front door and retrieved the newspaper. The Henrys batted around proposals on how to spend the rest of the day. James had to mow the lawn while Jane needed to do laundry, work on her summer class syllabus, and get groceries at the farmer's market.

"I want to build a fairy house!" Eliot cried and ran to his room. He returned with one of the library books he'd checked out during the week. "See? This girl makes one and the fairies love it. You have to use stuff from outside. If you buy stuff, that's cheating."

James examined the illustrations of the small structures crafted from pinecones, twigs, and stones. "I think we can make time for this project," James told his son. "It's going to be hot today, so let's take a walk in the woods after we get dressed. Maybe Snickers would like to come along."

Hearing his name, the miniature schnauzer raced into the room, his tail wagging.

Jane got ready and headed out for the farmer's market. James and Eliot went out back with both Snickers and Miss Pickles trailing after them. It was James's job to carry the hemp bag that would hold the fairy house materials.

"Okay, bud. Enough rocks," James protested as Eliot tried to add another heavy stone to the bag. "How about some lightweight sticks?"

It took another hour to construct the house. When it was done,

Eliot sat back on his heels and brushed the dirt from his hands. "When do you think they'll move in?"

James shrugged. "Fairies are very shy. They don't usually let people see them."

Eliot pouted. "Then how will I know if they liked my house?"

"Oh, they have a way of letting you know that they were here." He thought frantically. "Um, they might make a heart using flower petals or leave you some other gift."

"Like what?" Eliot's eyes shimmered.

Now James really was stuck. He glanced around the yard, stroking Miss Pickles as he tried to come up with a plausible answer. "A lucky four-leaf clover or an empty robin's egg. Something from nature."

"Cool." Eliot seemed satisfied. "When should we look for presents?"

Knowing he'd need time to sneak back to the fairy house and put an item there, James waved Eliot away from the edge of the woods. "Tomorrow. We need to give them time to discover their new house. Plus, I heard they come out with the sun. *Very* early. Let's go inside and see what Mom got from the market."

After a snack of celery sticks and peanut butter, Eliot went to his room to play with the train set Jackson had bought him. James donned a baseball cap and went back outside to mow the lawn.

"Take your shoes off before you come back in!" Jane warned. "I'm going to vacuum and mop since neither of my men are underfoot."

The Henrys passed an industrious morning. James finished with the front and side yards and stopped for a breather. His shirt was soaked with sweat and he'd emptied his water bottle. He wanted a refill and a bite of lunch before attacking the large expanse of lawn behind the house. He also wanted to check with Lucy and find out if Kenneth Cooper had been charged with a crime or had spent the night in the hospital, making phone calls to his firm and practicing the statement he'd make to the authorities.

Mindful of Jane's request, he kicked off his sneakers on the front porch and shook the grass from his socks. Frowning at the green tinge discoloring the ankle area of his white socks, James wiped his face with the old dishrag he used as a gym towel and stepped into the blissful cool.

In the kitchen, he refilled his water bottle, noting that an unfamiliar plastic pitcher containing a brown liquid had been left out on the counter. A tumbler with what James assumed was the tea given to them by Roslyn sat next to the pitcher. He picked it up and gave it a sniff. Normally, he wouldn't be suspicious of the holistic healer's odd visit the night before. After all, he lived in the South and it was an everyday occurrence for the townsfolk to help one another out, but why would Roslyn stop by when James had already purchased the products needed to cure Eliot's false cold?

He found Eliot still in his room. Train tracks snaked across the floor while library books, wooden blocks, and Lincoln Logs formed a series of tunnels. "Just a few more minutes," his son pleaded, assuming it was lunchtime.

"Where's Mom?" James asked, but Eliot just shrugged and continued to play.

Peering into the bedroom, James recalled that laundry had been on Jane's to-do list. He walked back down the hall to the tiny room next to the garage and found a pile of clean clothes partially folded on top of the dryer. The T-shirts had been placed neatly in the laundry basket, but the family's socks and underwear were scattered on the floor. The sight of the freshly laundered clothing dumped on the tiles caused a stirring of anxiety in James. He quickly checked the garage and, finding it empty, hurried out to the deck.

Jane was there, hunched over the railing, retching violently.

"Honey! Are you okay?"

She couldn't answer. Each breath was a desperate gasp as her body tried to inhale oxygen in between convulsions. One hand kept her balanced on the rail while the other clutched at her stomach.

"Oh, my God!" James stared at her in fear. "Did you drink the tea?"

Jane managed a nod and James flew into action. He raced into the house and dialed 911. With a tremulous voice, he told the operator that his wife had likely been poisoned by herbal tea.

"Which herb, sir?" the woman asked serenely and James was

exasperated by her calm. He wanted her to speak rapidly, to hastily tell him what to do, to promise that all would be well.

"I-I don't know," he stammered, picturing the shelves and shelves of products in Roslyn's storeroom.

The operator spoke again. It took a moment for her words to pierce the buzzing in James's head. "What are your wife's symptoms, sir?"

Suddenly, James felt that he was wasting precious time fielding questions from the composed woman on the phone. He slammed the handset down and yelled, "Eliot! Get in my truck!"

"But I wanna—" the little boy whined.

"Do what I said right now!" James so rarely shouted that his son responded immediately.

James grabbed a bucket from under the kitchen sink, ran back out to the deck, and gently lifted Jane into his arms. "You're going to be fine, baby." He rushed through the house, gently set Jane into the passenger seat, put the bucket on her lap, and belted Eliot in his car seat. He then raced inside once more, grabbed the pitcher of tea from the counter, and jumped into the truck.

The drive to the hospital was hell. Eliot sat in wide-eyed silence in his seat, his large pupils dark with fear. Jane retched several times but then dropped the bucket between her feet and grabbed her belly with both hands, moaning in pain.

Her agony made every red light and slow driver James's agony. Somehow, Eliot's mute presence in the backseat kept James from taking too many risks, but each passing minute filled his mind with torturous questions. How powerful was the poisonous herb in the tea? How much did Jane drink? Would he get her to the hospital in time?

James screeched to a halt in front of the emergency room entrance, unbuckled Eliot and told him to stay close. Lifting Jane out of the car, he left the Bronco where it was, doors open wide, the key in the ignition.

Ignoring the reception area with its enclosed desk, sliding glass window, and sign-in clipboard, James carried his wife right up to a man in scrubs who was loitering near the vending machines. "My wife's been poisoned!"

To the man's credit, he immediately leapt into action. He

slammed a nearby wall button, automatically opening a set of double doors leading to the treatment rooms. Gesturing for James to put Jane on the empty gurney in the hallway, he removed the stethoscope from around his neck and listened to Jane's breathing.

"Do you know what she ingested?" He spoke to James without looking at him.

"An herbal tea. I think it was deliberately brewed to do us harm. I have it out in the car."

The man gestured for a pair of his colleagues to come to his aid. "Go get it, please."

James took Eliot's hand to fetch the pitcher and then he stopped. "Thunder god vine," he said. "Check for thunder god vine."

The man removed the stereoscope stem from his right ear. "Thunder god vine?" His look of astonishment was quickly replaced by a nod. "Okay. But get the pitcher anyway."

Murmuring words of comfort to Eliot, James grabbed the pitcher of tea from the Bronco and handed it to the nurse stationed outside the double doors. "You have to move your car and check your wife in," she directed. "They're not going to let you back in here until you do."

Too blinded by worry to realize that Jane wasn't the only patient the emergency room team would see that hour, James hurried to move his car to the nearest lot. He completed the paperwork as fast as possible, his handwriting an anxious scrawl. Shoving the clipboard in the glass reception window's slot, he pointed at the double doors. "Can I go back now?"

"Your wife might have been moved, sir. Let me find out where she is." The woman picked up her phone and dialed a number. She then glanced back at James. "I've paged the doctor. I'll call you as soon as I have more information."

James controlled the rage surging through his body. He knew it stemmed from his feelings of helplessness and that he needed to press it back down. Only the warmth of Eliot's small hand in his kept him from erupting. He led his son over to the vending machines and bought him a bag of pretzels and an apple juice.

"What's wrong with Mommy?" Eliot asked, his lips quivering as he held his untouched snack.

Gathering the boy in his lap, James whispered, "She's sick, but the doctor's going to make her better. Don't you worry."

Deciding to funnel his anger, he called Lucy on his cell phone. "Roslyn must be the murderer you've been looking for! She tried to kill us! Me or Jane . . . maybe all three of us." The horror of his own statement sank in. "My God, she would have knowingly poisoned my son!"

"I'm on it," Lucy said after James ran through the details. "She must have been worried that you discovered something in her office and that you'd put two and two together and turn her in. Think about why you spooked her, James. When I catch her, I'm going to need as much information as possible to toss her in a cell."

Sensing Lucy was about to hang up, James called, "Wait! What about Kenneth?"

"He's denying everything. Says that he had the feathers in his pocket because he took them off your car." There was a smile in her voice. "Don't give him a second thought. He had cocaine in his system. First thing Monday morning, we get a restraining order for you and your family and go from there. He's never going to bother you again, James. I promise."

James saw the receptionist pick up the phone and then glance in his direction. She pointed at the wall button and gave him a nod of consent. "Gotta go," he told Lucy and moved toward the double doors.

A nurse took James and Eliot back to the treatment area and had them wait while she went inside a room with a closed door. Several minutes passed before a doctor emerged from within, explaining that Jane had been given activated charcoal and seemed to have successfully purged the contents of her stomach.

"The good news is that your wife ate a meal before drinking the tea, so the harmful qualities of the poison were absorbed at a slower rate." He peeled off a pair of clear disposable gloves. "We'll be watching her closely over the next few hours, but I believe she'll be just fine. Her throat will be sore and she may have other side effects such as headaches and cramping, but we'll make her as comfortable as we can."

"Can I see her?" James asked, his voice full of yearning.

The doctor flicked his eyes at Eliot. "You might want to wait a bit. Let her get everything out and get cleaned up a little. Trust me"—he clapped James on the shoulder—"no one wants to be watched at a time like this. It probably wouldn't help her to know you're in the room. She can only focus on one thing right now."

Heeding the physician's advice, James entertained Eliot by telling him as many Aesop's fables as he could remember. At the end of "The Fox and the Grapes" Lucy called again.

"Roslyn's gone. Anything of value has been removed from her house and her office." She cursed under her breath. "With all the money she got blackmailing Ned and Tia, she could be anywhere by now—on a first-class flight to paradise."

"I take it you didn't find a defibrillator under the floorboards either," James said with equal anger and dejection.

"I'm with the team at her house now, but Roslyn was no dummy. She was prepared for flight. Hold on, her phone is ringing." James heard Lucy speaking, but her low voice was garbled. After a rustle, Lucy returned. "That was a gallery in New Market. They called to tell Roslyn that her framing job was ready to be picked up. She'd commissioned custom frames for a series of ten nature photographs."

James stood up abruptly, nearly dumping Eliot on the floor. "Fern's? The photos Lennon bought for his *girlfriend*?"

"No, I'm thinking Roslyn is Lennon's mom."

A lightbulb went off in James's mind. "Lennon's new SUV! He told me a generous relative gave him a bunch of cash. Roslyn must have given Ned's money to Lennon. To her son . . ."

"He might have been involved in the murders too. Remember the prints on Tia's neck? The ones made by a large hand? And I could see her letting Lennon inside without worrying about being hurt. With his gentle hippie act, he might have fooled everyone. You sit tight," Lucy commanded. "I have to track down that rock-raking bastard!"

With no plans to leave the emergency room area, James and Eliot wandered back to the vending machines. He bought a package of Fig Newtons for Eliot and a granola bar for himself. The receptionist came out from her glass enclosure and gave Eliot a coloring book, crayons, and a sheet of rescue vehicle stickers.

"How's Mama doing?" she asked Eliot.

Putting a fire truck sticker on his shirt, Eliot said, "Daddy said she's going to be okay. He's always right."

The receptionist winked at James. "Enjoy that while it lasts."

Eliot had colored three pages when a nurse came out of Jane's room and told her husband and son they could go in and see her.

"She's a bit dehydrated and her throat hurts, but by the time she goes home tomorrow, she'll be good as new," the nurse said. Lowering her voice, she added, "The cops are going to want to talk to you."

"That's fine by me," James replied, and walked to his wife's bedside.

She smiled weakly and he felt the fear, which had clung to his chest like a parasite, release its grip and vanish from the room.

. . .

After Eliot was in bed and James had listened to the frantic phone messages left by his friends, he sat in the dark living room and thought. With his pets nestled beside him, he turned over all the details of the two murders. Pieces were still missing. How did Roslyn get Ned in her power in the first place? Who used the defibrillator? And where had it come from? Why would Roslyn perform such hideous acts of violence? As a means of providing for her son? And what hold did she have over Tia?

It was difficult to think clearly without experiencing spurts of rage and indulging in fantasies of revenge. After all, Roslyn Rhodes had poisoned his wife. If one little sip had been so harmful to Jane, James couldn't imagine what the tea might have done to Eliot.

"To protect her son, she would have killed mine," he whispered, the anger flooding through him like a fiery wave.

He'd saved his phone call to Lucy for last. When he reached her, he wanted to hear that it was all over—that the culprits had been apprehended. He wanted to be told that there was irrefutable proof that they'd murdered two townsfolk and had attempted to kill a third, and they'd be spending a lifetime in prison.

"I wish I had better news," Lucy said as soon as she heard his voice. "But the governor's pulling out all the stops on this one. He has the state and local police involved. Photos are being shown during every news broadcast, and for once, the media's skill at sensationalizing might work to our advantage. I already saw a segment about our manhunt during the six o'clock news."

"What about their cars?" James tried to rein in his frustration but failed. "Are they broadcasting their license plate numbers? Lennon's was pretty hard to miss. Green SUV with a vanity plate reading, VEG OUT."

"We found his car on a CarMax lot. Lennon sold the truck four days ago and deposited a check for over twenty grand in his bank account. He was smart," Lucy grudgingly admitted. "He waited for that check to clear and then withdrew all his funds. He's run off with at least forty thousand in cash."

James sighed and Snickers raised his head in concern. "That kind of money makes it easier to hide."

"Hey, my career is on the line here, so I'm totally invested in this case. If mother and son get away, I'll look totally inept! Trust me, James. I am *very* motivated to catch them. And I'll start tomorrow by going over every possession, every piece of mail, and every detail people can recall about Roslyn and Lennon. That means I'm giving you an assignment."

"Which is?"

"Think back on all the conversations you've had with both mother and son. If I gather enough data from enough conversations, I believe we'll get a clue as to where they've gone."

James smoothed the fur on his dog's neck. "That's what I've been doing for the last hour. I haven't come up with anything yet, but I will. I have scores to settle and I won't stop until mother and son are in cuffs."

Fuming, he hung up.

Outside, a summer thunderstorm was brewing. The wind curled around the treetops and clouds blanketed the moon. At the sound of a branch tapping against a window, Snickers cocked his head and growled. In the dark and silent living room, James growled too.

Chapter Eighteen

Gillian's Zen Cocktail

A week later, the Henry family arrived at Gillian's colorful Victorian for what their hostess had dubbed a "Union of Souls" fete. White and silver balloons bobbed from the porch railings and crepe paper sculptures of kissing doves dangled from the sconces by the double front doors. A little sign taped to the brass knocker directed guests to head to the backyard. Gillian had created an incredibly romantic atmosphere. She'd decorated her gazebo with more balloons and curtains of white streamers while twinkling white lights hung from the rafters in loose graceful swags.

It was a perfect summer night. The humidity was blessedly low, a soft breeze drifted down from the mountains, and the first fireflies of the season were speaking to each other in their magical language of light.

The women wore cool sundresses. The men, in shorts and polo shirts. The Fitzgerald brothers played croquet on the lawn as Lindy adjusted the volume on a battery-powered radio. Tony Bennett serenaded the partygoers, who exchanged small talk until Gillian asked them to gather for a toast.

The table she'd set was beautiful. Scott, Francis, Bennett, and Gillian had somehow wrestled her dining room table out the back door. Gillian had then covered it with a cloth so pristinely white that it glowed beneath the periwinkle sky like a new moon. Tall pillar candles protected by hurricane glass and posies of white roses in silver vases created a line of flickering light and sweet fragrance down the center of the table. Rolled white cloth napkins were fastened with ivy vines and a silver tray bearing glass tumblers filled with a bright green liquid and sprigs of mint rested at the head of the table.

"A green toast!" Gillian shouted. "To the bond between man and woman and parent and child! May your future be filled with joy, adventure, and an *endless* stream of love!"

The newlyweds clinked glasses with the other guests, and even Eliot, who was given limeade in a "grown-up glass," participated in the toast.

Bennett cleared his throat. "To James Henry, the best friend a fellow could hope to have. And to Jane, for bringing my man happiness. Lord knows he deserves it!"

"To the couple that makes me believe that love is forever!" Lindy cried.

The toasts continued for another five minutes. Most of the women had tear tracks on their cheeks and even Jackson's eyes were shining.

"What is this stuff?" he grumbled, holding out his glass.

Gillian interpreted his question as a cue to pour refills. "It's a Zen cocktail. I didn't want anything traditional like champagne. A whole family has been united by this marriage. By going green, I was able to include Eliot. I also wanted to celebrate how he's influenced his parents to embark on a healthier, vegetarian life-style."

Bennett gestured at the grill. "Is he the reason we're eating mulch burgers tonight?"

Gillian elbowed him roughly in the side. "You can have a nonvegetarian patty if you want. I prepared both, but I'm grilling the bean burgers first so they're not *tainted* by the meat."

"Leave the grilling to me," Bennett said. "I don't want to ingest any more carcinogens than I have to."

While the pair debated the cooking time and temperature of the burgers, Fern and Willow escorted Eliot away from the table and showed him how to play horseshoes. Gillian had thoughtfully purchased several lawn games perfect for a boy his age. However, it was the Fitzgerald brothers who got the biggest kick out of the putting green, the beanbag toss, and the croquet set.

The rest of the adults settled at the table and continued sipping their refreshing green cocktails. Eventually, the conversation led to the subject of Kenneth Cooper and the unsolved murders of Ned Woodman and Tia Royale.

"Kenneth is out of our hair," Jane explained. "We were granted a strict restraining order. I've heard he's also lost his job."

"I hope he gets disbarred," James murmured.

Milla rubbed her dimpled chin thoughtfully. "What about official charges? He's doesn't have to serve any time?"

Lucy fidgeted with the sprig of mint in her glass. "We couldn't charge him with possession. He didn't have any cocaine on his person or in his car—just in his body. And there wasn't much we could do about his affinity for leaving dead birds around Jane and James. But since no one wanted to see him go unpunished, we decided to put Murphy's idea into play."

"Her plan was to make the official inquiry public, right?" Lindy asked. "She splashed Kenneth's cocaine history all over the front page. Every news service in the country picked up that story. That jerk's law career is over." She grinned. "Luis was certainly at the right place at the right time! It's funny, though; he keeps telling me that he wasn't. He's being very mysterious about the big finale I missed. Even my students are acting weird. They won't even talk about the play! They must be focusing on their upcoming exams."

James nodded, recalling how uncannily quiet the campus of William & Mary could be during finals week. "How did Murphy ever get inside information from an employee in the rehab center?"

A wry smile spread across Lucy's face. "She never did tell me the whole story. All she'd say was there was a young orderly working there who dreams of becoming a writer. Apparently, he's now a *Star* employee."

"You see!" Gillian's voice was triumphant. "She made a personal sacrifice to come to our aid. Without her help, Quincy's Gap might never have been rid of Kenneth Cooper."

Bennett grudgingly agreed. "I suppose she's made amends."

Satisfied that her faith in Murphy's goodness had been proved true, Gillian put a hand over Jane's. "Are you completely restored after your ordeal last week? I'll never be able to look at my herbal teas in the same light!"

Jane laughed. "Don't give up on chamomile and peppermint because of me. Your teas aren't mixed with pure thunder god vine root. I'm fine, really. James saved me. He's my Superman."

"Speaking of the bad guys, are you getting closer to catching them?" Scott asked as he trotted over to the table and gulped down half his drink in one swallow. "Yum! I *love* going green!"

All eyes fixed on Lucy. "Roslyn and Lennon have not been apprehended. We've chased down dozens and dozens of false leads. Now that Tia's parents have offered a fifty-thousand-dollar reward, the phone calls and emails have been flooding in at a ridiculous rate. Even with other law enforcement agencies helping, it's taking all our manpower to sift through them. Despite the monetary incentive, we haven't received a single useful clue."

Lucy went on to give examples of the most preposterous tips the Sheriff's Department had received. These included a caller who swore mother and son had been abducted by aliens and another who claimed to have seen the pair, disguised as Elvis impersonators, dining on Grand Slams at Denny's.

When the laughter died down, Lucy began to toy with the ivy wrapped around her napkin. "Sheriff Huckabee's been breathing down my neck like a dragon. Sullie and I don't do anything but work. This is my first real break in a week." She glanced apologetically at James and Jane. "I've read the case files until I start seeing double, but when I lie down to sleep at night, I still feel like I've let everyone down. Even my dreams are focused on this case."

Gillian reached over and put an arm around Lucy's shoulders. "You're only human. Have faith in yourself. Someone will experience an unexpected moment of clarity and an answer will be revealed."

"I can't stop until I've set things right. You see, I made a mistake." Lucy looked at Gillian's kind face. "When I looked into the pasts of those working at the Wellness Village, I wasn't thorough enough. If I had been, I would have discovered that Lennon had changed his name at age eighteen. I concentrated on his adult years, calling former employers and such. He didn't go to college and has worked a series of maintenance jobs. No one had a bad word to say about him. I found no financial red flags. In my mind, he was low on the suspect list. Yet he was the killer!"

"You were researching backgrounds on dozens of people," James said. "What you did was logical."

The assembly agreed, soothing Lucy with their words and sympathetic looks.

"You'll get them, Lucy, even if they're out there preparing a new scheme and sniffing around for fresh victims to blackmail." Bennett's dark eyes flashed with anger. "You're going to make it right."

That being said, Gillian and Bennett excused themselves to

prepare the food. The partygoers agreed not to talk about the case anymore and, after another round of Zen cocktails, became quite jolly. Most of the company enjoyed Gillian's dinner of black bean burgers, fruit salad, and edamame. Bennett, Lucy, and the Fitzgerald brothers opted for traditional burgers, and for once, Gillian didn't chastise them for being unwilling to explore new tastes. Later, Willow and Fern served dessert. The group was treated to chilled white chocolate mousse garnished with a white chocolate dove. It was rich, creamy, and utterly decadent.

"Fern and I wanted to contribute in some way," Willow said, smiling shyly.

Fern handed Jane a square package wrapped in brown paper. "And here's the rest of our joint gift."

Jane opened the package, revealing the photograph of the purple rhododendron flower James had planned to buy for his wife.

"It's beautiful!" Jane exclaimed.

Gillian and Bennett gave them a gift certificate for a couples massage, Lindy had made them a stunning pottery fruit bowl, and Lucy presented them with a generous gift certificate to Dolly's Diner. The Fitzgeralds waited until all the other gifts and greeting cards had been opened before handing James a shoebox wrapped in the funny pages.

"Did you give them each a single shoe?" Bennett teased.

The box was stuffed with tissue paper and did not contain footwear. Nestled at the bottom was a glossy brochure featuring a cruise ship. Inside the folded brochure were two tickets for a five-day cruise from Norfolk to Bermuda.

James was flabbergasted. "You got us a *cruise*? To Bermuda?"

The twins bobbed their heads enthusiastically.

"This is too much!" Jane protested.

James quickly agreed. "Scott, Francis. We are *really* touched, but—"

"Nonrefundable, Professor!" Scott announced with delight. Francis gestured at Jackson and Milla. "We've lined up the dates with your babysitting service and worked it out on the library staff vacation calendar too."

"We also called your department head to see when your

summer semester would start, Mrs. Henry." Francis wore a mischievous grin. "He says to tell you 'Bon Voyage.'"

"I don't know what to say . . ." James broke off, too moved to continue. He and Jane bent their heads over the brochure, excitedly studying photographs of pink beaches. Next, they embraced the Fitzgerald twins several times until the younger men finally pulled away.

"Seriously, we're not going to be late on our rent because of this. We finally got our check from the gaming company," Francis explained. "It was a *big* check. Scott and I bought some awesome mountain bikes for off-road adventuring, a killer flat-screen TV, and new computers with more gigs than the Pentagon's entire database." He and Scott exchanged high fives. They waited for their boss to respond, but his eyes had turned distant. "Professor?"

Something Francis had said triggered James's memory. Suddenly, he gripped Scott by the sleeve. "Do you have a map of area mountain bike trails?"

"There's one online," the startled twin answered. "Why?"

James looked at Gillian. "Can we use your computer?"

The Fitzgerald brothers followed their boss inside and spent several seconds arguing over which site was best, but Francis finally won out and began typing. A map of Virginia covered by green bicycle symbols appeared on-screen.

"Can you zoom in on our area?" James asked and Francis quickly complied.

James read the names of the trails until he saw the one he recognized. "That's it!" he shouted. "Brandywine Lake!" Leaving the befuddled Fitzgerald twins staring at the computer screen, James raced outside. He found Lucy at the beanbag toss, engaged in an intense match with Fern.

"Brandywine Lake!" he shouted again, grabbing her elbow.

Lucy scowled. "Hey, you're throwing off my aim!"

"Lennon loved to mountain bike. Skye told me he went every weekend without fail. It's what he lives for. During one of our conversations, he invited me to ride with him one day. He said it's what he does to relieve stress. His favorite trail is Brandywine Lake."

Lucy squeezed the beanbag in her hand, her eyes glinting. "We need to circulate his photo around every trail in the region. We have a new composite showing him with and without the dreadlocks, so even if he's changed his looks, another rider might still recognize him." Her face shone. "Good work, James. This might be that obscure clue that catches those two fiends!"

Pausing briefly to thank Gillian for a lovely evening, Lucy jogged around the side of the house and disappeared from view. James returned to the table and explained what had transpired to the rest of the ensemble.

"There's something I don't understand," Jane said to James as everyone broke into animated chatter. "Why was Roslyn so anxious during the food festival if she was the one blackmailing Ned?"

James mulled over her question. "I don't know. Maybe Ned refused to pay her any more, which forced Lennon to get involved." He could see Roslyn's panicked face in his mind. "Could she have actually cared about Ned? Perhaps murder had never been part of her original plan."

Jane considered this theory. "Tia also looked scared when we saw her at the Apple Blossom Festival. If Lennon caused her to run away like that, she would have been too frightened to let him in her house later on. So what happened? Tia found Roslyn standing on the doorstep and invited her in with Lennon nearby hiding in the bushes?"

"Again, maybe Roslyn was trying to get money out of Tia without harming her. Tia would have viewed Roslyn as a potential friend—a vegetarian and animal rights sympathizer. She would have let the older woman into her home without having any idea that Roslyn was Lennon's mom. Nobody knew. After all, they don't look alike and they have different last names."

The couple fell silent. They watched Lindy, Willow, and Fern play croquet while Eliot and the Fitzgerald twins chased after fireflies. Milla and Jackson said their good nights and headed home. Jackson gave his son a brief hug and told him that he was still busy creating the couple's wedding gift. Thrilled over the thought of receiving one of his father's masterpieces, James teased, "You'd better get some rest then. I've got a blank wall in the living room that could do with a classy painting by Virginia's premier country artist."

James and Jane carried dishes into Gillian's kitchen, but she immediately shooed them away. "We are *not* going to waste this heavenly evening washing dishes. Out! Out into the night with you!"

So it was that they found themselves in a pair of wicker rockers on the back porch. Laughter floated up from the lawn as Eliot's high notes mingled with the low timbre of Scott and Francis's voices. The three women smacked mallets against croquet balls, their comfortable prattle circling lazily upward, where it caught in the tree branches.

Reaching for Jane's hand, James lifted his eyes to the indigo sky. "Gillian was right. This is heaven."

Epilogue

It took two weeks for a rider biking the Elizabeth Furnace Trail southeast of Strasburg to phone the tip line, saying that he believed he'd seen the man in the photograph a park ranger had given him the week before. The man he saw was unloading his bike from the rack of a dark green Jeep Compass.

"If he's your guy," the cyclist said to the officer fielding calls from the tip line, "you can catch him when he comes back out. It's a grueling thirteen-mile trail. Even the most experienced riders have to stop for a water break, so you have time. He might go for a dip in the reservoir too. It's a great way to clean off before pumping the pedals again. Just be careful, because if other riders see a bunch of cops hanging in the parking lot, they might warn your guy. Not because they think murder suspects are cool, but because they don't care for authority figures as a rule."

Lucy heard about the tip, and within minutes she and Sullie were in his Camaro.

"It's him. I can feel it in my gut," Lucy said, twisting her hands in anticipation.

"You're so sexy when you're on a manhunt," Sullie answered. He then focused his full attention on speeding around other vehicles, the magnetic siren on his roof screaming out a warning.

Upon arriving at the trail entrance, Lucy and Sullie had a quick conference with the local deputies and together came up with a strategy to ensure that the wanted man wouldn't slip from their grasp.

Later, Lucy would tell the supper club members how Lennon had dismounted in the parking lot, his young face flushed and satisfied from what must have been an amazing ride. The officers almost felt sorry for him, for it would be the last time he'd experience such sweet and invigorating freedom for many years to come.

Lennon's head was completely shaved, leaving only a hint of light brown stubble bleached gold by the sun, and he wore a pair of mirrored sunglasses. A sheen of sweat glistened on his smooth skin, and when Lucy and Sullie approached him, he bolted. Because a dozen local deputies and police officers were waiting for the suspect to flee, Lennon was quickly caught by a young deputy who'd been a track star in college. The two men struggled and Lennon's glasses flew off in the scuffle. He glared at the authorities, his eyes glimmered with rage.

Lennon—formerly Curt Snyder—denied everything, but his capture forced Roslyn to surrender of her own volition. The *Star* was loaded with photographs of her being escorted inside the sheriff's department by Huckabee himself.

"Roslyn tried to take the fall for both of them," Lucy told her friends. "She and Ned Woodman had a brief affair, and when he tried to break it off, Roslyn threatened to tell his wife and leak his indiscretions to the press unless he bought her silence."

"So that's how the blackmail began," said Lindy.

"Yes, but Ned wanted to come clean. He was going to tell Donna everything and then present himself to the authorities to confess the embezzlement of town funds. It was at the food festival that he told Roslyn he was no longer in her power. That's why she looked so frantic."

Bennett snorted. "She was losing her free ride—that's why she was sweating like a fry cook during the breakfast rush."

"Except she didn't keep any of the money," Lucy explained. "Every cent went to Lennon. She'd been struggling financially as a single mom and she was tired of the struggle. Go on, someone ask me why she was single."

"Because she's a duplicitous blackmailer?" James guessed.

Lucy paused, letting the dramatic tension build. "Because her ex-husband is spending thirty years to life in prison! He killed someone in a bar brawl. The fight started as an argument about sports. Punches were thrown, and Lennon's daddy took it to the next level by smashing his opponent's head into the jukebox."

"Ow!" several of supper club members said at once.

Gillian clucked her tongue. "I can't understand why that angry young man chose Lennon as his false name. John Lennon was an advocate of *peace*. It pains me that his memory is being disgraced by having his name associated with such a *twisted* soul."

"People won't remember this guy as Lennon," Lindy said in hopes of comforting her friend. "Murphy referred to him as Curt Snyder in her articles, and so has the rest of the media. I don't think anyone wants to use his fake name and the term 'double murder' in the same sentence." She turned to Lucy. "Tell us about the defibrillator."

"Roslyn purchased it years ago through an online medical auction. When hospitals or medical offices upgrade to new equipment, they often put the old stuff up for sale."

Bennett put a hand on her arm. "You mean I could just go online and buy a blood pressure machine? See what happens to my numbers after Mrs. McDougal's bloodhound chases after me like I'm wearing Milkbone aftershave."

"I think a stethoscope might be more handy in that scenario," Gillian said with a saucy wink. "Really, Bennett, you need to hire a dog whisperer. Perhaps I should look into that for you."

Before the couple could engage in a debate over befriending all the pooches on Bennett's mail route, Lucy continued her narrative. "Lennon was storing the device in the closet where Roslyn kept her refrigerated products. You were right to be suspicious of that locked door, James. Lennon lured Ned into Roslyn's office, saying that he knew about the blackmail and could show Ned where Roslyn had hidden the cash."

"Of course Ned followed him!" Lindy cried. "He could return the money to the town's account and avoid jail time, divorce, and public humiliation. So why believe Lennon?"

Lucy shrugged. "Because Lennon had access to all the buildings with his master key. Many of Roslyn and Ned's trysts took place in her office, which probably led them to assume that the young man knew about the affair. Lennon lured Ned into the bathroom by claiming that the cash was in the toilet tank. He then locked the door and used the defibrillator on the unsuspecting councilman. Afterward, he put the device back in the closet and returned to the festival."

The friends fell silent as each of them pictured the surprise on Ned Woodman face when he turned to find the person he'd hoped could rescue him wielding a pair of charged paddles.

James wondered what it felt like to be blasted with an electric current powerful enough to change the rhythm of a beating heart. Did death occur so rapidly that Ned had no chance to process the betrayal, or was there enough time for him to register shock and horror?

Sensing the mood shift of her audience, Lucy also grew more solemn "Roslyn claims to have been distraught over Ned's murder. She was concerned over her lover being killed, but she was far more distraught by Lennon exhibiting the violent tendencies she attributed to Lennon's father. She begged Lennon to leave Quincy's Gap right after the festival, but he'd already started blackmailing Tia and had genuine feelings for Skye."

"What hold did he have over Tia?" James asked. "We've never been able to figure that out."

Lucy shook her head. "You'll never believe this, but Tia was in a commercial for a fast-food restaurant when she was a teenager. I've seen the footage. Tia takes a huge bite of a cheeseburger and smiles at the camera."

"Where did Lennon see the commercial? It's gotta be older than my shower curtain." Bennett frowned in confusion.

"Online. Apparently, one of the other kids on the commercial went on to become a famous singer in a Grateful Dead cover band, so the clip was posted on a bunch of sites," Lucy said. "The second Lennon found out Tia was one of the rich Royale kids, he started digging around and stumbled across the commercial."

"Poor girl," Gillian sympathized. "She was probably afraid that no one would support her animal rights campaign if they knew about that silly ad, but she was wrong. She was a child when that was filmed!"

"She was a child when she was *murdered*," Lucy added with an undercurrent of anger. "Roslyn went to Tia's place to warn her to get out of town, but Lennon followed Mommy Dearest. Inside, Roslyn accidentally dropped Ned's fir tree charm, and because she'd had it in her skirt pocket, where she was also keeping a small wedge of cheese, Snickers swallowed it. Lennon snuck in when the two women were talking and hid in Tia's closet. He tried to get more money out of her, and when she didn't produce any then and there, he grew enraged. They struggled, and when she was weakened by strangulation, he zapped her with the paddles."

James felt his mouth go dry. "What a monster."

"Yeah, he's messed up. He and Roslyn have never had a healthy relationship. She said that all through Lennon's childhood, she went without so he could have nice things. She gave him too much power and spoiled him rotten, thinking that was how a loving parent acted."

"I feel a little sorry for her," Lindy admitted. "She has to live with the weight of so many regrets."

Lucy nodded. "At least she feels remorse. Lennon is just ticked off that he got caught."

"Well, that boy is in for a rude awakening when he gets to prison," Bennett said with satisfaction. "Not too much peace, love, and harmony in the slammer. Maybe he'll learn a little about the value of freedom when he only gets to see the sky through a barred window. Maybe he'll learn what he stole from Ned and Tia when the life he took for granted comes to a screeching halt."

There wasn't much to say after that and the supper club meeting broke up shortly afterward. The five friends were tired. Each of them felt glad to be welcoming the new season, as if the heat of the summer sun could burn away the damp, dirty residue left behind by a spring marred by stalking, blackmail, and murder. By mutual agreement, they all signed up for more sessions with Harmony. This time, however, no one was interested in treating sugar addictions. Instead, they wanted help in letting go of their repressed guilt for not discovering Lennon's foul deeds earlier. They also had another shared goal: to kick off the summer feeling in control of their bodies, their minds, and their futures.

"And I'd like to establish a sense of calm," James added when he made the appointment with Harmony's new assistant. Skye was long gone, and though James didn't know where the young woman went, he wished her a quick recovery from what was no doubt a deeply wounded heart.

A few weeks into the month of June, James was reading emails in his home office when Jane entered the little room. The walls were lined with bookshelves and books filled every available nook and cranny. There were books piled on his desk, on the side tables, and in boxes and chest-high towers within the closet.

Jane was smiling. "I forwarded you the email I received from Fay Sunray. Did I ever tell you that I'd written her to complain about how she'd upset Eliot during the Nashville show?"

"No, but I thought about writing her myself." He scrolled down his list of emails. "Here it is."

Dear Mrs. Henry,

I definitely owe you, your son, and everyone at that concert an apology. It was not the time, place, or the way to deliver my message about living a vegetarian lifestyle. In fact, my behavior may have done a cause near and dear to my heart more harm than good. The offending song has been cut from the DVD version of the show and I've mailed you a free copy of the edited work along with a signed photograph and a selection of Fay Sunray Friends puppets. I know these items can't make up for my poor judgment, but it is still my hope that I can bring a smile to your son's face.

Yours, Fay Sunray.

"She sounds very sincere," said James after he'd finished reading the email. "You know, she and Tia Royale would have gotten along well. But Fay seems to have realized something that Tia didn't. You don't have to be vulgar or crass to get your point across. A few farm puppets and a gentle manner can go a long way."

Jane laughed. "You need to shut down that computer and start packing. We have an early start tomorrow."

"I know," James said without moving. "I still can't believe we accepted a cruise from my employees. It feels so wrong and yet" — he glanced up at her with a smile — "so right."

"We'd better have a vacation while we can." She handed him a small package wrapped in white tissue paper.

"What's this?" James asked and began to tear at the paper. Parting the tissue, he saw that Jane had bought him an ebook reader. "Jane!" He looked stunned and not just a little taken aback. "I'm a librarian. I . . . I don't want to read books on a machine. I need to hold them, turn the pages, feel the cover, and leave a bookmark inside." His eyes were anxious and Jane could see that he was concerned about hurting her feelings.

"It's mostly for you to use on trips," she explained and gestured at the books. "And because we're going to need to get rid of all these."

James leapt from his chair. *"What? Why?"*

Ignoring him, Jane put her index finger on her chin and tapped. "A soft yellow paint would do nicely. Or maybe a calming moss green."

"Why do we need to paint this room? It's fine the way it is!" James spluttered.

Jane put her arms around her husband. "Beige is a bit boring for a nursery. I think we'll go with the green." She drew James's hand to her belly and smiled as his face began to glow with astonishment and joy. "Or we could just take a chance and paint it pink. I have a powerful feeling that this one's a girl."

Recipes

Dolly's Blueberry Dream Pie

4 ounces cream cheese, softened

½ cup confectioners' sugar

½ cup heavy whipping cream, whipped

1 (9-inch) pie shell, baked

2/3 cup granulated sugar

¼ cup cornstarch

½ cup water

¼ cup lemon juice

3 cups fresh blueberries

In a small bowl, blend cream cheese and confectioners' sugar until smooth. Gently fold in whipped cream. Spread in a pre-baked pastry shell.

In a large saucepan combine sugar, cornstarch, water, and lemon juice. Stir with wooden spoon until smooth, and then stir in blueberries. Bring to a boil over medium heat. Cook, stirring constantly, for 2 minutes or until thickened. Cool. Spread over cream cheese layer. Refrigerate until ready to serve. Garnish with a sprig of mint (optional).

Milla's Chocolate Mocha Cake

2 cups cake flour
2 cups granulated sugar
2/3 cup unsweetened cocoa powder
½ cup vegetable oil
2 eggs
1 cup buttermilk
1 teaspoon baking powder
2 teaspoons baking soda
½ teaspoon salt
3 tablespoons instant coffee powder
1 cup hot water

Preheat oven to 350 degrees. Grease two 9-inch cake pans

Measure flour, sugar, cocoa, oil, eggs, buttermilk, baking powder, soda, and salt into a mixing bowl. Dissolve instant coffee in hot water. Add to mixing bowl. Beat at medium speed for 2 minutes until smooth; batter will be thin. Pour into prepared pans.

Bake 35 minutes, or until a toothpick comes out clean. Cool in pans for 10 minutes, and then turn out onto racks to cool completely.

Frost with Milla's Coffee Icing. For garnish, sprinkle outside edges of cake with dark chocolate shavings.

Milla's Coffee Icing

4 cups confectioners' sugar
½ cup unsalted butter, softened
6 tablespoons strong brewed coffee
2 teaspoons pure vanilla extract

Beat together sugar, butter, coffee, and vanilla until smooth. To thicken frosting, add more confectioners' sugar.

Jane & Eliot's Vegetarian Pizzadillas

Package of flour tortillas or mini flour tortillas
Small jar of marinara sauce
2 cups mozzarella cheese, shredded (Jane and Eliot also enjoy the Italian blend available in the dairy aisle)
½ cup mushrooms
½ cup black olives
2 tablespoons butter

Spread 2 tablespoons of marinara sauce on each tortilla. Sprinkle ½ cup shredded cheese on top of sauce.

Add sliced vegetables (mushrooms, black olives, or any veggie you enjoy).

Place a plain tortilla on top and press down slightly.

Melt butter in skillet.

Place pizzadilla in a warmed skillet until cheese melts and tortilla turns golden brown.

Flip pizzadilla over to evenly brown other side.

Remove from skillet and allow pizzadilla to cool slightly. Cut each pizzadilla into quarters using pizza cutter.

Gillian's Zen Cocktail

Mix one part ZEN Green Tea Liqueur with two parts white cranberry juice.

Serve over ice with spring of mint as garnish.

Gillian's Black Bean Burgers

1 (15-ounce) can black beans, drained
1 small onion, chopped
1 tablespoon finely chopped jalapeño pepper
¼ cup bread crumbs
1 egg, beaten
½ cup shredded cheddar cheese
2 cloves fresh garlic, minced
¼ teaspoon pepper
¼ cup vegetable oil

In a large bowl, mash black beans. Mix in onion, jalapeño pepper, crushed bread crumbs, egg, cheese, garlic, and pepper. Divide into 4 equal parts. Shape into patties.

Heat vegetable oil in a large nonstick skillet over medium-high heat. Fry patties until golden, about 6 to 8 minutes per side. Top with cheese slices or a splash of taco sauce.

Gillian's Summer Fruit Salad

¼ cup honey
4 tablespoons lime juice
2 teaspoons poppy seeds
1 cup halved fresh strawberries
1 cup cubed fresh pineapple
1 cup fresh blueberries
1 cup cubed seedless watermelon
¼ cup slivered almonds, toasted

In a blender, combine the honey, lime juice, and poppy seeds to make dressing. In a serving bowl, combine the fruit. Drizzle with dressing; toss gently to coat. Sprinkle with the almonds.

About the Author

New York Times bestselling author Ellery Adams grew up on a beach near the Long Island Sound. Having spent her adult life in a series of landlocked towns, she cherishes her memories of open water, violent storms, and the smell of the sea. She now writes full-time from her home in North Carolina, which she shares with her husband, two trolls, and three keyboard-hogging felines. Adams loves coffee, champagne, kickboxing, 1,000-piece jigsaw puzzles, Pinterest, and black jelly beans.

Her traditionally published series include the Secret, Book, and Scone Society Mysteries; the Book Retreat Mysteries; the Books by the Bay Mysteries; and the Charmed Pie Shoppe Mysteries.

Her indie series include the Supper Club Mysteries, the Hope Street Church Mysteries, and the Antiques & Collectibles Mysteries.